W9-CHP-804

FIC
REY   #93-8641

Reynolds, Marilyn
Detour for Emmy

DATE DUE

Country High School
Vacaville, CA

E. C. I. A. CH. 2

Country High School
Vacaville, CA

DETOUR FOR EMMY

Marilyn Reynolds

Morning
Glory
Press

Country High School Library
343 Brown Street
Vacaville, CA 95688

26.70
ESEA
Chpt II
93-8641

Copyright © 1993 by Marilyn Reynolds

All Rights Reserved

No part of this publication may be adapted,
reproduced, stored in a retrieval system,
or transmitted in any form or by any means,
electronic, mechanical, photocopying,
recording, or otherwise
without permission from the publisher.

Library of Congress Cataloging-in-Publication Data
Reynolds, Marilyn, 1935-
        Detour for Emmy / Marilyn Reynolds.
            256 pp. cm.
        Summary: Emmy, whose future had once looked so
bright, struggles to overcome the isolation and depression
brought about by being a teen mother who gets little support
from her family or the father of her child.
            ISBN 0-930934-75-x : $15.95. -- ISBN 0-930934-76-8 :
$8.95
        [1. Pregnancy--Fiction.   2. Unmarried mothers--Fiction.]
I. Title.
PZ7.R3373De 1993
[Fic]--dc20

                                                            93-657
                                                            CIP
                                                            AC

                    MORNING GLORY PRESS, INC.
        6595 San Haroldo Way   Buena Park, CA 90620
                    Telephone 714/828-1998
                        FAX 714/828-2049
            Printed and bound in the United States of America

To Mike

Acknowledgments

Many thanks to the students of Century High School, and to my colleagues in the Alhambra School District, Judy Heitzenrader, teacher in the Pregnant Minor Program, Annette McCormick, the nurse for that program, and Bitsy Wagman of the Infant Care Center, for helping keep Emmy's story real. Thanks are also due Marilyn Mallow, Alhambra High School Librarian, and Barry Barmore, Century High School teacher, for their critical expertise.

To the Monday evening writer's group, I am grateful for hunks of time spent listening to and critiquing Emmy's story, and for general encouragement and good will.

A final thank you to that most unique bunch of cultivators, the Peace Ventures group.

Marilyn Reynolds

I tried to get closer. He was leaning against the back wall. I pressed my full weight against him and we kissed, long and full.

"Art," I said, crying, "I need you so much. I didn't know how much until now."

"All I could think on the plane was that I might never feel you in my arms again," he said. "I might die before we'd even really been together . . ."

1

When I graduated from eighth grade I felt important. I don't mean to sound conceited or anything, but my friends and I practically ran Palm Avenue School. We took district-wide championship in girls' soccer and softball that year. I was voted MVP of the soccer team. "Demon Em" my team-mates called me.

My best friend, Tammy Preston, got MVP for softball, and my other best friend, Pauline Molina, had the lead role in the school's spring play. It was a musical, and Tammy and I got to do a duet that left people gasping with laughter. Tammy couldn't sing very well, but what she lacked in musical talent she made up for in personality. One thing for certain about my friend Tammy. No one ever said she was shy.

The three of us were on Student Council, too. We volun-teered time to help out at the Senior Citizens' Center and we distributed free cheese. Our pictures were even in the *Hamilton Heights Times.*

Miss Cheng, the Student Council adviser, said we were an efficient, effective, but sometimes temerarious trio. It took us about ten minutes to find temerarious in the dictionary. I read the definition to Tammy and Pauline twice.

"Temerarious: reckless, rash; blindly, heedlessly."

"I think it means we've got balls," Tammy said.

"Yuck!" I said. "I'd rather just be temerarious, please."

"I'd rather speak English," Pauline said.

Pauline claimed not to like words with more than two syllables, but that wasn't really true. Hearing her deliver her lines in the school play, it was obvious she knew her way around the polysyllabics. When I told her that, she said, "Hmmmm. Polly Syllabic. Wasn't she that girl who was in Brownies with us and had to move away when her mom ran off with the plumber?"

"No, Stupid," Tammy said. "A polysyllabic is a baby frog with a big vocabulary—ribbit, ribbitum, ribbitimus . . ."

Sometimes, when we met someone new, we liked to pretend we were sisters. No one really fell for that, though. I had reddish hair, and freckles, which I hated. I was taller than the other two, and skinny. Tammy had long blond hair and blue eyes. She was cute, but she always worried about being too short. Pauline had dark hair and deep brown eyes, and she worried about getting fat.

We each had our pet worries, and we'd talk about them on and on into the night, piled together in Tammy's king-size bed on Friday night sleepovers. Tammy and Pauline and I had been friends since first grade, and we told each other everything.

Almost every boy at Palm Avenue School who was worth looking at twice was in love with Tammy. My mom said it was because of the way Tammy filled her softball jersey, but my mom always expected the worst from men. I thought Tammy's popularity had more to do with her personality than her early development. Anyway, *something* made the guys like her, and since the three of us were practically inseparable, it was only natural that Tammy's rejects would gravitate toward me and Pauline.

"I don't want any hand-me-downs," Pauline would complain to me when one of Tammy's exes would start hanging around. I liked it though. I didn't want to bother trying to find a boyfriend for myself. That would have been too much trouble.

To be honest, I wasn't all that interested in boys in the eighth grade, except to talk about. Being around them made me nervous. I liked the *appearance* of being popular with boys, though, which is where Tammy's discards came into the picture. They would stay near me and Pauline at after-school dances, or at the mall, hoping to get a second chance, or at least a look, at their true love. This one guy, Carl, really had it bad. He'd give me flowery notes to pass on to her because he was too shy to speak.

"He's a nerd," Tammy said, reading one of his many notes.

"He's a nice guy, Tammy," I said, feeling sorry for Carl.

"A nice nerd," she said, tossing the note in the waste-basket, laughing.

"He's a lot better than Gary, who probably won't even graduate from eighth grade!" Pauline said.

"But you've got to admit, Gary is *much* cuter."

"You're *so* shallow!" I accused.

"Yeah, well, I'm only fourteen. I'll get deep later. Just because you have depth and sensitivity doesn't mean the rest of us need it."

We laughed. Ever since our English teacher wrote on one of my papers that I showed depth and sensitivity beyond my years, Tammy and Pauline had been making fun of me about it. But it was true. I thought about things more than they did.

I guess I'm kind of smart. I don't try to be. It just happens. And I like doing some of the things Pauline and Tammy think are boring. Like book reports. I read all the time when I'm home. It's like I can go to a different world when I'm reading. I forget about how my mom and my brother, David, fight all the time, or how my mom's always complaining about money. I get to see more possibilities when I read about other people and places.

Pauline and Tammy read some, but not the kind of thing you can report on. They've practically memorized the "good" parts in that book *Forever* by Judy Blume. And Tammy found a book called *The Joy of Sex* in the bottom drawer of her mom's dresser. It had pictures and everything. I couldn't believe my eyes. The things some people do. I wanted to throw up, but I couldn't stop looking.

Tammy's mom works in the mornings at a real estate office. For the first two weeks of our summer vacation, Pauline and I would go over to Tammy's about 10 o'clock. Pauline would bring sodas and I'd bring chips, and we'd take turns reading from the sex book. We could hardly get past a sentence without screeching or laughing hysterically.

That summer, after the eighth grade, besides reading *The Joy of Sex,* we'd take the beach bus down to Huntington and hang out there with a bunch of our old Palm Avenue buddies. We'd swim and lay in the sun and talk about high school.

"What if we don't get classes together?" Tammy asked on one of those days.

"We will. We're taking all the same stuff," Pauline said.

"Yeah, us and about eight hundred other freshmen," I said. "We might not even get the same lunch period."

"We've eaten lunch together since first grade," Tammy said. "We're not going to stop now!"

"Yeah. First grade. Remember Em's ketchup sandwiches?" We all laughed.

"We were poor," I said. "It was easy to nab a little bread and ketchup from Barb and Edie's on my way to school."

Barb and Edie's is a little bar and sandwich place across from the big furniture warehouse down on Fifth Street. My mom is Barb. My mom's been part owner there for as long as I can remember.

"Speaking of Barb and Edie's," Pauline said, "let's get off at the Fifth Street stop when we go home. I'm dying for a big glob of Edie's onion rings."

"Let's not," I said. "I can do without seeing The Barb today."

"Are you and your mom fighting again?" Tammy asked.

"Not really. But she's mad at David, and I don't want to answer any of her nosy questions about him."

"What's new?" Pauline said. "She's always mad at David."

"Yeah, but this time he's messed up. He took her old wedding ring and some pearl earrings that were my grandma's, and he hocked them. He used the money for his friend's bail. She never wears that stuff, but for some reason she decided to last night."

"Oh, no," Tammy said. "I'm surprised I didn't hear her clear over at my place. Did she explode?"

"Like a nuclear bomb! She's given him until Sunday to get her things back or move out."

"What does David say?" Pauline asked.

"No problemo."

"What does *that* mean, anyway?" Tammy said.

"I don't know. That's just what David always says."

"So okay. We won't go to Barb and Edie's today . . . C'mon in the water!" Pauline shouted and took off running.

Tammy and I jumped up and ran after her. The three of us swam out past the breakers, laughing and splashing.

The great thing about being friends for so long was that it was like a lifetime of non-stop talking. We could tell each other anything without being ashamed or embarrassed. And we didn't have to go into all the background stuff. We'd lived through everything together so nothing took much explaining.

Like with David, they knew how he and my mom had been fighting since he was about ten years old. And they knew it kept getting worse. They knew how much I loved David, and also how angry I got with him for doing such stupid things—like this bail money thing. David's friends were real losers. Maybe if he'd had the kind of friends I had, he wouldn't always be in so much trouble.

The wave we chose to bring us back to shore turned out to be about twice as big as I could handle. We all started swimming, trying to catch it and ride it in. Instead, it caught us. I was tumbled over and over, my lungs burning for air, not knowing which way was up or down, my arms flailing, trying to stop the tumbling. Just when I thought I couldn't take any more, I felt my knees scrape the sand. I stood up and looked for the others. Tammy's cheek was scraped and Pauline was coughing and spewing salt water, but we were all there.

Before we could even really catch our breath, we were laughing. I could feel tons of sand in the seat of my bathing suit and I guess they were in the same situation. We walked back in a few feet, keeping a close watch on incoming waves. We rinsed the sand out of our cracks and crevices and went back to our towels. We lay on our stomachs, in a kind of star pattern, so our heads were together and we could talk. We spent the next hour on what was our number one subject after *The Joy of Sex*—trying to predict what Hamilton High School had in store for us in September.

"Hey, listen," Pauline said. "No problemo. Are we temerarious or what?"

About 3:00, some of the guys came down from the surfing section of the beach. They sat on their boards near our towels. We talked for a while and then they started doing stupid boy stuff, like trying to untie our straps and pour sand down our bathing suits. Really, guys were such cretins sometimes. Pauline and I just ignored them when they started that stuff. We weren't their main targets, anyway. Tammy put up with it for a while but finally yelled at them, "Bug off, Bozos!"

One of them, Carl, looked hurt. The others just laughed. Pretty soon they picked up their boards and went over by some seventh graders, and we heard squealing and giggling and high-pierced shrieks coming from the new centers of male attention.

"I know one thing," Tammy said. "I'm not going to have any of these baby boys hanging around me at Hamilton. Not when the place is filled with junior and senior hunks."

"I'll bet the good ones are already taken," Pauline said.

"I don't think so. I think there'll be plenty to go around. Think so, Em?" Tammy asked.

"Hmmmm. I don't really care," I said. "I'm too young to be worrying about such things."

"Yeah, right. That's why you've been glued to *The Joy of Sex* every morning for the past two weeks," Tammy said, throwing a handful of sand in my direction.

We argued about which of us was most interested in the "S" subject until time to go back to the bus. I think we were all really interested, but nobody wanted to admit it.

Back home I took a long shower. Usually I take short showers because of California's drought. I'm big on recycling, too. If we don't each one of us care about the earth, we're not going to have much of a place to live pretty soon. But this night I let the hot water pound my back and stream through my freshly-shampooed hair. That's got to be one of the best things about going to the beach—coming home and getting totally clean.

I took the book I was reading to bed with me. Mom was working and David was out, so everything was peaceful. I guess I must have fallen asleep reading because it was about 3:00 when I heard a tapping at my window.

"Em. Emmy. Open the window. I want to talk to you."

It was David. Mom had taken his house keys from him months ago. He had a key to his room, which was part of the original garage and not connected to the house. Other than that, he wasn't supposed to even come inside if my mom wasn't home.

I opened the window and loosened the screen, and David climbed in. He sat on the edge of my bed.

"I've got to get out of here for a while, Emmy," he said.

"Where will you go?"

"I can't tell you, Little Sister. The Mom-monster would probably shove bamboo splinters under your fingernails until you broke."

David and I had all kinds of secret names for my mom—names we'd made up a long time ago. We called her The Barb, because she could be so sharp and hurtful at times, and Mom-monster, or Mom-witch. I know it wasn't very nice, but when we were little we thought the names gave us a secret power over her.

"Come on, David. Where are you going? I won't tell."

"I know. She probably won't even ask. She'll be glad to be rid of me."

I couldn't argue with him about that.

"I'm not sure where I'll end up—I've just got to get out of here. I can't take anymore raggin', you know?"

I nodded my head. It wasn't the first time David had left home. He was eighteen, but he'd been leaving home off and on since he was thirteen—just after my grandma died, and there was no one left to be a peacemaker between him and my mom.

"Well, I wanted you to know," he said. "You and me, we're the only real family we've got without Grandma."

I sort of wanted to stand up for Mom—say she's our family, too. But I knew what he meant. It wasn't like she seemed to be on our side, or very interested in us.

"I wuv you, Em."

"I wuv you, too, Dabe," I said, repeating a ritual from when I was three. It was easier, I guess, to say it like little kids, than to just come straight out and say we loved each other.

I sat up and put my arms around David. He held on for a long time. I smelled the sweet aroma of marijuana coming from his clothes and hair.

"When will you be back?" I asked.

"I'll give you a call sometime when I know Mommie Dearest will be out."

"Take care, David."

"You too," he said, then crawled out the window and was gone. He left walking. His truck still needed a transmission, and he'd sold his bike just a few weeks ago.

I drifted back to sleep, wishing things were different. Tammy's older brother was in his first year of college, and I don't think he'd ever been in trouble except for little stuff, like not taking out the trash or forgetting to feed the dog. I never heard anyone yelling at her house, and I was around there a lot.

I pretended David just left for college, but I couldn't convince myself of that for long. I worried about him. What would he do for food? I knew for a fact he didn't have any money. And where would he stay? Maybe a friend would take him in—but his friends were such scumbags.

I heard Mom's car in the driveway, then, after a long time, I heard her poking the key around the lock. She must have had too much to drink. I knew I should get up and let her in. It could take hours for her to get the door unlocked. I didn't want to see her though. I didn't like the way she looked when she was drunk, and I hated trying to talk to her like that. And if I got up and let her in, she would insist on talking. So I stayed in bed and listened.

Finally the door opened and I heard her stumbling around in the living room. When I heard her in the hallway, I pulled the covers up over my head. She opened my door.

"Emmy—you asleep?" she asked, fuzzy tongued.

I pretended I didn't hear her. She tried one more time, then went back down the hall to her own room.

In the distance I heard the howling of a dog, sad and piercing. "Please take care of my brother," I prayed to a God I wasn't even sure existed.

2

Hamilton High—home of the C.I.F. championship Bull Dogs and nationally honored debate team, the pride of Hamilton Heights. We'd gone to some of the football games before, and Pauline and Tammy and I often walked past it. But nothing had prepared us for how crowded it would be.

I guess three thousand or so high school students in a school meant for two thousand is enough to make any place seem crowded. Even though I knew all ninety-six of the kids from Palm who were now at Hamilton, that was still only ninety-six freshmen out of a field of 822.

The first week there I was lost all the time. My Beginning Chorus class was about two blocks away from my geometry class. We had seven minutes between classes, and the halls were so crowded there were times when I could barely move, much less walk fast. And my locker was at the far north end of the campus, not near any of my classes.

Going to the bathroom was an impossibility. At Palm, that quaint little school where the temerarious trio had reigned, number one was easy—recess or lunch time, the bathrooms were never crowded, they were clean, and the stalls all had doors on them. In the event of the need for an embarrassing number two, all we had to do was raise our hand during class and ask to be excused. How civilized!

At Hamilton, two of the bathrooms were closed for repair. The rest were filthy. None of the stalls had doors on them, and just to walk in for an instant was enough to give a person lung cancer. You could see a cloud of smoke in the hall outside the girls' rooms, and you could smell it about twenty-five feet in each direction. They really were mainly smoking rooms, although now and then there would be a fight in one of them.

"I'm going to get some of those adult diapers that old movie stars advertise on late night T.V.," I told Tammy after my first week as a high school inmate.

"Oh, that'll be cute under your new tight black skirt," she said sarcastically. "I'm sure that will impress the boys."

"I don't *care* about the boys, Tammy. I want to be able to concentrate on history sixth period without worrying about am I going to wet my pants? I'm desperate."

Tammy was no longer listening. She was looking past me to where two older guys were leaning against the wall.

"Look, that's Greg Stewart," she said in a half-whisper. "He's *so* fine." Tammy had this dreamy look on her face that I was seeing more and more often as she pointed out one fine guy after another. I could see she'd totally lost interest in my bathroom problem.

Of course, like with everything else that first semester at Hamilton, I adjusted. I learned not to drink anything before 2:30 in the afternoon on school days. That way I could last all through school without going to the bathroom.

Another thing that was hard to get used to at Hamilton was the way people were divided into their own little groups. At Palm everyone hung around with everyone else. There were all different kinds of people, but nobody seemed to notice. But at Hamilton, the Asian kids all sat together in the cafeteria at lunchtime. The soshes and jocks took over a courtyard with benches down near the gym. Cholo gang-bangers hung out under the bleachers, smoking cigarettes and looking mean.

The heavy metal kids who wore only black with a few chains here and there always gathered in the far corner of the student parking lot. The druggies inhabited the steps of a church about a block away from school.

Our trio and about ten others from Palm Avenue ended up with a lunch spot on the grass near the flag pole where we watched the action from a distance, uninvolved except for Tammy who kept up a running commentary on which guys were fine and which were bozos.

By the end of the first semester, things were getting better. For one thing, we'd proven ourselves on the soccer field. At first, the coach didn't even play us. Game after game we sat on the bench and watched.

Then one day he got really angry with two of the star players. They'd been coming late to practice and he'd been warning them, but it kind of seemed like they thought they could get away with a lot because they were good. But he benched them for two whole weeks.

That mixed up the whole balance of things, and that's when Pauline and Tammy and I started getting to play more often. We weren't stars or anything. Most of the girls on the team were bigger and more experienced. But we were good dependable players, and our coach began to rely on us. It was nice to be noticed again.

In Beginning Chorus, at Christmas time, we'd had a caroling party and ended up back at this girl's house where we sat around a giant fireplace and drank hot apple cider and sang. I'd never been in such a big, fancy house in my life.

I'm used to going into houses that are nicer than mine—mine's small and sort of run down. But this place was like something you'd see in the movies. And there were even two maids, *dressed in uniforms*, who served us. The important thing, though, was that between soccer friends and choir friends, I began to feel like I belonged.

As far as older men went, Tammy wasn't having much luck. She was still the girl of choice with the old Palm Avenue crowd and with plenty of other freshman boys. But the juniors and seniors she'd planned to move on to hardly noticed her. All Tammy could think about were certain junior and senior boys. Pauline and I thought the boy-topic was generally boring. It's funny how things turn out.

I hadn't seen my brother since that hot summer night when he climbed out my window and disappeared into the darkness. He called every couple of weeks, collect, when he knew Mom would be at work. I liked talking to him, but it wasn't the same as seeing him.

He always said things were fine—"No problemo"—but sometimes he sounded kind of lonesome and sad. When he'd called in January, though, he was happier than I'd heard him in a long time. He'd found a great job with some cool people. Pretty soon he was going to send Mom some jewelry that would make the stuff he took look like Pic-n-Save.

"What's the job?" I asked.

"Farming," he said.

"Big bucks learning to be a farmer?"

"I'm a specialist, Em."

"So what's your crop . . . broccoli?"

He just laughed.

"David," I whined. "It better be legal!"

"No problemo."

David always made a big deal of my birthday—I think partly because Mom never did. So I was missing him big time when February 2 rolled around and I was going to turn fifteen without him. Mom was still asleep on the couch with her coat pulled up over her. I was pretty sure she hadn't been out 'til three in the morning buying birthday presents for me.

I was all depressed and feeling sorry for myself by the time I got to school. But there were Pauline and Tammy waiting for me by the flagpole. They each held three giant "Happy Birthday" balloons—the silver, helium-filled kind. The balloons even had my name on them.

"HAPPY BIRTHDAY," they yelled. They came running up to me, holding out the balloons and laughing. I got all self-conscious, but I wasn't depressed anymore.

Later in the day, the three of us were fooling around, waiting for Mr. Michaels to get class started. Usually he started us singing as soon as the tardy bell rang. It was like an obsession with him to start on time—not like my history teacher who made a twenty-minute project of taking roll.

But this time Mr. Michaels was gathering the Hamilton Harmonics together in the front of the classroom. The Harmonics were twenty of the school's top singers, mostly juniors and seniors. They were my heroes. Mr. Michaels had already told me and Pauline we were good enough to get into a capella choir next year. But when we'd asked about the Harmonics, he'd just given a non-committal "We'll see."

Tammy had already decided to give up her singing career and join drill team next year. "I've only got two notes, but I've got lots of moves," she'd said, when she told us she wouldn't be auditioning for a capella.

Every year the Harmonics went on a national tour. This year they were going to Boston where they'd sing at Paul Revere's church and at Harvard. I was sitting there day-dreaming about being with them in Boston when Pauline punched me.

"Pay attention when I speak. ATTENTION!" she demanded.

"Yes, Sir." I saluted.

"Pauline the Marine!" Tammy said.

"Yeah, a drill instructor," I agreed.

"Oh, shut up," Pauline said, laughing good-naturedly at our reference to her habit of barking orders.

"Hammy Tammy," I said, reaching over and poking her in the thigh. I don't like to insult one of my friends without insulting the other.

Pauline shrieked with laughter.

"Better than canary legs," Tammy poked back at me.

We got hysterical then, laughing and choking on our own words. It sounds stupid, but that's how we were when we were freshmen.

"**A**ll right, singers, let's pay attention now," Mr. Michaels said, standing in his usual place by the piano. He was tall and tan, and his hair was totally white.

"Sopranos, stand up, please," he said, looking at our section. "Isn't this a wonderful bunch of girls?" he asked the Harmonics.

The group of twenty singers clustered around the piano looked at us and shrugged in unison, like maybe they'd practiced it before.

Mr. Michaels laughed. "They're much more wonderful than you were when you were in Beginning Chorus," he told them. "Remember how you looked in the ninth grade, Veronica?"

A girl, Veronica, I guess, groaned and hid her face behind the shoulder of the boy next to her.

"Exactly!" Mr. Michaels said, then turned back to us.

"Now, sopranos. Listen carefully. This may be difficult, but I think you can do it."

Tammy and Pauline started laughing again. I didn't get it.

"Will every one of you who does not have a birthday today please sit down."

I felt my face grow hot as the others sat, leaving me standing alone in front of the whole class. I started to sit back down, too, but Tammy and Pauline quick stuck all six balloons behind me. *Everyone* was watching me. I wanted to turn invisible, or faint, or die even, when I saw Mr. Michaels put the pitch pipe to his lips and knew what would happen next.

"Happy Birthday to you. Happy Birthday to you . . ." They sang a jazzed-up version in clear, perfect harmony. Then, just when I thought it would end, one of the boys stepped forward and opened his arms to me. As the others hummed in the background, he sang, "Emmy, Emmy, it's your birth-day" to some old fifties tune, and then the whole class joined in at the end. I sat down, laughing, covering my burning face with my hands.

When I looked up, the boy who had sung the fifties thing was smiling directly at me. "Happy birthday, Emmy," he said on his way out of the classroom.

"That's Art Rodriguez," Tammy whispered excitedly. "He's to die for, Emmy, and he sang right to you!"

I was speechless, but Tammy and Pauline certainly weren't.

"He's the one that conceited Amy chick in our gym class is always talking about. Remember?"

That's all Pauline and Tammy talked about for the rest of the day. Art Rodriguez. Art Rodriguez.

"Did you see the way he smiled at you?" Tammy asked. "God, I'd chop off my baby toe for one of those smiles. He is fine, fine, fine."

"Watch out, Emmy, or Tammy's gonna get your man," Pauline said.

"He's not my man. I don't even know him. He was singing on *assignment*. I wish you two could talk about something besides boys. It gets boring!"

"Ha. Maybe sometimes, but I don't think you're bored right now, you tall, skinny vamp, you," Tammy said.

"Vamp?" Pauline asked, looking puzzled.

"VAMP!" I said. "You know, short for vampire—like that tall building in New York. The Vampire State Building."

But all the time I was pretending not to be interested in the Art Rodriguez talk, I was seeing his face before me and hearing his sweet tenor voice.

The day after my birthday, I saw Art standing near my locker, talking to Amy. When he caught me looking at him, he smiled. "Happy birthday, Emmy," he said.

What a smile he had. Dimples in both cheeks and the whitest teeth I'd ever seen outside a toothpaste ad. Butterflies fluttered around in my stomach and I looked away, embarrassed.

For the next two weeks I saw him everywhere—in the snack bar, on the way to gym, in the music room. Each time I saw him, he would smile that smile and tell me happy birthday. My heart would pound so hard I was afraid he'd hear it. I'd never even been out on a date, and here I was getting all weak in the knees and gushy feeling over this guy who half the girls in school lusted after. Who was I fooling?

On Valentine's Day Art was waiting for me after school.

"Can I talk to you for a minute?" he asked.

"Sure," I said, waiting for him to talk. Pauline and Tammy were staring. Tammy's mouth was hanging open. I swore it was, but she denied it.

We stood there, the four of us, for what felt like a long time. Finally Tammy and Pauline got the hint and walked on without us.

"I know this is a little late to be asking, Emmy. But are you busy tonight?"

Busy, I thought—not unless you call watching reruns busy. I shook my head no. I couldn't talk.

"There's a party at Bobby's house tonight. You know— Bobby Reyes from choir?"

I nodded my head yes, even though I had no idea who he was talking about.

"Do you want to go with me? It'll be a good party."

I nodded yes. I wished I could talk, but so far I'd only been able to communicate by head nods. What a dork.

"Where do you live? I'll pick you up about 8:00."

Where *did* I live? Finally it came back to me—my voice, my address, and I was able to give directions to my house. I admitted it earlier, didn't I? I am an absolute, black belt, social retard.

CHAPTER

3

"**T**AMMY!" I screamed into the phone as soon as she answered. "You go to the party with Art. I think I'm sick."

"I'd love to, but it's you he asked, remember? I don't know why, when he could have had me, but, men, who knows what moves them?"

"Don't go getting philosophical on me. I need HELP!"

"So, okay. It's jeans, the tight ones, and my black silk blouse."

"But Tammy, I can't even talk to him."

"Don't worry. He probably doesn't want to talk anyway."

"TAMMY."

"Okay, okay. My mom has to go to the market, and she said she'd drive me over so I could drop off the blouse. Don't worry. You'll look great."

I hadn't even thought about worrying about my looks, I was so worried about not being able to talk. Now I was really worried.

About 7:00 I heard Tammy and her mom walking up the driveway. They were laughing, like they were friends. My mom always took the late shift at Barb and Edie's. She worked from 4:00 to midnight. Edie took the early shift, 10:00 to 4:00, because she wanted to be home with her kids in the evening. My mom never thought about being home with us. As I heard the laughter in the driveway, I wanted some of that for myself.

"Hey, Kiddo," Tammy's mom said as soon as I opened the

door. "I hear you've got a date with a dreamboat."

I smiled. Sometimes Tammy's mom talked funny.

"Here," Tammy said, handing me her blouse. "Don't tell Pauline. She wanted to borrow it last week, but I wouldn't let her. This is important, though. Just promise not to sweat."

"Pretend the party is a Brownie meeting. You'll do fine," Mrs. Preston said.

That's how Tammy and I got to be good friends. Her mom was our Brownie leader in the first grade. I was always the last one there, after everyone else had been picked up. Sometimes my mom would call to say she'd be late, but mostly she'd just show up hours after everyone else was gone. I don't think I noticed at the time, but looking back on it, I think she probably shouldn't have been driving some of those times either.

I guess Mrs. Preston felt sorry for me, because she started asking me to stay for dinner and spend the night on Brownie nights. Tuesdays. Those were my favorite nights. I still spend the night at Tammy's on Tuesdays sometimes. Pauline used to stay now and then, but her folks were kind of strict and wanted her home at night.

"Did I ever tell you about my first date with Ron?" Mrs. Preston asked.

"Hundreds of times, Mom," Tammy said. "Besides, she's not getting married, she's just going to a party."

"Okay, don't listen to the wisdom of your first Brownie guru," Mrs. Preston said. "I just pray to God you girls learned all you need to know from *The Joy of Sex.*"

Tammy and I just looked at each other. I hoped my face wasn't as red as Tammy's. Her mom laughed.

"What? You think I don't know who's been reading that book? The pages are dog-eared, there's salt and potato chip grease all over page 127. . .

"Come on, Tammy, we've got to get to the market," Mrs. Preston said, still laughing. "Have fun, Emmy," she called to me as they turned to leave. When Tammy was almost to the car she turned and ran back.

"127," she whispered. "What was on page 127?"

"I don't know. Positions?"

"Oh, God," she groaned.

I'd changed clothes three times between when Tammy and her mom left and Art arrived to pick me up. We were quiet in the car, but somehow it didn't feel awkward. I don't know why. Not that I'd had all that much experience with boys, but whenever I was with a boy before it was like I was desperate for something to say. And I'd get really nervous.

Sometimes I'd have this overwhelming desire to stare at a guy's fly. And then I would force myself to look at the ceiling. Really, I had some serious social handicaps. But with Art, things were different from the very beginning. He said so, too.

"It's easy to be quiet with you, Emmy. I like that," he told me on the way to the party. "Some girls have to talk constantly. That wears me out."

I couldn't believe my ears. He liked the very thing in me that I was so worried about. And then, because he liked my silence, it became easy to talk.

We sat in the car for a while, across the street from the party, before we went in. Art pointed to the house where some kids were walking up to the front door.

"That's Bobby Reyes' house. He's my oldest friend since before preschool. And that's my house, right next door."

It was an average kind of neighborhood, maybe a little bit nicer than my street, but not as nice as where Tammy lived. Bobby's house was bigger than most of the others, and Art's was smaller. But Art's yard was amazing. Like a park or something, with all kinds of flowers and plants—the kind you only see at the arboretum. I thought of the brown lawn and torn-apart truck in my yard and felt embarrassed now that I'd seen where Art lived.

"I'd take you to meet my folks, but they're out tonight."

"Hey, Art? Are you coming in or are you going to sit in that insect you call a car all night?"

Art laughed as a short, dark guy came walking over to the car.

"Bobby," Art said. "This is Emmy."

Bobby leaned down and smiled at me through Art's open window.

"Happy birthday, Emmy," Bobby said. He and Art looked at me and laughed, but it wasn't like they were laughing at me. Art squeezed my hand.

"Everybody's out back," Bobby said.

We got out of the car and walked across the street with Bobby, following him through his empty living room and dining room to a big, glassed-in porch.

Absolutely everyone was older than I was—all juniors and seniors. It was a big party, with a deejay and kegs—not like the cake and ice cream birthday parties which were the only kind I was ever invited to.

"Do you want a beer or a soda?" Art asked.

I looked around. Nearly everyone there was drinking beer. I wanted to be like everyone else, but I was a kind of anti-alcohol freak because of not wanting to be like my mom.

"Root beer?" he asked.

"Okay."

He came back with root beer for us both.

"I don't drink," he said. "I don't care if anyone else does, but my brother got in some bad trouble and I think things would have been really different if he hadn't been drunk. I don't want to end up like him, poor guy."

"My brother's in trouble, too," I said. "But with him it's because of drugs. I don't think he's an addict or anything, but he's always getting fired from jobs, or sometimes these people call and leave scary messages. My mom kicked him out. He's a really nice guy, but he's just always in trouble."

We talked on and on, about our older brothers, and what it was like being the "good" kid in the family. It was as if we had known each other for years. It turned out that Art's brother, José, was lots worse off than David.

"One night he and some of his cholo friends were hanging out in front of our house, drinking and acting tough," Art told me. "If my dad had been home, he'd have sent Joey's friends on their way. But my folks had gone to Vegas for the weekend, so they were all hanging around my house."

It surprised me to hear Art talk about his brother's cholo friends. Art was about as cholo as my great-uncle Elmer. I didn't even know what a cholo was, except for the guys who hung out under the bleachers. They always wore baggy pants with army kinds of belts with silver buckles. Art wore jeans and sweat shirts and hung out with the jocks.

"So anyway," Art said, "I was in watching the Lakers and I heard all this noise in the garage. I went out and these guys, all of them drunk, were banging around under the dashboard of my mom's car. They hot-wired it and José got in the driver's seat. The other five crammed in wherever. I tried to talk José out of taking the car, but he just laughed at me. 'We'll be back before you know it, School Boy,' he told me, and they were gone. It was so stupid. I can't believe how stupid it was."

"So what happened? Did they get in trouble for taking your mom's car?"

Art took a big, slow swallow of root beer, then tossed the empty can into a huge plastic barrel that was sitting in the corner of the room.

"The whole school knows about my brother. I feel it when I walk down the hall. I feel them saying, 'There's José Rodriguez's brother.' Everyone knows."

"Not me."

He gave me a long look. I can't explain it, but the look in his eyes gave me a funny feeling—like the way my stomach feels when I'm in the front seat of the Cyclone at Magic Mountain, and we're paused at the very top of the highest incline. I want out but there's no way, and I know I'm going to plunge straight to the ground.

"C'mon, let's walk out back by the pool," he said, standing

and reaching for my hand.

I know holding hands is no big deal, but I felt special and like I belonged, walking hand in hand with Art across that room full of the older Hamilton High kids who seemed to have it all.

Amy was standing in the doorway between the den and the pool.

"Excuse us," Art said, guiding me past her toward the patio.

Amy looked great—she probably had the shiniest black hair and the bluest eyes of anyone I had ever seen. If I could have chosen to look like anyone else in the world, Amy Parker would have been my choice. I smiled at her but I guess she wasn't all that impressed with me. In fact, she barely glanced at me. But she sure flashed a killer smile at Art. He mumbled "Hi," and led the way toward the far end of the pool.

We sat cross-legged on the diving board. Our slightest movement gave the board a gentle spring. There was a perfect sliver of a moon, off to our right. We were the only ones out there. The sounds of music and voices were muffled, as if coming from far away. I felt good with Art—easy and peaceful.

I guess he must have felt the same way because he said, "I don't know why I'm telling you this. I never talk about it, not even to Bobby. We've been friends since preschool and we talk about almost everything, but not about my brother. Not anymore. When we were little kids, José was like some kind of god to us—always protecting us from the bigger kids. Bobby asked at Christmas if he could go with me to visit José, but I just said, 'No, Man. Think of him free.'"

"What do you mean?" I asked.

"He's locked up. Chino. Eight years. Six, maybe, for good behavior, but I don't think he can stay out of trouble there. I hope so, but I doubt it. There are fights every day, over nothing."

"Chino?"

"Yeah. The prison."

"What for?"

"For stupidity. God, I still can't believe how one stupid mistake can so totally mess up a person's life. His so-called friends, his *homies*," Art said sarcastically, "had more in mind than just the little joy ride they'd mentioned to José.

"Two of the guys in the car were known as Psycho and L'il Loco. I mean, God, do you follow the advice of people named Psycho and L'il Loco? . . . Anyway, 'Let's cruise the Flats,' they'd said."

"The Flats?"

"Yeah, you know, the barrio—gangbanger turf . . . José would have known better if he hadn't been so drunk, but he drove right to the corner where all the Flatters hang. 'Slow down,' they told him, and he did. José told me he knew he was in trouble when he realized the windows were down. He heard them call out 'Eighth Street.' He heard shots and thought they were being shot at. 'Jam it,' they told him, but he'd already pressed the pedal to the floor.

"He said it was funny, but all he could think about was he hoped Mom's car didn't end up with any bullet holes. It turned out that it was the guys in her car who were doing the shooting. José didn't even know that until the cops came to get him the next morning."

"But why? He was only driving."

"Yeah, but an eleven-year-old boy was killed. He'd gone to tell his older brother to come home—they were getting ready to cut their grandma's birthday cake. Eleven years old," Art repeated. "I don't care what neighborhood he lived in, he should still be out there, going to school and pitching for his Little League team."

"I think I saw something about that boy on T.V.," I said, remembering a story on the local news. "He'd just won some science award or something the day before he was killed?"

"That's the one," Art said. "Ramon Garcia. The baby of the family. Ramon Garcia. José prays for Ramon's soul every day, but I don't think the boy's family is impressed."

"Why did they do it—Psycho and Loco or whoever?"

"Getting even. One of their homeboys had been killed two weeks before. The guys from the Flats had shot up a party in Eighth Street territory. José had been at the party and he knew the guy who was killed. But even so, he would never have driven down to the Flats if he'd known Psycho and L'il Loco were packin'.

"My brother wasn't all caught up in that gang shit—just some of his friends were—you know, people he'd grown up with. He partied with them, but that's all. He would never have been involved in a drive-by if he hadn't been so drunk he didn't know what was happening.

"And now some poor kid is dead, and eight years of my brother's life are lost. Probably his whole life is lost because I think prison is going to ruin him for good. He's been out there for nine months, and already his eyes are going dead."

Art sat silently, holding my hand tight and staring down into the water. I didn't know what to say. I felt how he hurt. I thought about how I missed my own brother, and how I'd felt when my grandmother died. I knew how it was to not have someone around who had protected you as a little kid.

We sat for a long time, feeling the gentle spring of the diving board beneath us. "Do you visit your brother often?"

"Every Sunday morning. My dad and I go. My mom can't stand it. She goes to church and prays instead."

We talked on and on then, about school and friends and future. Art planned to go to Stanford and major in business. He had it all planned out through a program at school called Project Hope.

"What about you?" he asked.

"I don't know. My mom wants me to be a bookkeeper, but I think that might get boring. I know more what I don't want to do than what I want to do."

"Everybody knows that," Art said. "That's the easy part."

I laughed. "I'm just a kid," I told him.

"Maybe. Maybe not," he said, smiling the smile that gave me jelly knees.

About 11:00, when the first keg was emptied, some of the people at the party started getting crazy, jumping in the pool with their clothes on and doing ape screams like they were in the jungle. We got off the diving board just in time, or we'd have been dumped in the pool.

"Let's get out of here," Art said.

When we got in his car, he wanted to know what time I had to be home. It embarrassed me to tell him that I could be out as late as I wanted. Everyone else I knew had a curfew.

"But if I kept you out until 4:00 in the morning, I bet your mom would have the cops out after me."

I shook my head no.

We stopped at a deli and Art bought two sandwiches and some chips and sodas. He used the pay phone to call his folks. It was around eleven-thirty when we got to the beach.

I know it sounds silly, but we sang all the way down there—everything from "Itsy Bitsy Spider" and the Sesame Street song to "Dona Nobis Pacem," a song the combined choirs did at Hamilton's Christmas concert. Then Art finished our traveling duet show by doing his solo version of "Happy Birthday, Dear Emmy."

At the beach we walked out on the pier and watched ancient men fishing. Then we went down by the water and walked barefoot, letting the waves come up around our feet and ankles. We sat at the edge of the dry sand, watching the seagulls dive and strut.

The lights of a lone boat, far out in the ocean, captured our attention. Who was on it? Where were they going? Why? After the lights disappeared into distant blackness, we ate our sandwiches, together with plenty of wind-blown sand, and washed down with sodas. Art put his arm around me and, like with everything else that evening, it felt good, and natural.

"I have to be home by 2:00," he said, checking his watch. "After all my mom and dad have been through with José, I try not to give them anything to worry about. Usually I'm home by midnight, but I convinced my mom this was special."

He stood, brushing the sand from his clothes, and put his hand down to help me up. When I stood, he put both arms around me and pulled me close to him. I tasted the light salt spray on his lips as he kissed me once, then pulled away and looked at me. He leaned toward me again and kissed me longer. I felt the tip of his tongue at the edge of my mouth. Whenever I heard about people doing the tongue in mouth thing, I was totally grossed out. But it turned out that I liked it after all.

If I could relive one feeling, like for the rest of my life, it would be the feeling of those two kisses on the beach. It's sad to think that the very best feeling of a person's life has already passed by the time she's sixteen. But it has. No matter what kisses I may get in the future, they won't feel as good as when I believed in love.

CHAPTER

4

Art called Saturday morning, and we talked for a long time.

"Could you give it a rest, Em?" my mom yelled from the kitchen. "I'm expecting a call, and I don't want the phone tied up all morning."

She was so loud I guess Art heard her because he said, "I guess we'd better hang up . . . see you at seven?"

"Okay," I said. Tammy and Pauline and I sort of had plans to hang out at Tammy's—rent a movie and call out for pizza. Her mom and dad were going out and Tammy had to baby-sit her little sister, Bonnie. Bonnie was only six.

When I told them I was going out with Art, Pauline said, "My mom told me this would happen. Somebody'd get a boyfriend and that would be the end of our threesome."

"It's just for tonight," I said. "We're still going to the barbecue at your house tomorrow afternoon."

I felt guilty, though. I'd not even thought about our pizza/ movie plan until after I hung up from talking with Art.

"Don't be dumb, Pauline. Of course Em's going out with Art. Wouldn't you?"

"Not if I already had plans with my friends," she said.

"Well, I would!" Tammy said. "If some one of those fine junior guys asked me out, I'd drop our little social plans in a millisecond, and you should, too."

"But what about us—our trio?" Pauline whined.

"We won't stop being friends when we get boyfriends,"

Tammy said. "We'll just rearrange things."

"Well, I don't like it and I don't think it's fair," Pauline said.

"You're right, Pauline," I said.

Tammy threw her wadded-up old sweat shirt at me.

"Here I am, standing up for you, and you turn on me!"

"So are you going to break your date with Art?" Pauline asked.

"No, but I'll try to be more careful next time."

"Then you're a fool," Tammy said.

Later, sitting by the fountain at the mall, we laughed about our argument, but I knew we weren't exactly over it.

When Art picked me up for the movie, his friend Bobby and Amy were with him. We saw "Terminator Fifteen" or something. After, we decided to go to In-N-Out for hamburgers. There was a line of cars that was over two blocks long. Kids were out of their cars, talking in windows, checking out the scene.

"It looks like a long wait," Amy said. "You probably have to be home real soon, don't you, Emmy? I mean, being so young . . ."

This was the first thing she'd said to me all evening. I don't know what her problem was, but she was a real witch, if you know what I mean.

"No, I have plenty of time," I said. "But what about you, Amy, being so old and all? Don't you have to be home soon to apply your anti-wrinkle face cream?"

Bobby and Art howled with laughter while Amy sat statue-like, looking out the window to her left.

After hamburgers and cokes, we cruised around for a while. Art took me home last, and we sat out front in his car, talking. About 1:30 my mom came driving down the street in her beat-up old Chevy Citation.

"Is that your mom?" Art said, watching her car weave slightly turning into our driveway.

I thought about lying. No, it's a burglar—or our late night

cleaning lady—or an alien disguised as an earth person—
but I knew he'd meet her sooner or later, anyway.

"She's not a great driver, is she?'"

"Sometimes she's better than others."

My heart sank as I saw The Barb walking back down the
driveway toward us. She went over to Art's side of the car
and tapped on the window. When Art rolled it down, she
stuck her hand inside.

"Hi," she said. "I'm Barbara, Emmy's mom."

"Art Rodriguez," Art said, shaking her hand, "pleased to
meet you, Mrs. Morrison."

"Barbara will do. Mrs. Morrison makes me feel eighty
years old, especially when spoken by such a handsome
young lad." She laughed her loud, gravelly laugh as I sank
low in the seat.

"All right, Barbara," Art said. I could tell he was embarrassed to use her first name.

"Well, good night, kids," she said, and walked back
toward the house. "Remember, love is blind but the neighbors ain't."

"I like your mom," Art said.

"She gets kind of carried away sometimes."

"At least she's friendly. Not like my mom. If that had been
my mom, she would have yelled at me to get in the house,
and she would have pretended you weren't even here."

"Is Amy your mom?" I asked.

Art laughed. I liked that I could make him laugh. In all
of my previous life, the only ones who had laughed at my
jokes had been girls. Well . . . David, but brothers don't
exactly count.

Soon, Art and I were seeing each other all the time. He
picked me up for school and took me home after. I still ate
lunch with Tammy and Pauline, but the rest of the time it
was Art, Art, Art. When Art walked me to class, with his
arm around me or holding my hand, I felt protected and like
I was part of the Hamilton High inner circle. And where

before the only people who said hi to me in the halls were my old friends from Palm Avenue, now people whose names I didn't even know would smile and say hi and call me by name. It was a trip how things changed so fast.

Usually my mom and I only saw each other on weekends. I left for school before she got up, and I was in bed long before she got home. Even if she came straight home from work, which she usually did not, she still didn't get home until 1:00 or so. I will say one thing for my mom. She worked hard at the cafe and she always paid our bills on time, but she wasn't exactly a big part of my life, like some moms are with their kids.

I'd signed my own report cards and permission slips for so long, the school would probably have accused me of forgery if I started bringing notes with my mom's real signature. It wasn't that I *wanted* to be a forger, I could just never get her attention long enough for her to sign anything. She hardly ever even looked at my report cards. "Oh, I know they're okay," she'd say, waving my hard-earned "A"s away without so much as a glance.

I don't know how I'd have turned out if it hadn't been for my gramma and Tammy's mom. When we were little and it was raining, or we stayed late at school for sports or rehearsals, Tammy's mom was always there to pick us up. If I needed help with a costume or supplies for a project, Tammy's mom helped, and she never made me feel like I was a bother.

As for my gramma, she'd lived in the house next door until she died. She taught me and David to love music and to bake cookies, and she took us to the mountains every year after the first snowfall. She taught me always to ask myself "What if?" whenever I had a big decision to make. "Think about what will happen if you do this—what will happen if you don't. Remember, Emily there are no easy answers in this life."

But the best part was how she loved us. Her face would

light up, and her eyes would sparkle when she saw me
walking up her steps. She had the same light and sparkle
for David, too.

Even after four years, I still cried for missing her. It had
been an accident on the freeway. One of those multiple pile-
ups. She was crushed by a semi-truck. She'd gone to the
other side of town to get a special deal on boots for David for
Christmas, and then she was gone.

At the funeral he kept sobbing, "I don't want boots, I want
Gramma," over and over again. And then weeks later, a
policeman showed up at our door with a package containing
Gramma's purse and the boots. That was the first time
David ran away from home.

One morning, after Art and I had been going together for
a month or so, I was surprised to see my mom sitting at the
kitchen table when I wandered out for my morning juice.
She was sipping coffee and smoking a cigarette. At thirty-
five she was younger than most of my friends' moms. When
she went to work or out with friends, she looked pretty and
almost young. But in the mornings? She could have been an
ad for a scary movie—"Moms from Hell." Her hair, "bottle
blonde" her friend Edie called it, stuck out all over. She had
double bags under her eyes, and I could smell her stale gin
and cigarette breath from across the room. I preferred that
she stay in bed in the mornings.

"Emmy," she said, in her hoarse, morning voice, "Mrs.
Dugan called yesterday."

"Oh? How is she?" I asked, taking a carton of orange juice
from the refrigerator and pouring some into my glass.

"We didn't discuss her health. She wanted me to know
that 'that Mexican boy's car is here for hours every day.'"

"Yeah? So? I hate when people are prejudiced."

"That's not the point. She thinks the two of you shouldn't
be here together unsupervised, and she's probably right."

"Mom. Art brings me home from school. We study. Sometimes we listen to music. Then he goes home for dinner."

"Well, you shouldn't be here without an adult."

I groaned. "It never bothered you before," I said. "And what about Pauline and Tammy? You don't care when they're here. And nosy old Mrs. Dugan doesn't care either, I guess."

"That's different. They're girls."

"Oh, so because of a racist neighbor and a sexist mom, I'm not supposed to have a friend over?"

"No. Because it doesn't look right, that's why," Mom said.

"How do you think it looks when you have your so-called friends sleep over?"

"THAT'S ENOUGH, EMMY," she yelled. "YOU'RE NOT TO HAVE HIM HERE WHEN I'M NOT HOME, AND THAT'S FINAL."

"But, Mom . . ."

"AND BESIDES, NO ONE HAS SLEPT OVER HERE SINCE JEROME AND I BROKE UP. I'M KEEPING MY LOVE LIFE AWAY FROM HOME. AND THAT'S NONE OF YOUR BUSINESS, EITHER!"

"But . . ."

"And another thing. Stop taking collect calls from David. It's getting to be entirely too much. And it wouldn't hurt you to vacuum around here every few days or so, either."

That's my mom. She'd go for months without complaining, and then once she got started, she'd come up with a whole list of things. When she got mad, she'd start using phrases like "That's enough. That's final. That's entirely too much."

"What does Mrs. Dugan care, anyway?" I asked

"Oh, I don't know, Em." Mom said, "She's probably just jealous because you don't go over there after school anymore. You know, she's old and lonely, and she doesn't have anything to do but sit and look out her window all day long."

Mrs. Dugan was the lady who moved into my gramma's house after the accident. I'd been so in the habit of going to that house that I continued, even though my grandmother no longer lived there. I think maybe I was looking for a replacement, and Mrs. Dugan liked me.

Until the eighth grade, I would stop by Mrs. Dugan's almost every day after school. She always had something sweet for me, and she'd ask me about school and tell me about how things were when she was a girl.

She had thousands of slides from trips she and "the mister" took before he died. When she got out her slide projector, we made a party of it with tea and little cakes and linen napkins.

Pauline and Tammy went with me once to see the slides of Egypt. I was fascinated by Egypt, the pyramids and the Great Sphinx, but my friends were bored by Mrs. Dugan's detailed stories. Not me. Honestly, from about the fifth to the seventh grade, I think I probably learned as much from Mrs. Dugan's slides and stories as I did in school.

But then she started telling the same stories over and over. And I noticed her house smelled funny. Then she started complaining constantly about how awful the world had become. She got extra locks on her doors, and she always kept her blinds closed. She'd sit in a chair by her front window and lift one blind with her crooked index finger, but other than that, the blinds were closed tight. She was still always nice to me, it just stopped being fun going there.

I rinsed my glass out and turned it upside down in the drainer.

"Use soap, Emmy."

"Why? I use this same glass every day," I said, holding up a glass Art had bought me at the swap meet. It had my name engraved on it in fancy old-English lettering. "You don't have to worry about my germs. Just don't use my glass."

Mom sighed. "I'm going back to bed for a while. I mean what I say though, Em. Don't bring Art here after school," she said. "I mean it!"

The advantage to having a neglectful, disinterested parent was that no one ever told me what to do. Then all of a sudden my mother thought she could boss me around? No way.

After school that day, Art parked his car in the church parking lot around the corner from my house. We walked to my house. Art took the long way so he wouldn't pass Mrs. Dugan's place. When he got to my driveway, he crouched low and ran next to the fence which divided the two properties. I held the front door open for him, and he stayed crouched until he got inside. We sat on the floor, laughing. Sneaking Art into the house felt like a challenge—an adventure.

"What if your mom decides to check on you?" he asked.

"She won't. They get real busy at the cafe about this time when the warehouse workers get out. You're safe."

"But what if she came anyway?"

I laughed. He was frowning so hard his eyebrows were practically meeting in the middle of his forehead.

"Where would I hide?" he said, glancing around the house. He walked to the back door and looked outside.

"There's no place to hide," he said, still frowning.

I laughed even harder. "Why do moms worry you so? You're always worried about doing stuff just right for your mom, and now my mom's got you all worried, and you've only met her once."

"I know. Most guys would just say, 'Cool, Emmy's sneaking me in, who cares about the mom.' But I can't. This thing with my brother really gets to me, Em. I've seen my mom so hurt, the life practically crushed out of her, and all she ever did was try to do right by me and José—I don't want to be a part of hurting anyone's mom, mine or yours."

"Okay," I said. "I'm sorry I laughed. I think my mom wouldn't care that much."

"Bobby says I shouldn't worry so much about pleasing my mom. He thinks I let her run my life. But I'm all she's got now and I want her to be proud of me. It's like now I've got to be twice as good, because of José. That's just how I feel."

I leaned my head on his shoulder and kissed his neck

lightly, one kiss after another at that soft place just below
his jaw. He lifted my chin and returned my kisses, neck,
chin, lips. My insides got all warm and mushy, and when I
looked in his eyes, they had softened. His frown was gone.

"I know a place with an escape hatch," I said.

"Where?"

"My brother's old room. We could study in there, and if
my mom ever did come check, which she won't, I could crawl
through the window into my bedroom and you'd just stay in
David's room."

We spent the afternoon cleaning out the old garage room.
It smelled dank and musty, but we opened the window and
door and I shook out all the linens. Art dusted and swept and
did all of the inside chores just in case Mrs. Dugan decided
to look out her back window instead of the front one. By four-
thirty the old place looked pretty good. We had two Mom-
drills.

"Okay, she's just opened the front door," Art said in a
whisper. "Now she's inside."

I quick slipped through David's door and around to my
own slightly opened window. I crawled inside, silently,
without a hitch. Then I went back to the garage room.

"Mission accomplished," I said.

"Roger," Art laughed.

It reminded me of when the trio built a secret clubhouse
behind Pauline's garage. We used two giant refrigerator
boxes that we dragged all the way from the furniture
warehouse to Pauline's. It was great, until the first heavy
rain. Dave's room didn't leak though. Besides, it never
rained in California anymore. (That was another theme of
Mrs. Dugan's. The communists were emitting anti-rain
signals from their satellites.)

We sat side by side on David's bed and worked on math—
me on geometry and Art on Algebra II.

"How come you're taking geometry? I didn't get geometry
until tenth grade."

"I told you. I'm smart," I said.

"I am, too," he said.

"Not smarter than me," I said.

"Than *I*, Smarty," he corrected.

"Well then, I'm stronger than you," I said, throwing myself at him and pinning him to the bed. He rolled over, but he couldn't hold me down. We laughed and wrestled and tickled and laughed some more.

"I give up, Emmy. You're too much for me," Art gasped, holding his sides, trying to protect his most ticklish spots.

"Darned right," I said, worming a finger into a rib and watching him squirm.

"Shhhh," he said, suddenly serious. "I think I heard something. Mom drill!"

I listened. Nothing.

"Gotcha!" he said, pouncing on me and pinning me down.

"Say uncle," he ordered.

I laughed.

"Uncle, uncle, uncle," he demanded.

"Art! Look!" I said, jerking my head in the direction of the clock on David's chest of drawers. "Six o'clock!"

He jumped and I squirmed away.

"Gotcha," I said, pointing at the clock that said 5:20.

"Yep. I better go pretty soon, anyway." He stacked his books neatly on the bed and stood to leave. Dinner was at six at his house, and he and his mom, dad, and grandmother all sat at the table and ate together. I wondered what that would be like.

"Come here, Sweet Em," he said, pulling me up and toward him. He kissed me long and hard, his tongue teasing the tip of my own. I felt the warmth of his body against mine and pulled closer, tighter against him. He reached for my hand, guiding it. "Feel how hard, Emmy. For you . . . Do you ever want more?"

"Yes. Sometimes. Do you?" I whispered.

"Always."

"I get scared."

"I love you, Em. I would never do anything to hurt you."

"I love you, Art," I told him. "I can't believe we're together. I'm afraid I'm dreaming."

He kissed me again, then picked up his books and was gone.

Later in the evening, when David called, I told him about Art. I'd already told him a little, but now I admitted to being in love.

"I wish I was there to watch out for you. Maybe I should come home."

"Come home, please. I'm dying to see you. Art and I even cleaned up your room."

"What do you mean? Why'd you do that?"

I told him all about it, including the Mom drills. I thought he'd laugh his head off, but he didn't.

"I don't like it, Em. You'd better not be having sex with this guy. If he hurts you, I'll come down there and cut off his nuts. You can tell him that for me!"

"David, I love him. I'm happy. I thought you'd be happy for me," I said, choking back a sob.

"I'm sorry, Em," he said. "I guess it's hard to think of you growing up and me being so far away."

"You'd like him if you could only meet him."

"Okay, okay. I guess not every guy's like me. But Em, most of them are. They're sex crazed and they'll say anything. I'm serious, Em, hang on to your virginity until you're about thirty-two. And don't forget about AIDS. Do you know about AIDS? Shit, I really ought to be there."

"So come home. Mom'd probably let you back by now."

"It's just that I've got this deal going, Em. I can't leave right now. I've got too much at stake."

"I think I've got a lot more to worry about with you than you do with me," I told him.

"That's all *you* know," he said.

The last thing he said to me was, "Stay out of my room with this Art guy."

I finished my homework and talked on the phone to both

Tammy and Pauline. "Get me a date with one of Art's friends," Tammy asked for about the hundredth time.

When I talked to Pauline she complained about how boy crazy Tammy was, and how we didn't have as much fun as we used to. Nothing like someone saying you're not having fun together to make it impossible to have fun together.

I wanted the trio to be as important as ever, but it wasn't. Tammy and Pauline and I would always, for sure, be special friends. But the person who held my thoughts and attention was Art—sweet, handsome, loving, intelligent, sexy Art.

When I undressed for bed that night, I stood naked before the mirror in my room. My body was lean and muscular from years of athletic activity. My skin was very light—too light in places where you could see the outline of veins near the surface. My pubic hair was red.

The first week at Hamilton High, one of the older, snotty girls in gym made a remark about my red "bush" when I was getting out of the shower. I was so embarrassed I got some trumped-up excuse from gym for the next week. But now I don't think I'd be embarrassed by that remark. I mean, who wants one of those ugly black patches, anyway?

I quick grabbed my nightgown and pulled it on. What was wrong with me anyway, standing naked in front of a mirror? Was I turning into some kind of pervert?

In bed, I thought about Art. I ran my hands across my body, pretending they were his hands, wondering how it would feel with him inside me. The thought of such a thing had repulsed me just months ago, when we were reading *The Joy of Sex*. Now I tingled at the thought of me with Art, doing IT.

I was scared, but I knew it would happen soon. God, how I loved him. How I wanted to please him. How I wanted to be totally his, and to have him be totally mine.

CHAPTER

5

In May, Art was gone for five days to Boston on choir tour. We had seen each other every day since Valentine's day. Every day I had seen his dimpled smile and felt his warm touch.

I knew I would miss him, but I didn't know how much. I was numb without him.

He called twice while he was away. He was filled with news of Boston—dinner and dancing at the Hard Rock Cafe, their concert in Boston Common, seeing the church that had held lanterns warning the revolutionaries that the British were coming. I desperately wanted to be there.

Even though he told me he missed me and loved me, it was scary to hear how much fun he was having without me.

"Next year, Em, you and I will be on choir tour together. Mr. Michaels is already talking about it—maybe New York— there's a music festival there next May."

"What if I don't make it?"

"Don't make it?" he yelled into the phone. "You sing better than any soprano in the Harmonics right now, and most of them are graduating. Michaels will beg you to try out. You'll see."

I laughed at that idea. Then Art told me again he loved me, and I got all choked up.

"I'm bringing back a surprise for you."

"What?"

"It's a surprise."

I'd been to Art's house for dinner a few times. His grandma and his dad made a big deal over me. "Muy bonita," his grandma would say, running her hand softly across the top of my head. "Roja." Her English was limited and so was my Spanish—I was taking Spanish I, but mostly I knew how to count and say, "El burro es un animal." This was not a very useful phrase at the dinner table.

Art's dad made me wish I'd had a dad. He spent hours every evening working in his garden after he'd already worked a full day in other people's gardens. Azaleas and camellias filled their back yard with color, and he was planting vegetables, too.

"Wait until you taste my tomatoes, Roja."

Roja, Spanish for red, was what Mr. Rodriguez and his mother called me. I had never liked anyone calling attention to my red hair, but somehow Roja was okay with me.

"One taste of a Joe Rodriguez tomato and you'll throw rocks at those pretend tomatoes in the market." He had a gentle, bubbling laugh like Art's, and I knew from the beginning he liked me.

It was different with Art's mom. She was polite enough, but she never had much to say to me. I felt as if she were watching me from a distance, measuring me in some secret way. She talked to me about Art, that was all.

"You know Arturo's very smart," she would say. "The teachers have told me that since preschool. He's going to Stanford, you know. His counselor says there's no doubt he can get a scholarship."

Her eyes would warm when she looked at Art, but they turned cold when she looked at me.

"Jealous," Pauline said, when I told her how Art's mom was. "We talked about it in psychology. Mothers don't want to let go of their sons—something to do with sex."

"Pauline! That's gross!"

"All I'm saying is she's jealous."

"You're nutso."

I was really surprised when Mrs. Rodriguez called the night the choir was due to arrive back.

"Do you want to ride to LAX with us to meet Arturo?"

"I'd love to, Mrs. Rodriguez," I said, stunned.

"I'm sure we're not the only ones he's missed," she said. It was the first time I'd heard her refer to any feelings Art might have for me. Maybe she liked me after all.

"We'll pick you up about 7:30," she said.

I gave her the directions to my house and told her I'd be waiting in front. I was ashamed to have them see my house. Their yard was neatly trimmed and filled with flowers. My yard was overrun with weeds, and David's partially dismantled Toyota pick-up was sitting in the yard exactly as he'd left it when he took off last summer.

Once, when I'd told Bobby I was afraid Mrs. R. didn't like me, he'd said she probably didn't. She had plans for Art to marry a nice, rich Hispanic girl. I didn't qualify.

At the gate where we were supposed to meet Art, the screen said Flight 255 from Boston had been delayed.

"Oh, my God," Mrs. Rodriguez groaned.

Mr. Rodriguez put his arms around her. "It's just late, it's nothing," he said soothingly.

"No, something's wrong. I feel it,"

"Please. Relax."

Art's grandmother began rubbing Mrs. Rodriguez's back.

Other choir parents and friends were milling around. I went over to talk to Bobby Reyes' sister, who I knew from chorus.

"It looks like we'll be here for a while," she said.

"Do you know why it's late?"

"Something about mechanical trouble in Boston. They were two hours late taking off."

I began to get nervous. Maybe Mrs. Rodriguez was right. I went back over to where Art's family was sitting.

"They were late taking off," I said. "There was some kind

of mechanical difficulty."

"And it's not fixed yet," Mrs. Rodriguez said, sobbing. "I know it isn't. My baby's in the air in a plane that's got something awful wrong with it!"

Mrs. Reyes came over and sat beside Mrs. Rodriguez.

"They're okay, Karla," she said, patting Art's mom's hand. "They're just late."

"You don't know, Toni. I feel the same way I did that horrible morning when they came to get José. I know about my sons. I only have one left, and I'm going to lose him." Tears mixed with mascara rolled down her cheeks in dark, murky streams.

Mr. Rodriguez took his wife's purse and riffled through it. "Where are her pills?" he asked his mother. "Do you know?"

Art's grandmother unzipped an outside compartment and took out a bottle of capsules.

"Would you get some water, Mija?" he asked, turning to me.

I ran to the bar and asked the bartender for a glass of water.

"We don't serve minors here."

"There's a sick woman out there. She needs a glass of water to take a pill with."

"You'll have to get it somewhere else, Kiddo."

"I'LL GET IT HERE OR I'LL SCREAM MY HEAD OFF!" I threatened.

"Nope," he said.

I took a deep breath, filling my lungs the way Mr. Michaels taught us to do before we had a long phrase to sing. I used my fine soprano voice for the most high-pitched scream this side of the movie, "Psycho." Everything stopped. The bartender looked at me like he couldn't believe his eyes. When I ran out of breath, I took another deep breath, and opened my mouth wide.

"Stop. Okay?" he said, filling a glass with water. "Bring back the glass, you hear?"

"No problemo," I said, rushing out of the bar.

"Gracias," the old Mrs. Rodriguez said, taking the glass and handing her daughter-in-law a capsule.

"Valium?" Mrs. Reyes asked Art's dad.

He shook his head. "She's not the same, you know, since José—very nervous. Very, very nervous."

The pill seemed to quiet Mrs. Rodriguez some. After an hour or so, the room was pretty much filled with people waiting for choir kids. I guess singing runs in families, because I saw a lot of the Beginning Chorus kids there, waiting for older brothers or sisters who were in a capella choir, or in the Harmonics. Some of us went into the snack bar and got sodas. We sat at a big table, getting silly, but underneath it all I was uneasy.

I glanced over by the waiting area and saw that everyone was up and gathered around the agent's desk. I ran out to join them.

"...just a precautionary measure," the agent was saying. "We're clearing the runway and alerting emergency equipment. Your friends and family are completely briefed on emergency procedures and every effort is being made to assure their safety."

My stomach clenched, and I swear my heart stopped. Until now, I hadn't let myself think it was even possible that Art and the others were in real danger, but emergency equipment? God. God, God, God, kept flashing through my brain.

Everyone was talking at once—Why wasn't the plane checked out more carefully in Boston? Why hadn't they changed planes when they found this problem? When would it land? Was the pilot experienced?

"I'm sorry. I've told you all I know. Please sit down, stay calm. I'll let you know when I get new information."

Family groups were knotted together, faces tense with fear. Some were crying. Every airplane accident I'd ever heard of came back to me—explosions, fire in the cabin, holes in the fuselage, passengers sucked into space. Art's face floated before me, and then the others, too. Dear God, let them be safe. Even Amy.

"He's gone. My baby's gone." Mrs. Rodriguez's words were muffled against her husband's shoulder. "My life is over," she exclaimed, her sobs intensifying, her whole body shaking.

"Please, Karla. Karlita, we must hold them all in our love. We must not bury them yet."

"YOU!" she shouted, turning on him. "YOU HAVE NO RIGHT. I WOULDN'T HAVE LET HIM GO, BUT OH, NO. YOU INSISTED. I KNEW THIS WOULD HAPPEN. WELL, HIS BLOOD IS ON **YOUR** HANDS."

Everyone turned to look at the screaming woman. Mr. Rodriguez turned away. I went over and put my arms around his ample waist.

"It is so hard for me, Roja. So hard," he said.

Just then the agent announced, "Flight 255 is approaching the runway."

We rushed to the windows, jockeying for a view. We stood close, silently watching, barely breathing. It was an eerie sight. There was no activity on any runway. Fire trucks and ambulances lined the area, safety-suited personnel stood, hoses at the ready, looking like creatures from a science fiction movie.

"There!" Mrs. Reyes said, pointing northwest. "Be safe, Bobby," she whispered. "God help him."

"Please. Please," I begged.

Behind me I heard Mr. Rodriguez's quiet voice, "May our love protect you—every one of you."

The plane touched down on a foam-filled section of the runway, bounced, skidded, and turned. Mrs. Rodriguez screamed, "My baby. My son!" Old Mrs. Rodriguez gripped my arm, her eyes closed, lips moving.

One more complete turn on the runway, and the giant metal craft slid to a stop. Chutes snapped into place and emergency doors opened. There they were, sliding down the chutes and running just as soon as they hit the ground.

Emergency workers pulled the slower ones out of the way so they didn't fall all over each other.

As the first passengers came into the waiting area, a cheer went up. People cried and laughed and jumped up and down. I threw my arms around Art's grandma and we laughed, rocking back and forth.

Mr. Rodriguez had his arms around his weeping wife. He looked gray and tired.

Mr. Michaels was standing near the agent's desk, clipboard in hand. Had he kept that with him as he slid down the chute?

"Singers, please. Let's be certain we're all accounted for, and then we can fall apart with our families in any way we deem appropriate." He started calling names, alphabetically. He'd already called Rodriguez once when I saw Art walking through the double doors. His mother ran to him and threw herself on him, practically knocking him down.

"Aye, Mijo," she said, still crying.

"It's okay, Mom. It's okay."

"You're never flying again, Mijo!"

"We'll see," Art said, noticing me for the first time.

"Em!" he called out to me. His mother was still hanging on as he slowly made his way in my direction. I couldn't get past her to hug him. I planted a kiss on the back of his neck, and was suddenly overwhelmed by relief. Tears warmed my cheeks as I felt Art's hand grasp mine.

"ALL HERE!" Mr. Michaels called out. "ALL HERE!" He beamed at the screaming, applauding crowd. Then he sat down on a hard plastic chair, put his hands over his face and cried. I could see his shoulders shaking from clear across the room.

No one could get any luggage yet. They had to wait until ten the next morning for the plane to be completely checked out and the baggage unloaded.

On the way home, Art sat in the back seat between his mom and grandma and I sat up front next to his dad. It was after one in the morning when we got to my house.

"I'll walk Emmy to her door," Art said, climbing over his grandma to get out.

"It's late, Mijo. We'll just watch Emmy from here to see she gets in okay," his mother said.

"No, she has to go around back and it's very dark there," he insisted, walking over to meet me.

We went around back, to the door I never used and didn't even have a key for.

"I had to have a minute with you, Em, to feel you close to me," Art whispered.

I put my arms around him.

"I was so scared," I said.

"*You* were!"

I tried to get closer. He was leaning against the back wall. I pressed my full weight against him and we kissed, long and full.

"Art," I said, crying. "I need you so much. I didn't know how much until now."

"All I could think on the plane was that I might never feel you in my arms again. I might die before we'd even really been together . . ."

There were three short beeps of the horn.

"I'd better go," Art said, "or they'll wake up all your neighbors . . . Bye."

"Bye," I said, moving reluctantly away from him. I waited until I heard their car start down the street, then walked around to the front door.

6

None of the choir tour kids were in school on Monday, and half of Beginning Chorus was out. Even Mr. Michaels was absent. They must all have been exhausted, and they still had to get their baggage straightened out.

We had an ancient sub, so we fooled around all third period. We passed newspapers around that told of last night's emergency landing. It's a good thing we had something in print because rumors were rampant. A guy I didn't even know came up to me first period and said a hijacker had a bomb on that flight, and he'd shot two kids who tried to wrestle a gun away. I just laughed.

When I walked past the church parking lot on my way home from school, I saw Art's car parked there. I took off running, around the corner, down my block, up the driveway to David's room.

I flung open the door and there was Art, sitting on David's bed, grinning his all-time great grin. I dropped my books and pounced on him, laughing. We rolled around, and kissed, and laughed, and rolled around some more.

"I've never felt more alive," Art said. I knew what he meant. Just thinking about death, having it so close, made this ordinary day precious beyond words.

"How's your mom today?" I asked.

"Okay, I guess. I wish she wouldn't get like that."

"She was blaming your dad for letting you go. I felt sorry

for him."

"I know. She blames him for José being in jail, too."

"Why?"

"I don't know. She just does."

We sat quietly for a while, then Art said, "Hey! Want your present?"

"Of course."

He pulled a sack out from under the bed. It said "Hard Rock Cafe" on it. He took out a black T-shirt with the Hard Rock logo on it and handed it to me.

"I love it," I said, holding it up for size.

"And me?"

"I love you, too, most of all."

"So where's my present?" he said, drawing me to him.

"Ummmm. I don't have a present for you."

"Yes, you do, you just don't know it . . . Lie down beside me and we'll talk about it," he said.

We stretched out on the bed, facing each other. I kept looking at his face, his eyes. I got all teary, thinking how lost I would be if his plane had actually crashed.

"What?" he said, wiping my tears gently with a warm, clean-smelling finger.

"That was so awful last night," I said. We held each other close for a while, then Art began kissing me, running his hands across my body in ways he had not done before. He unfastened my bra and jeans, and I felt the warmth of his hands on my skin.

He unbuttoned his pants and moved my hand down to touch him. Every part of my body was tense, alive, straining toward him. He slipped his hand inside my pants, between my legs.

"God, Emmy. You're ready. Don't tell me you're not ready. I need you so much. Please."

"Yes," I said, hearing my voice strange and throaty.

He reached into the Hard Rock Cafe bag which was on the floor beside the bed and pulled out a foil wrapped condom along with a package that said "Spermicide" on it.

"I told you I'd take care of you," he said. "Here, take this stuff in the bathroom and insert it. We're going to do this right." He handed me the package. "I'll be right here, waiting for you."

While I was in the bathroom putting foam stuff in the applicator and trying to figure out how to get it in me, I got scared again. Maybe if I stayed in the bathroom for a long time, Art would forget what we were doing. But then I thought how I'd almost lost him. I looked at the diagram one more time, then managed to insert the foam. I took a deep breath and went back to Art.

"Are you okay?" he asked.

"I think so."

He slipped my clothes off, kissing each new exposed spot. Then he stood and stripped. He turned his back to me and I knew he was fumbling with the condom. When he lay down beside me, I felt the latex shield against my leg.

We kissed and caressed each other, gently at first, then frantic and fumbling. He pushed and pushed until I felt a jab of pain. I tensed and cried out.

"Okay. It's okay now," he assured me in short gasps.

He was pushing hard, calling my name. It hurt like anything, but I didn't care. He was inside me. We belonged to each other.

Suddenly Art groaned, again and again, and there were these spasms. I thought he was dying. What had I done? Had I moved wrong?

"Em, Em, Em," he said, laying full on top of me, breathing heavily into my sweaty-wet hair.

"God, how I love you. There'll never be anyone else for me, I swear."

He pulled out, gently, and went into the bathroom to get rid of the condom. When he came back, he asked, "How are you?"

"Fine," I said.

"It'll be better for you next time," he promised, handing me a washcloth to clean myself up with. There was blood, but I guess I should have expected that.

We stretched out next to each other again, skin to skin.

I must admit I was kind of disappointed in this sex stuff. The beginning was great, but actually doing IT didn't do much for me. It sure did for Art, though.

"I've never felt so close to anyone in my life as I do to you right now," he said.

I liked that. Even though no bells had rung, I felt close to him, too, and it seemed that now we were together in a way that was more certain and concrete.

"Look," he said, "I'll show you my secret identification mark."

He turned his back to me and pointed to a small, dark spot on his lower left cheek.

"Female eyes have never cast their gaze upon this sign of distinction."

I bent to look more carefully. It was a small, triangular-shaped mole, slightly raised.

"Cute," I said, leaning to kiss it. "But I bet your mom and grandma have seen it."

"Oh, but that doesn't count. Only you count."

We continued to meet in Dave's room most days after school. We'd do a little homework, make love, and do some more homework. Art was right. It got better.

With softball practice for me and track for Art, some days we didn't get there until five or so, so we only made love. But most of the time we studied, too. Art was serious about Stanford. He was a good influence on me in that way. I'd always gotten good grades, but I'd never thought much about my future. With Art, and all his plans for the future, though, I started thinking about my future more, too.

"Go to Stanford with me, Emmy."

"You must be crazy," I told him.

"No. When you graduate from high school, come to Stanford. Maybe we'll get married and live in student housing."

"I'm only fifteen!"

"Yes, but you're growing up fast, and we know we want to stay together," he said, kissing and nuzzling my neck.

Tryouts for the Hamilton Harmonics were on the first Wednesday in June. Pauline and I both auditioned. We had to sing not just for Mr. Michaels, but for the Harmonics singers, too, solo. Art kept telling me I'd do fine, but I wasn't sure.

When it was my turn, I got so nervous I lost my place and had to start all over. There goes New York, I thought. But at six o'clock on Thursday morning, a car full of kids came barreling down my driveway. Bobby Reyes pounded on my front door.

"Emily Morrison. You've got exactly five minutes to get out here, and then we're coming to get you."

I grabbed a pair of jeans and my new Hard Rock T-shirt, brushed my teeth, washed my face, and ran to the car carrying shoes, hairbrush, and lipstick.

"Congratulations," kids screamed from the car. "You're a Harmonic."

There were two others in the car from Beginning Chorus, but no Pauline.

It was a longstanding tradition to kidnap the new Harmonics the day after auditions and take them to breakfast. I knew I looked awful, but so did everyone else. I kept watching the door, hoping another group would show up and Pauline would be with them, but it didn't happen.

Mr. Michaels congratulated us all and said he thought this could be the best group ever.

At lunch, Tammy was bubbling with enthusiasm over my acceptance into the Harmonics, but Pauline was quiet.

"I really hoped we'd both get in," I told her as we made our way through the crowded halls down to the gym.

"I guess I just don't have the right boyfriend," she said.

"Do you honestly believe that?" I asked.

"Yeah. Don't you?"

"It never occurred to me," I said.

"Oh, grow up, Emmy. Michaels thinks Art is God's gift to the music program. You think he doesn't want to keep Art happy?"

I got a sinking feeling. What if it was true? Pauline walked straight to her gym locker without looking back. But I *was* a good singer. Wasn't I? But Pauline was good, too.

After school I went to the music office.

"What can I do for you, Emmy?"

I told Mr. Michaels what Pauline had said.

"What do you think?" he asked.

"I don't know."

"Well, you can tell Pauline, or for that matter, I can, that the Harmonics are chosen based on their singing ability first and foremost, then their ability to work with a group, their dependability, and their general attitude. Who is going with whom is the least of my concerns, though young love running the rough course it often does, I would rather my singers *not* be romantically involved with each other."

I smiled, relieved.

"You're a good singer, Emmy. You know that."

I nodded.

"Don't sell yourself short. Believe in you. You're talented and smart."

I could feel myself blushing.

"Now, about your friend. I'd be happy to talk with her about why she wasn't chosen. She sings well, and frankly, I considered her seriously. There's a strong possibility for her next year. But she doesn't read music as well as some of the others and she's moody. Sometimes she tries, and sometimes she doesn't. In a group that performs as often as the Harmonics, we need people who are willing to try hard consistently. Okay?"

"Okay," I said. "Do you think we'll go to New York?"

Mr. Michaels groaned. "After that horrible airplane experience in May, I thought I would never ever take another group anywhere. But yes, I think there's a chance. Ask that question in September," he said, smiling. I wished he was my dad.

When report cards came, I had all "A"s. I'd never done *that* well in school before. Even my mom noticed. There was also a letter from my counselor, Mrs. Werly, with my grades. She said there would be a meeting June 22 for outstanding students and their parents to discuss possible involvement in Project Hope. I didn't know if I wanted to go or not.

"Of course you'll go!" Art said when I showed him the letter. "Project Hope—that means you can get your whole college education paid for."

"But it's a night when my mom works."

"Emmy. Make her take off. One of the project's requirements is parent involvement."

"She's never gone to any of my school stuff."

"This is different. She's got to go, at least to the first meeting. It's like somebody is willing to hand you $60,000 worth of education and all you've got to do is get good grades and attend a few meetings."

I was surprised that my mom wanted to go to the meeting. She traded shifts with Edie, so it worked out. During the question and answer period at the meeting, my mom said, "I'm a businesswoman, and I see the necessity of bookkeeping and accounting in all economies. Don't you think those are excellent fields for women?"

The picture of my mom in her short waitress skirt and vinyl boots as a businesswoman made me laugh. But she wasn't exactly lying, either. She did partly own a small business.

"Mrs. Morrison, I'm sure that bookkeeping and accounting are important and lucrative endeavors. However, *these* young men and women," Mrs. Werly said, making a sweeping gesture toward the group of forty or so students scattered among parents and other school counselors, "are our hope for the future of America. Let's challenge them to be the M.B.A.s, the doctors and scientists, the leaders in art and politics."

There was applause, and my mother nodded her head, as if in agreement. I hoped this would get me off the book-keeper hook.

There were about thirty freshmen in the room. The only ones I knew were Becky, who was also one of the Harmonics, and twin brothers from my Honors English class.

There was a slide presentation showing scenes from colleges and universities around the nation, then there were graphs showing earning power as it related to education, then Mrs. Werly gave a talk.

"Project Hope is part of a state program, combined with funds from private industry, to open doors for gifted, talented students who might otherwise have difficulty financing a university education.

"You students qualify for the project on the one hand because of your strong capabilities, and on the other because you are dealing with one or more risk factors—racial minority, low income, single parent family, physical handicap—things which sometimes seem to get in the way of advanced degrees. Project Hope is your key to the future. You must work hard and plan, but each of you has already shown a strong capacity for success. Congratulations!"

Then there were forms to fill out, and pamphlets explaining what Mrs. Werly had already told us. There was a time line for Project Hope activities during the summer. Everything was color-coded and filed in slick folders. Cool.

When I stopped in at Barb and Edie's the next day for a quick lunch, I saw my report cards displayed prominently on the bulletin board by the telephone. I couldn't believe it.

"I hear you're the hope of America," Edie said, ruffling my hair. I smiled, embarrassed.

A man at the end of the bar looked me over and said, "America could do worse. Yes siree, Sister."

Edie laughed. So did I.

"He's harmless," she whispered to me.

The trio got together for a beach trip, but it wasn't the same. It was hard to believe that just last summer we had pored over *The Joy of Sex* and now I was practically living it. I didn't talk to Pauline and Tammy about any of that, though. That was a promise Art and I made to each other. What went on in Dave's room was private, between us.

Tammy and Bobby Reyes had started going around together, and sometimes the four of us, Tammy, Bobby, Art and I, did stuff together. I had refused to set them up, in spite of Tammy's begging, because I liked Bobby and I knew how Tammy was. She was obsessed with a guy until he started liking her, and then she lost interest.

But finally she got Art to set her up, and all of a sudden it seemed that she and Bobby were all settled down. She hardly ever even talked about other guys anymore. Her mom called it the miracle of Bobby Reyes.

Pauline often complained that we put boys ahead of the trio, and she missed the old days. But it seemed like whenever the three of us did get together, Pauline was sullen and grouchy and we didn't have much fun.

Sometimes, when I called Pauline and asked her to do something with me she'd say something sarcastic like, "What's the matter, lover-boy Art busy?" So I kind of gave up.

The "Hope of America" group, as my mom called us, went to a three-day session at Hamilton High. They gave us interest tests and I.Q. tests, and then each of us got individual career and college counseling. It was really thorough. I knew more about me after those three days than I ever thought possible.

Besides all the testing, they had us do these weird things called guided imagery. They showed us a bunch of pictures of college campuses, and then had us close our eyes and imagine ourselves in one of the pictures. What were we doing? What were we sensing?

I really got into it. I imagined myself by the duck pond at Sonoma State, up in northern California. I was studying the poetry of Emily Dickenson, analyzing rhyme and rhythm. The sun was sinking slowly behind the hills, casting a reflective glow on the water.

A group of students walked past on their way to the tennis courts. I closed my book and sauntered toward the library, then the student lounge, in the shadow of giant trees, to my dormitory. My roommate was waiting for me, with tickets to a concert in San Francisco . . .

When the timer buzzed the end of guided imagery, I felt as if I'd really been away.

After all our tests had been evaluated, we met individually with a Project Hope counselor.

"You're a very bright, well-rounded young woman," Mrs. Werly said, shuffling through the collection of tests and worksheets spread out on her desk. She showed me this graph that she interpreted as meaning I could be whatever I wanted to be.

She asked a lot of questions about my goals and dreams, and then talked to me about ways to achieve them. It gave me a lot to think about.

"Consider all we've discussed today, talk it over with your parents—is it just your mom?"

I nodded.

"Then talk it over with your mom and come to my office at 11:00 tomorrow. We'll make a plan. You'll change it, over and over again through high school and probably college, too. But you must have a plan—that's a main requirement for this program."

She put all my stuff in a folder and handed it to me. "Maybe this will help," she said.

When I showed it to Tammy, she said, "I want to do that. How do you get to do that?"

"Get all 'A's, I guess."

"Oh, well. Never mind," she laughed.

At home that night, I started listing the things I would like to be. A forest ranger, because I loved the outdoors; a teacher—probably English and P.E. because I loved books and sports; an environmental engineer because I didn't want us to keep messing up our environment; a singer, just because; or a horticulturist because Mr. Rodriguez had shown me how interesting plants were.

When I read my list to Mrs. Werly, she laughed.

"See, I told you you were well-rounded."

She asked me a bunch more questions, then began another worksheet with me.

"Education goals?" she asked.

"Well . . . I don't know if I can or not, but I'd sort of like to go away to college," I said.

"That's good. I think it's important to have the experience of living away from home."

"We don't have much money," I said.

"That's the glory of Project Hope," she said. "With a combination of jobs, loans, and outright scholarships, your way will be paid wherever you choose to go. Just keep up your end of the bargain by getting good grades and taking part in extracurricular activities."

For educational goals she put "Advanced degree."

"What does that mean?" I asked.

"It means longer than four years of college, and you end up an expert in your field."

"What if I don't want to go more than four years, or I can't afford it?"

"Then change your goals. But Emmy, live to your greatest capacity. Use your intellect, your body, and your sensitivities to the fullest.

"Career goals?" she asked.

"I don't know. They all sound good."

"Let me look again," she said. She paused at singer.

"Opera?"

"No, just regular," I said.

"Madonna?"

"Not exactly."

"Now, a forest ranger is rather specialized. You might do better with a major in environmental studies, with a strong emphasis on natural sciences. That way you could go either direction."

What we finally ended up with was a plan to major in environmental studies, with the possibilities of being a forest ranger, a teacher, or a consultant to industries. Mrs. Werly mapped out a basic eight-year plan—courses to take in high school and what to do when. I would minor in music or English, I wasn't sure which.

"In your junior year we'll get specific about colleges."

I was jazzed. I had a plan. When I told Art, he said, "That's great, Em," but he didn't sound very enthused.

"What's wrong?"

"I worry that you'll be far away from me."

"But Art. You're going to be the first one to go away," I said.

"That's different. I'm the guy."

That was the first time he'd ever said any of that "I'm the guy" stuff to me. I didn't like it.

"What's that mean, anyway?" I asked.

He just laughed. "Listen to us, Em, starting to fight over nothing. We've got over a year together, right now. What say I come over and we enjoy it?"

I know exactly when it happened. Art and I, and Tammy and Bobby, had planned to drive down to Laguna Beach in the afternoon, after Bobby and Art got off work at 2:00. Art was a lifeguard at Hamilton Heights Park, and Bobby worked as an equipment supervisor. We were going to be beach rats for a while, just lounge around and swim some, and then in the evening we planned to roast hot dogs and marshmallows. But when we got to Tammy's house, her mom was sick—high fever and all, and Tammy had to stay home with Bonnie.

"I'll stay and help," Bobby said. "We can take Bonnie back to the park later."

"I don't want to go to the park," Bonnie whined.

"Go on to the beach, Bobby," Tammy said. "I don't want to spoil your fun."

But Bobby ended up staying, and just Art and I went to the beach. In the evening we sat around the campfire and talked about our families and us and the world. When the fire died, we took our towels and blankets to a little cove, private and protected, and listened to the constancy of the waves.

"Remember that first night at the beach?" Art asked.

"It seems like a long time ago," I said.

"But we knew right then, didn't we? We knew we'd be together for a long time."

"I knew I wanted to," I said.

"And I knew we would," Art said. "Emmy, you've got to know, you're the best thing that's ever happened to me."

"I don't want it ever to end, Art. I think I'd die without you."

"I'm here, Em. I'm always here."

He gave me a sweet, salty kiss. The rhythm of the waves, the moon on the water, the smell of the soft sea breeze, made me want him more than ever. We began fumbling with each other's clothes.

"Maybe we should go back to the drugstore first," I said, pausing.

"It'll be okay, Sweetheart. I know what to do," he said in that breathy voice he got when he was excited.

I wasn't convinced, but he was kissing my breasts, rubbing his hardness against me, and everything in me wanted to feel him inside. I tugged at his shorts, pulling them down, as he slipped my bikini bottoms off.

He kneeled over me, thrusting. His eyes shone in the near darkness and I was close to feeling those amazing, mindless convulsions when he suddenly pulled out, and I felt his warm wetness against my belly. He kissed me and rubbed me, and in an instant I had reached my peak, clutching him close to me.

We lay in silence for a while. How peaceful and natural it was in our little cove.

"Let's go rinse off," he said. "No one's around. Let's run."

We ran naked into the ocean, catching our breath with the cold shock of it. We swished water over our bodies, splashed our faces, and then ran back to our cove. We dressed and wrapped the blanket around us.

"That's maybe not the best way," Art said, rubbing his head against my shoulder. "But better to be safe. We'd really be messed up if you got pregnant."

"That's so stupid," I said. "I can't believe how stupid some of those girls are. You know Maria, from my soccer team?"

Art nodded.

"I heard she was pregnant."

"I'd never do that to you, Em. I love you too much for that."

"What if it *did* happen?"

"I won't let it."

"But what if?" I said.

"It won't, I'm telling you. No what ifs."

But what if, I thought.

7

With the money I'd earned during the summer helping out at Barb and Edie's, I bought some really cool clothes. As I waited for Art to pick me up the first day of school, I stood looking in the mirror. I was a different person than I'd been a year ago. I was taller and, although I was still thin, I had become more womanly looking. Maybe it was love, or that I had a plan for my future. Whatever it was, I was no longer the scared little freshman who didn't know how to find her way around or talk to people.

"My senior year. I can't believe it," Art said. "My mom made waffles and bacon for me this morning and cried when I told her goodbye—just like in kindergarten," he laughed.

"My mom groaned and rolled over when I stuck my head in to say goodbye. Just like in kindergarten," I said, laughing, too.

"Your mom's a trip," Art said.

"Yeah, well, so's yours," I laughed.

Art's face clouded over. I should have known better. Where his mom was concerned, Art had no sense of humor.

"Where were you this morning?" Pauline demanded when I saw her at lunch time. "Tammy and I waited and waited out by the flag pole, and you never showed up."

"I have Harmonics before first period, remember?"

"No, am I supposed to be so impressed with Harmonics

that I memorize the whole schedule?"

"Oh, get a life!" I said, and walked away. I was sick of Pauline always being on the rag.

"**W**hat's wrong with her, anyway?" I asked Tammy when we talked on the phone that night.

"I think she's just jealous. She's like that with me, too. Always complaining that I spend too much time with Bobby, and that I'm obsessed with drill team. She needs a man."

Tammy made me laugh. Her answer for everything was simple: Get a man.

"She's a good friend, though," I said, mellowing some.

"Remember how we used to get the giggles in Mrs. Kline's room, and how mad she'd get?"

"And the madder she got, the more we giggled?"

"And when she sent us to the office, we were still laughing uncontrollably, and the secretaries started laughing, too?"

"Let's go back and visit," I said. "The trio—tomorrow?"

We decided to try harder with Pauline, and then we drifted on to talk of our favorite subjects—Art and Bobby.

Art called at 9:45. "I've been trying to call all evening, Emmy," he said, sounding annoyed. "Who've you been talking to?"

"Tammy."

"That long?"

"Yes."

"Well, you know I'm not supposed to use the phone after ten. It seems like you could have saved me a little more time—especially if it was only Tammy."

"It was Tammy," I said. "Not *only* Tammy. It was Tammy."

"Yeah, okay. I just wanted to talk to you. That's all."

"What did you want to say?"

"I forget."

We laughed, but neither of us could think of much to say, and it was kind of a relief when, at 10 o'clock, I heard his dad in the background saying, "Come on, Artie. Let's not have a fuss."

Sometimes I couldn't believe how much everyone in Art's family tiptoed around his mom.

What had seemed like a great idea the night before didn't seem so great the next day. Tammy had drill team practice and Pauline wasn't all that enthused, so we didn't go visit Palm Avenue School after all.

When Mr. Michaels chose me to do a solo in the Harvest Concert I was scared, but I said okay. I sang, "You Are the Wind Beneath My Wings," and although I could never look at Art when I sang it, everyone knew I was singing to him. It went "Did you ever know that you're my hero . . . I can fly higher than an eagle, you are the wind beneath my wings."

I believed it. Art had helped me grow up and take my life seriously. He brought joy and laughter to me. And, maybe best of all, the secret fears I'd had about sex were gone.

After I sang my song the night of the concert, there was a long silence. Then the audience started clapping and whistling and stomping their feet. They chanted "EM-MY, EM-MY," over and over again.

At the party afterwards, I felt like a star. People crowded around me and told me how good I was. Mrs. Michaels said what a pure, true voice I had, and that I did the song better than Bette Midler or Kenny Rogers. It blew me away.

Bobby and Tammy motioned me over to where they were sitting in the Michaels' living room. "Where's Art?" Bobby asked.

I looked around, but didn't see him anywhere. I walked out to the kitchen where a few of the kids were still pigging out on a giant pizza, but he was nowhere around.

"Anyone seen Art?" I asked.

"No, but I'd like to," Amy said in that sleazy manner of hers.

"Fat chance," Carl said. "After 'Wind Beneath My Wings,' I bet Art's signed on for life."

I wished I hadn't seen such a wad of pizza in Carl's mouth

when he was talking, but I liked him a whole lot for what he'd said.

I looked out front. Art's car was still there. I walked around back. There he was, sitting all in the dark, on the patio swing.

"What's up?" I said.

He was quiet, just looking at me.

"What is it?"

"I don't know, Em. I'm happy for you and all, but I hate seeing all those people fawning over you. I mean, you're *my* girl. I'm the one that discovered you, and now everyone else wants to latch on."

"What do you mean, discovered me?"

"Well, you know. Nobody even knew you were around until we got together."

"Excuse me, Mr. Big Shot Arturo," I said angrily, "but, believe it or not, there *was* life before you!"

"Oh, so if you liked life so well before me, maybe you'd like to go back to that life!" he said, his voice harsh and angry.

"Fine with me!" I said.

"Fine with me, too!"

He grabbed my hand and pulled me, half-running, to his car.

"I'll get a ride with Tammy and Bobby," I said. "You don't need to bother with me!"

"No you won't. My mother taught me always to take the girl I brought home, no matter what!"

"Oh, your mother, your mother. Why can't you think for yourself, instead of being such a mommy's boy?"

He opened the car door and pushed me inside, then got in. He peeled out down the street as fast as his car would go. I was trembling with anger. His hands were clenched white-tight around the steering wheel. By the time we reached my corner, my face was soaked with tears.

"Please don't take me home yet," I whispered.

He drove past the corner and turned down a darkened cul-de-sac. We parked near the end of the street and sat, turned away from each other. Finally Art said, "God, I'm sorry, Em."

"Me, too," I gasped, turning to him, clinging, shaking with sobs.

"What happened?" I said. "I don't get it."

"I don't know. I don't know. Sometimes I get scared that I'll lose you, and tonight, when you looked so beautiful up there and you sounded so great, and everyone thought you were so wonderful, I just kept thinking, 'She's *mine*. That's *my* song.'" he said, burying his face in my hair.

"It *is* your song. You *are* my hero. I think that all the time. But it was different when you said it—not like you loved me, but more like you were better than me . . . I'm sorry about what I said about being a mommy's boy," I whispered.

Later, in Dave's room, after we made love, we promised never to fight again, and to never forget that we were the wind beneath each other's wings. But our fight had lessened the pleasure that should have been mine for my brief singing triumph. It took days for me to shake off a feeling of deep sadness.

CHAPTER

8

"Emmy Morrison and Carl Saunders, you're half-way there," Mr. Michaels announced at the beginning of class one morning as he reviewed student fund-raising accounts. "Bobby and Art, you're somewhere hovering over Colorado . . . Hmmm, let's see," he said, running his finger down the income column. "Amy, you haven't even made it to Palm Springs yet."

"My parents will pay my way," she said, tossing her long, black hair. "I *hate* selling greeting cards and cookies like some kind of little Girl Scout," she said, sending one of her superior looks in my direction.

After class, Carl caught up with me.

"Don't let Amy get to you," he said. "I've known her a long time. She's a natural bitch."

I laughed. "Thanks," I said. "But I don't care what she thinks. I'm going to New York no matter what. I'm going to climb to the very top of the Statue of Liberty, and sing in St. Patrick's Cathedral, and see a Broadway play, and I've got to raise my own money to do it."

"Me, too," Carl said. "My mom said she'd try to help, but I don't think she can really afford to."

"I like doing that stuff anyway," I said.

"What stuff?" Art asked, moving in between us and taking my arm.

"See ya," Carl said, heading toward the science building.

"I think he's got the hots for you, Emmy," Art said.

"Don't be stupid," I said. "He's just being friendly. I've known him since the fifth grade."

"He wants to meet you in Dave's room," Art said, grinning.

I punched him in the arm.

"Dave may be coming back, anyway," I said.

"What?"

"My brother may be coming home. He talked to my mom last night, and she said they could try it for a while."

"Well, he sure can't use his old room," Art said.

"Art. It *is* his room."

"Well then, where will we go after school?"

"Sometimes I think all you care about is sex," I accused him.

"That's not true, Em," Art said, acting offended. "It's your fault anyway if I do."

"Why is it my fault?"

"Because you are so totally, awesomely, sexy," he said, kissing me just below my ear in a place he knew always got to me.

I couldn't concentrate in algebra. I'd never even been out of the state of California, and in a few months I would be going to New York City, clear on the other side of the country. At first, I was afraid I wouldn't be able to go because of the money, but if I'd already earned half of it, and it was only mid-October, the rest should be easy.

Besides choir tour, I was also distracted from algebra by the possibility of David coming home. I hadn't seen him for over a year, and I still missed him something awful at times. Art and I talked about a lot of things, but the family stuff, like trying to deal with Mom's drinking habits, or sharing memories of our grandmother—Dave was the only person in the whole world who understood those things. I could hardly wait to see him.

It wasn't only choir tour and seeing David that were keeping my mind off algebra. It was the big "what if?"

Halloween night, as I was putting the finishing touches on my Marge Simpson costume, the doorbell rang.

"Trick or Treat!" I heard a gruff, male voice.

I went to the door and there he was. My long-lost brother.

"David!" I screamed, throwing myself at him.

He hugged me so hard I could hardly breathe.

"God, I've missed you, Little Sister," he said, pulling away and looking me up and down. He lifted the wig off my head and tousled my hair.

"Wow!" he said. "Look at you. You're all grown up!" He laughed and hugged me again.

He looked great. When he'd left, that long ago summer night, he'd been skinny and pale and his hands always shook. But now he looked strong and healthy. I squeezed his upper arm.

"Have you been working out?" I asked, then grabbed his gut.

He laughed. "I've got so much to tell you . . . stuff I didn't want to talk about on the phone."

He sat on the edge of my bed and watched as I finished my Marge Simpson make-up and readjusted the wig.

"I've been in rehab, Em."

"Rehab? But I've been talking to you almost every week," I said, puzzled.

"It was a modern place," Dave said, laughing. "You know, toilets, stoves, phones . . ."

"But . . ."

"I couldn't tell you over the phone. But it's absolutely the best thing that ever happened to me. For the first time in a long time, I have some hope for my life."

I sat next to him while he unraveled the whole story.

"I'd been staying wasted most of the time. The only time I even made an effort to be straight was when I wanted to call and talk to you. And then, one night I was so strung out on PCP a friend dumped me at a hospital emergency room."

"PCP?" I said, shocked. "I didn't think *anyone* was stupid

enough to use that stuff." I looked at him carefully. The pictures I had in my mind of PCP users were of crazed monsters. But this was definitely my gentle brother David sitting beside me.

"I know it was stupid. I'm lucky I'm alive and still have a few brain cells left," he said.

We heard three short beeps from the driveway, Art's signal that he'd arrived. David followed me out to the living room and stood watching as I greeted Art with a kiss. He was a strange-looking Bart, with his dark skin and his funny blonde wig.

"Art, this is my brother, David. He's here," I said.

"I see," Art said, smiling and extending his hand.

The three of us talked for a few minutes, then Art said, "We'd better be going, Em."

"David and I still have a lot of catching up to do," I told him.

"No, go ahead," Dave said. "I've been traveling for a long time. I'm going to crash hard, and then tomorrow sometime you and I are going to have a long heart-to-heart."

Art and I left to go to Hamilton's Haunted House.

"Is he staying in our room tonight?" Art asked.

"He's staying in *his* room."

"Did you get our stuff out?"

"What stuff?"

"You know, Em. The condoms and foam."

"No. I didn't even think about it."

Art groaned. "This is going to be very embarrassing."

We sat talking, arms around each other, parked in my driveway. We had felt the usual peeled grapes and pretended they were eyes, and danced to the monster mash, and figured out whose face was behind each mask. Maybe I was getting too old for Halloween, but it hadn't been as much fun as I had expected.

"You've been quiet tonight, Emmy. Anything wrong?"

I took a deep breath. "I hope not."

"What do you mean?"

"I'm late."

"It's only one-thirty. Your mom never cares anyway."

"That's not what I mean," I said, feeling all fluttery for even saying anything.

"What then?" Art asked.

"You know. Late. Late. My time of the month late."

"So, what are you saying?"

"I don't know. I'm not very regular, but I've never gone this long without a period before."

"How long?" he said, sitting up straight and looking at me intently. I knew I had his attention.

"The middle of August."

"Well, you don't have to worry about being pregnant. You're not worried about cancer, are you?" he asked, suddenly alarmed.

"I'm worried about being pregnant," I told him.

"But Emmy, you can't possibly be pregnant. We've never even had a condom break, and if it had, we'd still have had the spermicide back-up."

"Remember the night at the beach when we didn't use anything?"

"I pulled out in plenty of time, Em. You do know you can't get pregnant without sperm, don't you?" he said, sarcastically.

"Well, I've heard that method's not really safe," I told him, remembering the birth control chapter from my health and safety class.

"It's as safe as a condom, except for disease, and we know neither of us has a disease because we've only been with each other."

Although Art always told me I was first, I was never quite convinced. He already knew a lot by the time we got together in Dave's room.

"If it's so safe, how come we always used condoms?" I asked.

"Because it takes too much control. I like to let go," he

said, leaning over and kissing me, long. "I wish your brother hadn't come home," he said, kissing me again. "We've got to find another place. Soon."

As his kisses became more impassioned, I tried to respond, but couldn't.

"C'mon, Sweetheart," he said in that whispery voice. "You'll be okay. Don't worry," he reassured me. But I couldn't help it.

The next morning I woke feeling queasy. I hadn't told Art about that, how I felt sick all the time now when I first woke up. It was probably my imagination. All of this was probably just my imagination. Everything was going great for me and here I was, worrying about nothing.

I felt better around noon, and walked down to the little neighborhood market where I bought sausage and eggs. Back home, I left the door open for David. I started frying up some potatoes and sausage while I set the table, complete with place mats and a rose. I wanted David to know how happy I was to have him home.

"Do I smell sausage?" he said, padding barefoot into the kitchen. He was wearing jeans and my Hard Rock Cafe shirt. "Look what I found in my room," he said, smiling.

"Art gave it to me."

"I see," he said, giving me a look full of questions. A look I'd nearly forgotten during his long absence.

"I found some other things, too, that I suppose Art gave you?"

I felt my face grow hot, but concentrated on turning the eggs rather than answering.

"Well . . . at least you're being careful," he said.

I nodded, not meeting his eyes, and placed the food on the table. We sat down to a breakfast feast.

"Thanks, Emmy," David said, taking a big bite of sausage. "Where's Mom?"

"I guess she didn't come home last night," I said, glad for a change of subject.

"I hate the way she does, leaving you alone all night."

"I don't mind," I told him. "It's not like I'm a kid and scared anymore. And I can always catch her afternoons at the cafe if I need her, or if we're out of food. Besides, when she's home we fight about stupid stuff."

"Do you think she'll let me stay for a while?"

I nodded.

"She's stayed pretty angry," he said. "I was wrong, I admit that."

"Tell her. I think she's missed you a lot but she's too stubborn to ever say so."

"Yeah. I've missed her, too. I've missed you most—you're my number one, but honestly, I had a lot of thinking to do in rehab. I learned to take responsibility for my own problems. She's got plenty of problems, too, but she's always kept us fed and clothed. I know that's pretty basic, but a lot of those dudes in rehab with me hadn't even had that much."

"I know," I said. "Some of my friends' families look really good to me, but then I kind of like that I can make all my own decisions without anyone else butting in."

I told David how important Art was in my life, and he gave me the gory details of life in a drug treatment center. I told him about the choir tour to New York, and how the concert audience had cheered for me when I sang my solo. He said he was planning to get his high school diploma through adult school, and then try for a civil service job.

"No more broccoli farming?" I teased.

"I'm through with that stuff, Emmy," he said.

We both knew broccoli was a joke. I was sure he'd been "farming" marijuana, but he'd never come straight out and said so. Maybe that was part of his protectiveness.

"How about school, besides choir?" he asked.

I told him about being first string soccer this year, and Project Hope and my eight-year plan. He laughed.

"I'm proud of you, Em. I don't know how you've done it. Your friends have these super-moms and super-dads who are like Ward and June Cleaver, and here you are with no guidance at all, and you run circles around them.

"I've had you, David, and Grandma when I was little. That's been better than any T.V. look-alike family."

David looked down at his plate, frowning. "I'm gonna do better by you now, Emmy," he promised. "I'll be here when you need me, not like before when I was half stoned all the time."

"But I've always known you loved me," I said.

He looked up, smiling. "It's great to see things come together like this for you, Em. I wish I'd taken school seriously. I guess you have to be the family success story," he laughed. "Have you told me everything?"

"The whole enchilada," I lied. I don't know why, but I couldn't bring myself to tell him what was most on my mind. It was the first time I could remember ever consciously keeping something important from him.

We did the dishes, blowing bubbles with the soapy dishwater like in the old days. Mom came home about 3:00 to get ready for work. I thought maybe I should leave them alone for a while, so I stuck some money in my pocket and went for a walk.

I passed the drugstore where I usually go, and where they know me, and went to one about five blocks farther away. I bought one of those home pregnancy-testing kits like they advertise in magazines. By the time I got home, Mom was gone and David was out in the garage washing clothes.

I slid the test kit under my bed. I stretched out on the bed and wondered if I should take the test or not. I decided to do it and set my mind at ease.

9

"**I**'m pregnant," I said, as soon as I got in the car with Art. It was Sunday, and we were going to his house for dinner.

"Emmy. How many times do I have to tell you? You *can't* be pregnant."

"I took a home pregnancy test. It turned out positive."

"Well, you can't be pregnant," he said, his jaw set. "Unless you've been with someone else . . ."

"Art!"

"Well?"

"You know I've never been with anyone else. How can you even think that?" I asked, tears welling in my eyes.

"I don't know what to think," he said, looking straight ahead. "You insist you're pregnant, and I know I didn't do it. My mom always tells me not to let any girl trap me, I've got my whole future in front of me. I don't know what to think. My cousin Roger got trapped with a baby."

"Roger?" Art had more cousins than anyone I'd ever known.

"Yeah, down in Pico. One day he was a football player and the next he was a hamburger-flipping, diaper-changing dropout. I'm way too young for the baby trap, and I've taken care not to mess up that way."

"I'm not trying to trap you. I'm just telling you I'm pregnant. How do you think I feel? Don't you think I feel trapped?"

I looked out the window to my right, crying silently. The

street, the houses, the trees, the flowers, were as familiar to me as my own face, but now they were dull and colorless, where only yesterday they had been bright and beautiful.

Art parked around the corner from his house and turned off the engine. I couldn't look at him.

"Emmy. Listen," he said, pulling me toward him. "You need to go to a doctor and get this thing straightened out. Those tests aren't reliable."

"But I haven't had my period since August, and I feel awful in the mornings." I clung to him, sobbing.

He held me close for a long time while I struggled to catch my breath. He handed me a tissue.

"Wipe your face," he said gently. "We've got to get going. I told my dad I'd help him move some stuff to the garage before dinner . . . It's going to be all right, Sweetheart. Believe me."

I dabbed at my eyes and blew my nose. I tried to believe him, but deep inside I believed the pregnancy test, not Art.

Tuesday morning, in Harmonics, we were all gathered close around the piano, working on a new song, when I suddenly felt so dizzy I could no longer stand. I reached for the piano. Everything went black. The next thing I knew, I was on the floor with everyone crowded around me. I heard voices, faint and distant.

"Stand back. Stand back!" Mr. Michaels was saying. "Give her air! . . . Carl, go into my office and call the nurse—there's a directory on my desk."

Open your eyes. Say you're okay, I told myself. But nothing happened. I knew I should move, but I couldn't. I felt a warm hand against my neck.

"Her pulse is okay," I heard Mr. Michaels say. "Has she been sick, Art?"

"No. Nothing like this has ever happened before," he said, so close I could feel his breath on my face.

I finally managed to get my eyes open. "I'm okay," I said weakly. I tried to get up.

"No, no, you just stay here for a while," Mr. Michaels said, gently but firmly holding me down.

"The nurse is on her way," Carl called from the office.

Things were coming clearer to me. Mr. Michaels and Art were both kneeling beside me. The rest of the group were hovering about four feet away. I was mortified.

"**C**an we clear this room out? It's almost time for the bell," a voice boomed into the room.

"Out! out!" I heard heavy footsteps getting closer.

A short, stocky woman in a khaki skirt and blouse knelt down beside me. She took my pulse, felt my hands and forehead, and looked closely into my eyes.

"I'm fine, now."

"Ummm. You're probably right, but we'll take it slow. Do you have a class coming in next period, Mr. Michaels?"

"No. This is my conference period."

"Good. Then if you and this other young gentleman will just go about your business elsewhere, this young lady and I will stay here for a few minutes."

"Sure. And thanks for getting here so quickly," Mr. Michaels said, walking toward his office.

The nurse looked over at Art, who was now sitting on the floor beside me.

"You too," she said. "Scoot. Vamoose. Make like a tree and leave."

"She's my girlfriend," Art said.

"Congratulations. Now go to class."

Art didn't move.

"Really. Go. She'll be okay."

"I'll find you at lunch time," I said, feeling like such a fool over all the fuss.

"Now tell me exactly what happened," the nurse said. I told her. She asked a bunch of questions. Finally she said,

"Think you're pregnant, Emmy?"

I nodded my head, feeling the familiar tears start again.

"This is not good news for you?"

"No," I whispered.

"Let's see if we can get you up," she said, putting her arm under my upper back and helping me to a sitting position.

"Okay?" she said.

She helped me to my feet.

"Steady?"

"Yes. I'm fine."

"Good. Let's go down to my office and talk." She picked up the jacket my head had been resting on and took it to Mr. Michaels.

"She'll be fine," I heard her say.

On the way to her office she introduced herself.

"I'm Mrs. Gould," she said. "And you're Emmy Morrison?"

I nodded yes.

We sat in her office and talked for over an hour. I didn't know *anyone* could think of so many questions to ask. But it was a relief to be able to talk about it. She told me how I could get a MediCal card that would cover basic medical care for the pregnancy, or for abortion if I decided to do that. She was gruff, but I liked her.

"What have you been using for birth control?"

"Condoms and foam," I told her.

"Good for you. Ever have unprotected sex?"

I told her about the time at the beach. She laughed.

"The old pull-out method," she said. "The world is full of cute little pull-out babies. I could name seven from this school alone, just last year. Of course I wouldn't betray any confidences, but take my word for it, they're all over the place . . . Does your boyfriend know you're pregnant?"

"I've tried to tell him, but he doesn't believe me."

"He believes in screwing around and not taking the consequences? Is he one of those?"

"No," I said, feeling defensive for Art.

"No?"

"Well, maybe. I don't know."

"I guess you'll find out soon enough. But from what you told me about your mom and your boyfriend, it doesn't sound like you'd get an abundance of support from them, and as a teen mom, you'll need plenty of help."

She gave me the names of some doctors who accepted MediCal as full payment, told me to get my buns in to one of them, and said she wanted to see me next week, or after I saw the doctor, whichever came first.

"Remember, Emmy. You're not the only one with this problem. It's tough, but it's not insurmountable."

"Even with not much support?"

"Well, that makes things harder. We can talk more about that after we know for sure whether or not you're pregnant."

I got an appointment for Wednesday afternoon with a doctor close to Hamilton High. I'd never, ever experienced anything so embarrassing. I had to climb up on a high table, with nothing on but a flimsy paper thing open all down the back. Then I had to put my feet in these stirrup things, leaving my most private parts wide open and exposed.

Then the doctor put this metal tool inside me and poked around. She was nice, but how nice can a person be who does that kind of stuff all the time?

At the end of the examination, Dr. Kirkpatrick confirmed what I already knew and what Art didn't want to believe.

"We'll send a urine sample to the lab, just to be sure, but everything indicates you're pregnant. You'll probably deliver around May 15, although it's hard to predict right now because you've been so irregular. We'll know more later, as we track the development of the fetus," she said.

She gave me several pamphlets about pregnancy, the importance of good nutrition, and what to expect during labor and childbirth. Yuck. She also talked about abortion and gave me a pamphlet explaining the pros and cons.

"If you're having an abortion, the sooner the better."

"I just don't know yet."

She handed me a bunch of vitamin samples, talked again about the necessity of good nutrition, regular hours, and no tobacco, drugs, or alcohol.

Back home, I stretched out on the couch and read each pamphlet. Gross. The pictures of a fetus inside its mother were scary. How would it ever fit? And then, the pictures of it coming out. Impossible. I remembered how much it hurt when Art and I first had sex. How could a baby possibly come out that little hole? I really, really didn't want to go through that.

I read and reread the pamphlet about abortion. That sounded awful, too. How I wished I could go back in time and undo that night at the beach.

Friday, while David was at the Adult Center taking classes for the G.E.D., Art and I were stretched out on his bed, talking. Even though we knew he wouldn't be back for hours, the room no longer felt like it was our secret haven.

"I have something to show you," I said.

He smiled his dimpled smile. "I love surprises."

"Right," I said, taking my lab report from my pocket and handing it to him. My heart pounded in my chest as I watched him read it over and over again.

"I don't get it," he said.

"Like I've been *trying* to tell you, I'm pregnant."

"But Em . . . How?"

I told him about how Mrs. Gould said there were lots of little pull-out babies running around.

"She says that way before a guy comes, there's fluid with sperm that seeps out. She says it only takes one of those little devils, and they're strong swimmers."

Art just lay there next to me, staring at the ceiling.

"I never heard of that happening," he said.

"Well, it was you, Art. I've never, ever done it with anyone else—I've never even wanted to. This is *our* baby I've got growing inside me."

"I don't know. Maybe. You're going to get rid of it anyway, aren't you?"

"You mean have an abortion?"

"Yes. Have an abortion."

"I don't know yet."

"Emmy, we can't ruin our lives with a baby. Someday we'll want babies, but my God, not now. We've got college, and beginning careers ... Besides, it would kill my mom if I didn't go to Stanford in September."

"Could we for once leave your mother out of this? I've just found out I'm pregnant—or to put it another way—we've just found out we're going to have a baby, and all you can think about is your mother!"

"*We're* not going to have a baby, Emmy. *You're* going to have an abortion. We're not ruining our lives over one little mistake."

I turned to him, trying to get close. "I don't want to fight," I whispered. "I'm just so scared."

Art put his arm around me, lightly, and went back to staring at the ceiling. "I love you, Art. I need you."

"Love you, too, Em," he said coolly.

I hardly slept all that week. I'd wake up in the middle of the night, crying. Sometimes I was crying over a tiny, not-a-chance-to-live, aborted baby, and sometimes I was crying over my own aborted life—no choir tour, no sports, no college. What should I do? What *could* I do?

I kept hearing my Grandma's words, "Remember, Emily, there are no easy answers in this life." How I longed for an easy answer.

I fantasized that the tests were wrong, and that on my next doctor's visit she would tell me it had all been a huge mistake. But I knew. Besides being sick in the mornings, my breasts were getting bigger, and very tender.

How had I ever let myself get into such a mess? I was supposed to be so smart.

10

"**Y**ou've got to tell her, Emmy," David said. "*I'll* tell her, if that would be easier."

We were sitting at the kitchen table the night before Thanksgiving, cutting up fruit for the jello mold I was supposed to take to Art's house the next day.

"She's got to know, Em, before she hears it somewhere else."

"I keep thinking maybe I won't have to say anything. Maybe she'll just notice. You know?"

David peeled and cored another apple and began cutting it into small, even pieces.

"It's still possible to get an abortion," he said.

I shook my head. "For a while that sounded like a pretty good idea," I told him. "That would make Art happy. I could go on choir tour, I'd stay with my eight-year plan, and I could continue to be one of the Project Hope kids. Mom wouldn't even have to know. But I waited too long," I told David.

"Don't be silly. You're only about three months along, aren't you? You've still got time."

"Officially, there's still time. But David, I've already felt those little butterfly moves inside me. It's alive and it's . . . it's . . . part of me," I said, choking on the words. "And what if Mom had had an abortion when she was pregnant with you? She was still in high school, you know."

"Yeah, but you can be sure she was *not* a person with an eight-year plan. If I know old Barb, I'll bet her plans didn't go beyond whatever party was happening that night."

"But at least she *had* you, Dave. That's one good thing she did."

"Maybe. I'm not so sure she did me such a favor."

"I hate when you say things like that."

"Yeah, well, that's just how I feel sometimes. And life may not be so great for that little sperm/egg combo you've got started, either. In a way, I think your idiot boyfriend may be right about the abortion thing. Do it so you can get on with your life."

"I just don't know. One day I think I'll get an abortion and be done with it, and then I feel those little flutters . . . "

David threw the last little piece of apple in the bowl and sat looking at me for a long time. "I don't know why this had to happen to you of all people. Your stupid little schoolboy should have known better," he said angrily.

"C'mon, David. Art didn't mean to get me pregnant. He was being careful."

"Shit," David said, walking out of the room and slamming the front door behind him.

By the time I finished stirring the jello into a pan of hot water, he was back, perched on the counter next to the stove.

"Sorry," he said.

"Okay."

"Whatever you decide, however this whole thing turns out, I'm here for you, Little Sister. I want you to know that."

I felt my throat tighten. My brother was saying what I wanted to hear from Art. The only thing I was hearing from Art these days was a lot of silence with an occasional demand for abortion.

Besides turkey and ham and all the traditional Thanksgiving food, Art's family made tamales and a giant pot of red beans. There were aunts and uncles and cousins. Art's cousin Roger and his girlfriend, Yolanda, were there with their six-month-old baby.

"Is that what you want?" Art said to me, jerking his head

in Yolie's direction.

We were in the kitchen, stacking plates and silverware and setting up serving dishes for the buffet-style meal.

"She's seventeen, she's quit school, she's home all day with her baby, and look at her. God, Emmy, think about it."

I glanced over at Yolie. She was holding the baby, absently rocking back and forth as he squirmed and fussed. She looked tired, and older than seventeen.

"Where'd Roger go?" I asked.

"He's outside drinking beer with the uncles. Trying to escape the baby trap," Art said disgustedly. "You know how that goes."

"No, I don't know how that goes," I said. I walked quickly, angrily, past Art and out back, where his father was cutting flowers for the table.

"Hi, Mija," he said, smiling at me. "Here, a beautiful flower for this beautiful lady. How lucky my son is." He took a pure white camellia and tucked it into my hair, behind my ear. I turned away quickly to hide my tears.

After dinner the men stood around outside, drinking sodas or beer, laughing and telling stories in a mix of Spanish and English. The women did the dishes and cleaned up the kitchen and told their own stories, but without so much laughter.

I don't know why, but the women in Art's family seemed sad to me—not just Art's mom, but his aunts, too. I looked over at Yolie, still sitting in the rocker. I wondered if she would be sad, too. It looked as if she had a good start on the family sadness. I pulled up a chair next to her.

"How old is your baby?" I asked. I already knew the answer, but I couldn't think of anything else to say.

"Six months," she said.

"When are you going back to school?" I asked.

She gave me a sideways glance. "I'm not going back to school," she said. "I don't have nobody to watch my baby."

"But don't they have a place at that special school where

they take care of students' babies?"

"Yeah, but I don't want to leave him with strangers," she replied.

"But how will you ever get a good job if you don't even graduate from high school?"

She looked at me as if I were from another planet. The baby fussed, and she jiggled him on her knees.

"I'm not lookin' for no job," she said sullenly. "Roger's working and I take care of the baby."

"But what about when he's older? Won't you want to work then?"

Yolie shrugged and looked away. I tried to think of something else to talk about, but nothing came. After a while I went back toward the kitchen to see if I could help with the clean-up. Art's mom was sitting at the table with her head resting on her hands.

"I miss my Joey so much on days like this," she sighed. "I don't know what I'd do without Arturo. My life would be over."

The kitchen was full of women working busily, washing and drying dishes, putting food away, but no one seemed to have heard Mrs. Rodriguez. I walked over to where she was sitting and put my hand on her shoulder. She looked up.

"You can't know," she said coldly. "Only a mother can know."

I drew my hand away. There's a lot you don't know, too, I thought, walking through the back door and out to where the little kids were playing badminton. I sat on the edge of Mr. Rodriguez's potting bench and watched the game.

"That was out," one of the little cousins yelled.

"Was not!" came the cry from the other side.

"Was *too*!"

"Was *not*!"

The game stopped while yells of "too" and "not" bounced across the net. I got a glimpse of Art, out by the curb, laughing with one of his uncles. I thought how we had laughed together all the time, before we got into our own word game. It all boiled down to my claiming he got me pregnant and he claiming he did not. Not, too, not, too—like the little kids, our game had stopped, too.

When I looked back at the badminton game, they were playing happily again. I didn't think it would be that easy for me and Art. He had hurt me too much, with his talk about how if I was pregnant it must have been with someone else. I didn't think he really believed it, but still, it hurt a lot to hear him say it.

And he was much more worried about how his mother might react to my pregnancy than he was about anything I was going through. Even if I got an abortion and life went on as usual, I didn't think I would ever again feel as safe and loved with Art as I had at first.

"See you tomorrow," Art said, giving me a quick kiss as he leaned across me to open the door. I got out without a word, slammed his car door, and ran into my house. He peeled out the driveway and down the street. I couldn't even say exactly why we were mad. But we were. There was an iceberg building between us that was bigger than the one that sunk the Titanic.

The light was on in Dave's room, so I put the jello dish down on the kitchen counter and went in to see him. But instead of finding my brother, I found my mom, curled up on her side, staring at nothing. My mom never cried, and I was shocked to see that her eyes were red and puffy.

"Mom? What's wrong?"

She didn't say anything. I looked at her carefully and took a few deep breaths. I didn't think she'd been drinking.

"Mom?"

She let out a deep sigh and pushed herself to a sitting position. I sat on the little camp stool and waited.

"Those damn cops, and your damn stupid brother," she said.

"What? What happened?"

"They came and got him. On Thanksgiving. Damn them!"

"But why?"

"Thanksgiving. I know we never make a big deal of holidays, but I was going to take Dave down to the Fish and Fowl for a good old-fashioned turkey dinner. And just when we start liking each other, they have to take him away," she said, making little choking sounds.

"Mom. Why? Tell me why."

"They had a warrant for his arrest. Something from up north," she said.

"Where did they take him?"

"I don't know. Bastards. They won't tell me anything."

"But he was doing great, Mom. Working and going to school, and he wasn't getting high even on weekends."

"I know. This was from a long time ago."

"Well, it's not fair!" I said, wanting to scream and pound walls, call the president and my senator, something—there had to be something we could do.

"I know I'm not the greatest mother, Em. I drink too much and I've always left you kids on your own a lot, but I swear I love you both—I'll admit there have been times when I've been so mad at your brother I could have killed him, but since he's been home this time things have been different. But now I'm really worried about him. What will this do to him?"

I shook my head. We sat in that little room, which still had the feel of David about it, thinking our own thoughts. I'd never guessed my mom even noticed that she wasn't a great mom, and it was the first time I'd ever heard her say she loved us. I started to move closer to her when the phone rang. I ran for it, hoping it would be David.

"Emmy?"

It was Art.

"Who is it?" my mom yelled from the other room.

I held the phone away. "Just Art," I yelled back.

"Just Art?" he asked.

"I didn't mean it that way. We were hoping to hear

something about David. He was arrested earlier today."

"Tough break," he said. Somehow I expected more, but Art had other things on his mind.

"I've been thinking about us a lot," he said.

"And?"

"This is hard, Em, because you were my first love and all, and I thought we would last forever . . ."

I felt the catch in my throat, the gaping emptiness, before he even said what I knew was coming.

"I don't think we should be together anymore for a while," he said, "at least until you get your problem worked out."

"Art . . ." I started, but found I had nothing to say. What *could* I say?

"I mean, I want us to still be friends. We'll always be friends," he said, "but I can't handle this other stuff right now."

"But Art. I need you. I love you. How can you just change overnight? I thought you loved me," I said, choking back tears.

"I did love you, Em. I do love you. But I just can't handle this right now. Maybe, if you get an abortion, things will be good again. But I really can't handle having a pregnant girlfriend."

"So you're just turning your back on me?" I screamed. "What about me? How do you think I like being pregnant?"

"I'm telling you, get an abortion. Don't stay pregnant."

I hung up the receiver and sat in front of the phone, staring at nothing. Some time later, minutes, hours, I couldn't say, my mom came in.

"Come on, Em. Sitting here in the dark won't help David. Do you want to go get some ice cream at Baskin Robbins?" she asked.

"No thanks, Mom," I said, rousing myself and walking toward my bedroom. She was trying to be nice, but it had been years since a trip to the ice cream parlor could solve my problems. Did she really think my life was that simple?

I crawled into bed and pulled the covers up close around

my chin. Then something strange happened. I started shaking and I couldn't stop. Like in those old movies with guys in the jungle fighting malaria. My teeth chattered and my legs jumped. My whole body jerked uncontrollably. I was cold and sweaty, all at the same time.

"Mom," I tried to say, but nothing would come out. I thought I was dying, and I knew I didn't want to. As bad as things were, I prayed not to die. I swear, my soul left my body and floated somewhere around the ceiling. I could see myself shaking and jerking around on the bed, my hair wet with sweat and kinky the way it gets with the least bit of moisture. I struggled to get back into my body, lowering slowly, rising, then lowering again, each time coming closer.

The next thing I knew, I was fighting to wake up, to place myself somewhere in the familiar, real world. The glowing numbers on my alarm clock told me it was 3:20 in the morning. It was that eerie time when all but the most distant street sounds have quieted, and the smallest movements of insects and night creatures can be heard.

I felt the vast emptiness within me. Art, who had received my most fervent love, was gone from me. My brother, my most loyal and trusted friend, was in trouble, somewhere far beyond me. My mother thought my problems were insignificant enough to be eased by an ice cream cone. Tammy and Pauline were still good friends, sort of, but lately we'd been drifting apart. And besides, no matter how close a person is to her friends, it's not like family love, or the true love of a guy.

I was alone, in the dark, with no one. I cried with loneliness for the Art I thought had loved me, and for my missing brother, and for the mother who didn't care enough to know me. I cried for my dead grandmother, too. How I wished I could look into her sweet, calm face and talk with her again, just for a few minutes. What would become of me?

By morning, I knew what I would do. I would have the baby. Maybe it was a stupid thing to do. It wasn't that I thought it was a sin, or some kind of murder, to have an abortion. That's not why I decided to go through with the pregnancy.

It was more that I thought maybe this was my only chance to have someone who was truly mine, someone who I could pour my love out to, and who would love me back.

It wouldn't be easy. I worried about how I would tell my mom, and what Tammy and Pauline would think of me. But my mind was made up.

I went back to sleep and slept through until 8:30. I awoke rested and not feeling sick at all. I waited, listening in my room for sounds that my mother was awake. I knew what I was going to say.

CHAPTER

11

"What do you mean, you're holding him until his hearing? What are the charges?"

I guess I must have dropped off to sleep again, because it was 9:15 and my mom was already on the phone. I pulled on some sweat pants and an old T-shirt and went out to the kitchen in time to hear my mom slam down the phone.

"What'd they say about David?" I asked, sleepily.

"They're keeping him in jail until his hearing. That's unless I can come up with $20,000 bond. Where would I get $20,000? Besides, he got himself into it, I guess he can get himself out."

"But why did they arrest him in the first place?"

"I don't know. Some drug thing from up north. They may be sending him back up there."

My heart sank. My poor brother. In jail. I knew he'd been doing illegal stuff up there, but really, he was the nicest guy I knew. Being nice and trying to turn your life around ought to keep you out of jail. But it wasn't working for David.

I watched my mom fussing around the kitchen. I was three inches taller than she, which gave me a bird's eye view of the dark brown roots preceeding her latest bleach job. There was no easy way to say it, so I just blurted out, "I'm pregnant."

"You're *what*?" my mother screamed at me.

"Pregnant," I said, watching her drain the grease from the bacon which would go into her standard mid-morning

BLT breakfast.

"I don't believe this," she said, turning to look at me.

I shrugged. "So believe it or not," I said. "That's how it is."

"For Christ's sake, Emmy, I thought you were smarter than that!" she said, still screaming.

"As smart as you were, I guess."

"I was eighteen when I had David, not *fifteen*!"

"I'll be sixteen by the time I have the baby."

"God. I suppose you and Art are going to get married and live happily ever after," she said sarcastically.

"Not exactly," I told her, turning away from her gaze.

She slapped a glob of mayonnaise on one slice of bread, mustard on the other, and cut a thick slice of tomato.

"Want a sandwich?" she asked.

"No, thanks."

"So. Are you sure, Em?"

"Yeah. I'm not hungry."

"Not that!" she said, piling bacon on one side of the bread, then adding the tomato and lettuce. "I *mean* are you sure you're pregnant?"

"I'm sure," I said. Then I told her about fainting at school, and my talk with the nurse, and seeing the doctor. She sat at the table, eating her sandwich, with a cigarette burning in an ashtray beside the paper towel she was using for a plate. She was thirty-six. When my baby got to be my age, I would be thirty-two.

"How far along are you?" she asked.

"About three months."

"So what does Art say?"

"Art and I aren't together anymore."

"You were just out with him yesterday," she said, looking me in the eye for the first time since I'd said the "P" word. "What do you mean, you're not together?"

"We broke up," I said, going to the sink to rinse my juice glass. Don't cry. Be strong. Don't let her see you cry, I repeated to myself over and over, trying to concentrate on other things. I reached under the sink, took out the cleanser, and started scrubbing the week's coffee stains away. I felt my back grow hot under the intensity of my mother's gaze.

"I never did trust that little wetback."

"Mom!"

"Really, Em. He gets you pregnant and then he's out of here? Is that it? I told you, you ought to stick to white boys."

"That's got nothing to do with it," I said, scrubbing at a stain that had been in the yellowed enamel sink since the day we moved into the place. Why did she always have to go off on some tangent? All I wanted to do was tell her I was pregnant, and she had to dump her stupid prejudices on me.

There was a long pause. Then she said, "I can help. My hands are tied as far as David is concerned, but I'll help you."

"You will?" I was stunned. I couldn't remember a time my mother had ever said the words "I'll help you." Suddenly my defenses were down and tears came pouring down my cheeks. I turned to find her standing behind me. She put her arms around me, holding me stiffly in an unfamiliar embrace. The heaviness of stale cigarette smoke overcame me, and I pulled away. She went to the phone on the wall and dialed a number by heart.

"Sheila?. . .You know the clinic you went to a few months back when you had that little problem? . . .Yeah . . . Can I have the number?. . . No, it's not for me," she said with a laugh. "I took care of that business a long time ago when I got my tubes tied . . . I tell you, it's the only way to go." She laughed again, a coarse laugh that made me uneasy. "Just a friend," she said, with a conspiratorial wink in my direction. She wrote down a number, thanked Sheila, and hung up. I watched her dial the number she had just written as it slowly occurred to me what she was doing. I reached past her to the phone and pressed the receiver down.

"What are you doing?" she asked.

"I'm not having an abortion if that's what you think."

"That's what I *know*, Emily. You're for sure not having a baby!"

"Yes, I am. I've already made up my mind!"

"Well, unmake it. It's not going to happen. I'm not going to let you ruin your life with a baby."

"It's *my* life. And it's *my* baby."

"How can you possibly take care of a baby? You're just a child yourself."

"I thought you said you'd help."

"I *will* help. I'll help you get an abortion. But, Emily, I can't afford a baby, and you for sure don't have any money. And who would take care of it? You've got school. It's not a doll that can sit on your bed all day while no one's at home, you know. And don't even *think* that I'd be hanging around here taking care of some squalling kid."

"Why would I think that?" I screamed. "You never even took care of your own kids. You left that all up to *your* mother."

"Yeah, well, I'm not like my mother, so don't you go thinking you can turn some half-breed baby over to me!"

I ran out the front door and down the driveway.

"You come back here right now," The Barb yelled at me. "Don't you go anywhere until we get this settled!"

I just kept running. I'd had all the help I could take from her in one day. I must have run three blocks before it occurred to me that maybe running at top speed wasn't on the list of things pregnant women should be doing. I slowed to a walk. One of the pamphlets I'd picked up in the doctor's office recommended walking as good exercise for expectant mothers. Something about that term, expectant mothers, amused me, and I found myself smiling through tears as I walked, almost without thinking, the two miles to Tammy's house. It wasn't until I opened her front gate that I remembered the whole family was visiting her uncle in Fresno for the Thanksgiving holiday.

I walked on another mile or so to the park where the three of us, Tammy, Pauline, and I, had first played AYSO soccer. I sat on the deserted jungle gym and looked out over the grass. How I longed for those simpler days when one of my friend's parents would drive us to the game, all suited up with chin guards and knee pads. After, we'd usually go to McDonald's, or Pizza Palace, and relive the game.

Over by the little slide, there was a mom and dad with a baby who could barely walk. They would lift her gently to the top of the slide and then, one on each side, hold her under her arms while she slowly slid to the bottom. The baby laughed with delight each time she started the slide, and then her parents laughed, too. It seemed that none of them would ever tire of it. I tried to picture myself by the slide with my own baby, but I couldn't make the picture seem real.

A shiver ran through me as a cool breeze swept autumn leaves in little flurries. I wished I had grabbed a sweatshirt in my hurry to leave. According to the clock on the restroom wall, it was only 10:30. I couldn't go home until at least 3:00, when I knew for sure my mom would be gone.

I walked over to the recreation center in hopes that I could find a warmer place to sit, but the sign said they wouldn't be open until Saturday morning. Oh, well. That's how things had been going for me lately, anyway. From the big stuff to the little stuff, nothing went right.

By the time I finally got home, I was frozen. I turned the gas wall heater on in the living room and stood in front of it, rubbing my arms and legs until I felt warmed clear through.

On Friday nights Art and I usually went to a movie or to a party at a friend's house. Even though I remembered everything he'd said the night before, as in "I don't think we should be together for a while," I got ready anyway. I took a steaming hot shower and washed my hair with a vanilla-scented shampoo. Art loved the smell of my hair when I used that shampoo.

I put on fresh jeans and a teal blue sweater, and sat in front of the T.V. waiting. Once I thought I heard his car, but it turned out just to be the man across the street. The phone rang about 8:30. Art apologizing for being late—he'd be right over, and then everything would be okay. That was my hope. I let it ring three times, so he wouldn't think I'd been sitting around waiting.

"Hello?"

"Hello. Is Benny there?"

That was it. One phone call—wrong number.

Mom came in around midnight—early for her. I pretended to be asleep, but she insisted on talking. She turned on my light and poked me until I had to respond.

"I was telling Edie today about the mess you're in," Mom said.

"Thanks a lot. Maybe you'd like to put it on the bulletin board down there, too."

"Drop the sarcasm, would you?" Mom said, pushing my legs over and sitting on the edge of my bed. "It just came up because she was telling me about her niece who announced at their Thanksgiving dinner that she was pregnant. Rhonda, remember her?"

"Rhonda? The one who used to tag after us whenever she came to visit? Isn't she a lot younger than I am?"

"She's thirteen."

"And pregnant?" I moaned.

"That's how I feel about you," The Barb said. "Really, seriously, I don't want to fight with you, but I want you to get an abortion. It's the only thing that makes sense."

"I don't want to fight either," I said, "But I know for sure I'm going to have the baby." I turned my back away from her and stuck my head under the pillow. She sat there for what seemed like a long time, then left. She didn't bother to turn the light out on her way.

Tammy called about seven Sunday evening.

"Am I ever glad to be home. Fresno's got to be the deadest town in the world."

"Not as dead as this one if your name happens to be Emily Morrison," I complained.

"Dead? I bet you and Art have more excitement in one evening than all of Fresno has in a year."

"Not anymore," I said. "We broke up."

"What? Why? I bet it's that Amy witch."

"No. It's just Art. It's what he wants."

I was glad to be talking to Tammy on the phone rather than in person. It always embarrassed me to have people see me cry. I think she knew anyway because my voice wasn't very steady, but at least we weren't face to face.

"He just thinks we shouldn't be together for a while." I tried to explain without explaining.

"There's something you're not telling me, Em," she said. "Remember me? Your Brownie buddy? Your blood sister?"

"I've got big problems," I told her, and then it all came out. There was a long silence after I confessed that I was pregnant. Finally she said, "How can you be pregnant? I didn't even know you were doing it."

For the first time in days, I laughed.

"You didn't have to know we were doing it for me to get pregnant, Tammy."

"But *doing* IT? I thought I would be the first to do it."

We laughed again. Nothing like a crisis to send good friends into fits of hysterical laughter.

She asked me all the details. Did I know for sure? What did Art say? Had I told my mom? What was I going to do?

"Are you scared?"

"Really. Scared and confused."

"You're coming to my house after school tomorrow," Tammy said. "My folks go square dancing on Monday nights and my sister goes to Granny's, so we'll have the house to ourselves. We'll eat pizza and talk all night. God, I can't believe I'm going to be Aunt Tammy within a few short months. Shall we invite Pauline over, too?"

"I don't know. I'm afraid Pauline is going to be all uptight. You know how she's been acting lately anyway."

"You mean the Miss-I-Can-Do-No-Wrong-You're-Never-Right attitude?"

"Exactly."

"Well. I'll leave it up to you. You're the bad girl this time. Call her if you want, otherwise it'll just be you and me and baby makes three," she laughed.

"Tammy?"

"Yes?"

"Don't tell your mom yet. Okay?"

"Okay. But why not?"

"I don't know. I guess I'm just embarrassed."

"My mom'll love you anyway, don't you think?"

"Well, she has so far. But I'd just like to wait a while. Okay?"

"Okay. You're the boss."

I thought I would call Pauline, but somehow I never got around to it. I guess I wasn't quite ready to talk to her about my situation. But I was happy to be going to Tammy's the next night. The great thing about Tammy was that she never seemed shocked by anything, and she always liked me, no matter what. And I sure could stand some time away from The Barb.

Tammy called back about midnight. "I can't sleep," she said. "I'm worried about you. I laughed and joked around about being Auntie Tammy, but then when I really thought about it . . . This isn't funny, Em. It's awful."

"I know."

"I don't know how you can do it."

"I don't know either. I only know I have to."

"Well, we can talk more tomorrow night," Tammy said. "Good night, Emmy."

"Thanks, Tammy. 'Night."

CHAPTER

12

It didn't take long for me to know who my true friends were. From the first night I told Tammy, she stood by me. When my mom threatened to kick me out, Tammy offered to share her room with me, and when I started crying after choir one day, hearing Art's silence one too many times, Tammy joked me out of feeling sorry for myself.

Pauline was another story.

"I never thought one of *my* friends would be a teenage mother," she said. "I think it's really stupid. And you of all people!"

"So does this mean my baby can't call you Auntie Pauline?" I asked. Tammy and I both laughed.

"I don't think it's very funny," she said, scowling at me.

"It isn't funny," I admitted. "But I can't cry all the time. I'm tired of crying."

"Well, you've ruined your life."

By the time I was showing, December to the careful observer, January to everyone else, Pauline was avoiding me at school. She still called now and then, but at school she kept her distance, like maybe pregnancy was contagious.

Teachers were funny, too. I began to feel invisible in some of my classes. In history, where Mr. Garner used to always call on me for the hard answers, I could hold my arm up until my fingers went to sleep and he'd call on everyone *but* me. He was the worst, but Miss Rosenbloom, in English, now seemed a lot less interested in me, too. I was still getting "A"s, but as far as class discussion went, "A" stood for anonymous.

Mr. Michaels moved me from the front row to the back for Harmonics performances. He moved a lot of others around, too, but I thought it was mainly because he wanted my growing belly to be hidden from public view. Maybe I was just getting paranoid, though.

When we got back from Christmas vacation, Mrs. Werly called me into her office.

"It looks as if you need to make some changes in the planning part of your portfolio," she said, pulling her copy of my goals form from a file drawer.

"I guess so," I said, not meeting her eyes.

"What do you mean, you *guess* so, Emily? Don't you think your condition demands some changes? Or do you just think you'll have a baby and park it somewhere and not be at all inconvenienced?"

I looked up, surprised by the anger in her voice. Her face was tight and stern looking. "I doubt that you'll be going off into the woods to be a forest ranger if you've got a child to drag along and care for," she said, sarcastically. "And I doubt that you'll go away to college if you've got a baby to take care of. So think about it. Maybe you want to go back to your mother's bookkeeping plan for you."

"But I still want to go to college," I said.

She looked at my goal sheet again, shook her head, marked "REVISE" across it in huge letters with a yellow highlighter, then put it back in the file cabinet.

"When is the baby due?" she asked.

"May 20."

"You can start at Teen Mothers the first of February. That's the beginning of second semester."

"I'd rather stay here."

"Maybe you should have thought about that four or five months ago," she said.

"But why can't I? There's a girl in my Algebra II class, Josie, I think her name is. She's a lot farther along than I am and she's still here."

"Legally, we can't force you to go to Teen Mothers," Mrs. Werly said. "But if you stay here and have your baby in May, you're going to miss so much school you can't possibly pass your classes. The Teen Mothers program is set up so that you can pass your classes even though you have to be out for several weeks."

"But I could make up any work I miss," I pleaded.

"It doesn't work that way, Emily. This is not a correspondence school, and your teachers are much too busy to give you your own little individualized month's worth of work. No. If you want to pass your classes next semester, Teen Mothers is the place for you. Besides, you'll learn a lot of practical things about how to take care of a baby and what to expect during childbirth. History and Algebra II are probably not as important to young mothers as how to bathe and diaper a baby."

I listened as she outlined the program for me—a van would pick me up and take me home each day. I would work on basic requirements, English, history, math, along with preparing for childbirth and taking child development classes.

"You may want to finish high school through the continuation program, rather than trying to return here. Most girls find that works best for them. That way, when you have to miss school because your baby is sick, or for doctor's appointments, you can easily work things out with your teachers."

"I'm coming back here in September."

"Ummm," she said. "Maybe so. We'll see."

When I left Mrs. Werly's office, I had the feeling she was erasing me from the memory bank in her brain.

The choir room was filled with posters of New York City. There was a chart on the wall with all our names on it and little paper airplane cutouts. How ironic that my airplane had already landed on the New York space. I had sold enough candy, sung enough concerts, got enough sponsors for the walkathon, that my way was totally paid for. Too bad I would be about nine months along by then.

Carl's airplane was right behind mine, and Art's, though I tried not to notice, was over Pittsburgh. The rest were strewn out across the United States, with Amy's still being closest to home.

Now that we were finished with our Winter Concert and Christmas performances, everything we did revolved around the New York trip. We were learning "New York, New York," and "East Side, West Side (All Around the Town)." We were practicing "East Side, West Side," complete with choreography, one mid-January morning when Mr. Michaels yelled, "Freeze. Hold it right there."

We stopped and turned to face him.

"No. Get back exactly the way you were. Girls—hands on your partner's shoulders. Boys, arms around your partner's waist."

It just so happened that Art and I were partners in this section of the dance. Mr. Michaels never paired us up, but in this one song, we shifted partners eight times, and there was no avoiding a short six steps with Art.

Usually we moved through it so quickly that it hardly seemed real. But on this day we were frozen, my hands resting lightly on Art's shoulders, his arms around my alive, thickened middle. There we all stood, listening intently to Mr. Michaels' instructions, touching, yet trying not to, when the baby gave a mammoth kick. Art jumped back about three feet, as if he'd been jabbed by a red-hot poker.

"Art?" Mr. Michaels said, looking at him with his "I'm close to annoyed" look.

"Sorry," Art muttered, and stepped back into position, but holding his hands out a little, not touching me. There were snickers from the others. Suddenly, I felt like a leper.

I ran from the room and down the hall. The reality of a

five-month pregnant body forced me soon to slow from a run to a walk, but I went, fast as I could, out the front gate and headed home. One of the narcs came running after me, insisting that I get back to class, but I yelled at him that I was sick, and I kept walking.

At home, I crawled in through David's window and threw myself on the bed, crying. How could my life have changed so drastically in such a few short months? I could still sense Art's presence in the little room. He had been such a part of me, we had belonged to each other. Now, the body he had loved so fully repulsed him.

I lay on my back, hands resting on my stomach, watching a spider at work spinning a web near the ceiling light fixture. Was it the same spider we had watched one sticky afternoon last summer as we lay close, weary from lovemaking? We had talked then of the wonders of nature— the thin silken thread of the complex patterned web—the dragline that offered quick escape and a safe return. I wished for a dragline of my own, but I was beyond a quick escape. I ran my hands over my stomach, trying to remember what it had felt like, flat.

If I had had an abortion, like my mom and Art wanted me to do, it would all be over by now. I would be trying to figure out how to get enough money together to buy a dressy outfit for the night the Harmonics were scheduled to see a Broadway play. Instead, I needed to add another extra-large sweat shirt to my limited wardrobe.

The baby kicked, another strong one. It made me laugh now, thinking how it had kicked its disbelieving dad. Already, I thought, this kid has a mind of its own. As I lay there, feeling the life within me, watching the spider working away at its own life, I heard the comforting sound of rain, tap, tap, tapping on the roof overhead.

I remembered those rainy-day forts David used to build with me when I was so little I still wanted our mother to come home to us. He would throw blankets over kitchen chairs and we'd hide there, protected from the bogey-man.

And we would run outside in the rain, our heads thrown back and our mouths wide open, pretending we had been lost in the desert for months, and this was the water from God that would save our lives.

The picture of David smiled down at me from his dresser. He had ten more months to go—maybe only six with good behavior. We wrote every week. If my baby was a boy, it would be David. If it was a girl, it would be Rosemary, after my grandmother. I wanted to name my baby after a love-filled person. I wanted my baby to be surrounded by love.

The rain was coming harder now, steady and substantial. I walked outside, out in the middle of the yard. I stood with my head back and my mouth open, letting the water wash over me.

I stood for a long time, then held out my arms and slowly turned in a circle, looking up at the gray sky until, dizzy, I flopped down on the rain-dampened weedy grass.

The baby kicked, and I laughed. "Little Rosie-David," I thought, "you'd better be a kicker for this life." I got up, still laughing, and went back to the house.

I saw a thin sliver of light coming from a separated blind in Mrs. Dugan's house as I walked up the driveway. Spying on the pregnant bad-girl, I thought, but I didn't mind. Mrs. Dugan had entertained and educated me for so many years when I needed something more than I had, I couldn't be angry with her now. In fact, maybe I should give my baby a middle name after her. David Dugan? Rosemary Dugan?

I laughed again as I grabbed a towel from the hall closet and started drying my soaked hair. I can't explain it, but somehow I felt cleaner, lighter, than I had for a long time.

I waited until 3:00, when school was out. Then I went back to the music room to pick up the books I'd left there when I rushed out. Mr. Michaels was working with two freshman boys, trying to get them to match pitches. I couldn't imagine what it would be like, not to be able to hear a distinction between a C and a C sharp, or an A and an A flat, but these guys sounded like they couldn't tell an A from a Z.

When Mr. Michaels saw me, he said, "Stick around for a few minutes, would you, Emily?" then turned back to his tone-deaf students and told them he thought they'd all worked hard enough for one day.

"Have a seat," he said, motioning me toward a desk next to the piano. As the boys left, they slammed the door shut behind them. Mr. Michaels walked back over and opened it wide. I got all paranoid again. Like maybe he thought if he was alone in a room with me, with the door closed, I'd accuse him of being my baby's father. I know Art told his soccer coach that I'd lied about him being the father of my baby. Maybe he'd given Mr. Michaels the same story.

Mr. Michaels sat down across from me on the piano stool.

"Emily, I'm sorry you're having difficulties in Harmonics," he said. "I know this has to be a hard time for you in many ways."

I nodded.

"I can't choreograph everything around trying to keep you and Art separate, you know. That was very disruptive this morning. I'm not blaming you, but I can't have people running out of the room in the midst of rehearsal."

"I know that," I mumbled.

"We need you in the group. You're very talented—a strong singer and you work well with the others. Try to keep your personal problems out of it."

"Okay," I said, wishing the words would come to explain my feelings, but they didn't.

"What shall we do with the $650 you've earned for the trip? You can donate it to the group to offset costs, or I can maybe figure out a way to hold it over for you for next year. I can't just hand it to you because, officially, it's money earned by the whole choir."

"Could I donate it just to Carl and Becky?" I asked.

"Nope—all or none."

"You mean I would be helping to pay Amy's expenses? And Art's?"

"Yes, and Monica's, and Bobby's, and Eric's, and . . ."

"No. Hold it over for next year then."

"What if you don't come back next year?"

"I'll be here. And if I don't get accepted back into the Harmonics, then just pass it on to next year's group."

"You'll be accepted back, unless you lose your voice in the labor room."

"Does that ever happen?" I asked.

"Not that I know of. I would think that would be the least of your worries."

I smiled and picked up my books. "Thanks, Mr. Michaels."

On the way out I caught a glimpse of Art and Amy at the end of the hall. I guess he was on his way to soccer practice. He didn't see me, but I think Amy did. She looked straight at me, then looked back at Art and blew him an exaggerated kiss.

"Bye, Mr. Mole," she said in her sickening, insinuating way.

"Bye, Babe," he said.

My stomach turned flip-flops, and this time it wasn't the baby. It was something deep inside me, in my lonely inner being, getting lonelier. Mr. Mole, I thought. If ever there was even the slightest hope that Art would love me again, it was gone with those sing-songy words that Amy had just sent out into the hallway.

I walked home in the rain, trying to get back the clean, free feeling it had brought earlier, but I felt tired and heavy as I trudged along to the rhythm of "Good-bye, Mr. Mole. Good-bye, Mr. Mole." I pictured the little triangular shaped mole on Art's butt, saw, as in a movie, how I had kissed it lightly, playfully, back when his love felt true and safe. I heard his old words, "Only you, Em. First, last, and always. Em and Art."

Once home, still soaked from the rain, I opened my English textbook and read and reread the assigned poems. Emily Dickinson. Everything touched me, like I was raw and undefended. There is one that ends "Parting is all we know of heaven/And all we need of hell." I agreed with the hell part, even if I didn't understand about heaven. But the one that got me was a short, rhymed poem titled "A Word." It went:

A word is dead
When it is said,
Some say.
I say it just
Begins to live
That day.

I was afraid that's how the "Mr. Mole" words would be for me, always alive, eating at my roots, stealing my strength.

13

I finished the semester with all "A"s. But in two of my classes my citizenship grades had dropped from excellent to satisfactory. It wasn't fair—I was behaving the way I always had in class. I went to see my counselor.

"They just don't like me since they know I'm pregnant," I told Mrs. Werly.

"Oh, I doubt that. Your mind is on other things now. You've probably not been as attentive in class as usual," she said, shuffling through some papers on her desk.

I choked back tears of frustration. "No. *I* haven't changed. They have. Mr. Garner and Miss Rosenbloom act like I'm not even there."

Mrs. Werly looked up. "Teachers are human, too," she commented, "although I doubt that either Mr. Garner or Miss Rosenbloom have been unfair, no matter how disappointed they may be."

"Disappointed?" I asked.

"We all hate to lose a bright, capable girl to pregnancy. It seems such a waste."

"I'm not lost. I'm coming back. I'm going to college!"

"You'll come *half* back, if at all. You can never again fully apply yourself to school once you have a baby."

"You'll see," I said, awkwardly rising from the chair.

As I walked out the door of the counseling office, Mrs. Werly called after me, "Good luck to you at Teen Mothers."

The first day of second semester I stood waiting on the curb in front of my house, in an extra large sweat shirt that hung over my partially unbuttoned jeans. I groaned when I saw the yellow van round the corner. It was the same as all those other school vans that carried the kids I'd always felt sorry for, like the retarded kids and the deaf kids. I never thought I'd be riding in such a van, stared at by curious eyes as we made our way toward the little "special" school.

All of the window seats were taken. I sat next to a girl I had seen around Hamilton, but hadn't really known.

"When's your baby due?" she asked.

"May 20," I said. "How about you?"

"April 12."

She looked huge. Her blouse was pulled tight across her belly, and she was resting her hands on it, like it was a shelf or something.

"You're Emily, aren't you?"

I nodded.

"I heard you sing at the Harvest Concert. You were really good."

"Thanks," I said, embarrassed.

"I'm Monique."

"Hi, Monique."

I didn't know what to say after that, and I guess Monique didn't either, because we rode on, watching traffic, not talking. I wondered if we would be friends. She had a dark, pretty face and a friendly smile.

I wasn't usually sick in the mornings anymore, but the van ride was getting to me. Finally, we pulled into a long driveway and stopped by two large metal buildings which were sitting in the middle of a big asphalt parking lot. I followed Monique inside.

It looked more like kindergarten than high school, I thought. There was a bulletin board along half of one wall that was crammed with pictures of babies. A teddy bear mobile hung from the ceiling. Each of the bears had a big red heart with a baby's name and birth date written inside.

There was a row of paper cups lined up along the window, and little green sprouts were shooting out of each one.

There were toilet paper rolls, string, colored paper, glue, rulers, and scissors all over two big tables on the other side of the room. A tall black woman in bright African-looking clothing greeted me.

"You must be Emily," she said, reaching out to shake my hand. "I'm Camille Dodson." Her smile was broad and welcoming, and I immediately felt at ease with her.

"Sit down," she said, patting the back of the chair next to a desk cluttered with books and folders, markers and coffee cups. "Take a minute to fill out this emergency card."

I carefully printed my mom's business address and phone number, but I didn't have that information for my doctor.

"Bring it tomorrow," the teacher said. "Come join us for class meeting. Just drag that chair over and find a spot in the circle."

Monique scooted over to make a place for me.

"This is Emily Morrison," Ms. Dodson said. "Now let's go around the circle and introduce ourselves—name, due date, and something you did this weekend. Let's start with you, Monique."

"Well. I'm Monique, and my baby's due April 12. Me'n Julio got pizza and watched 'Silence of the Lambs.'"

"Ugh. How could you eat and watch that movie?" one of the girls asked. The others laughed.

"No comments when we go around the circle, remember, April?"

"Sorry, teacher," she said in a teasing way.

"Okay, you're next, Bertha."

"I'm Bertha. My baby's due next Friday, and I fought with my boyfriend all weekend."

"I'm Candice. My baby's due March 23, and my mom and I rearranged my room so we can get a crib in there soon."

A shy, pretty girl with hair as shiny black as Amy's said softly, "Veronica. May 28th."

There were fifteen girls and two teachers sitting around the circle. The other teacher was Mrs. Prim, a little gray-haired lady with a soft voice. Her name fit her perfectly. The girls all called her Mrs. Prim, but the younger teacher they called Camille. It seemed strange to me to call a teacher by her first name.

When it came my turn, I said, "I'm Emily. My baby's due May 20. This Saturday I went up to Ventura to watch my soccer team in the playoffs."

I felt my face grow hot with embarrassment. Here I was, six months pregnant, talking about "my" soccer team. My world had passed me by, but I still didn't get it.

After class meeting, we sat two or three to a table and worked on our individual programs. I would continue with Algebra II, Honors English, and U.S. History. But I couldn't get a lab science and there sure was no music program at Teen Moms.

We only were in school from 9:00 to 1:00. I was used to starting at 7:30, for the Hamilton Harmonics, and getting out at 3:10—4:15 during soccer and softball. Four hours was nothing.

Camille brought a composition book to me. "Every day in class we set aside fifteen minutes for moms to write to their babies. You can spend more time if you want, but at least fifteen minutes."

"What do you mean?"

"Well, sort of a journal. Tell your baby how you're feeling, what plans you're making for it, anything. Just start communicating. Your baby will love having it read to him or her later on, and for now, unborns sense messages that are coming in from their mothers. You know, down 'n dirty, tell it like it is, from the gut feelin' stuff, girl."

It amazed me that Camille flipped back and forth between talking like a Ph.D. sociologist one minute and a street-gang hoodlum the next. I'd never had a teacher like her before.

The whole journal thing sounded silly to me, but as soon

as we got back from lunch break, everyone took out their composition books and started writing, so I did, too.

Dear Baby,

Today is my first day at Teen Moms. I'm here because of you. You're not even out in the world yet, and already you've changed my life. I love your little kicks. I think maybe you'll be a soccer player, like your mom. Try not to worry because, even though my life is a little messed up right now, I'm going to be a really good mom. Love, your mom, Emily Morrison

On the way home, Monique said, "Why have you got so many books?"

"'Cause . . . I don't want to be behind in school when I go back to Hamilton."

"I don't think I'll even go back. School's never done that much for me," Monique said.

"Not go back? You mean be a dropout?" I couldn't believe it. I thought the only people who were dropouts were my brother's friends.

"Julio doesn't want me to leave the baby with anyone else. I don't think I'd like that either. I mean, why have a baby if you're going to go off and leave it?"

"But not even finish high school?"

"What's the big deal about a diploma? I'm having a baby. Julio will help with money. And I can get welfare. My mom wants us to stay with her, so we won't have to worry about rent."

The van stopped in front of a run-down house with bars on its windows. The paint was chipping and peeling and the porch steps were broken, but the yard was green and pretty, with a peach tree in front and lots of flowers bordering the front and sides. The whole place was surrounded by a high chain link fence and the front gate was padlocked.

"See you tomorrow," Monique said. She pulled herself up and walked/waddled down the steps of the van to her gate.

As we slowly pulled away, I watched Monique. She was

fumbling in her purse, I guess for the gate key, when a heavyset woman wearing tight pants and a T-shirt came out of the house to greet her.

I couldn't hear what they were saying, but as Monique unlocked the gate and walked toward the woman, they seemed happy to see each other. They met on the front walk and hugged, then walked hand in hand back up the broken steps and into the house. I got that lonely, empty feeling again.

I couldn't concentrate on my homework. I went to the fridge for a soda, but then I remembered that junk food wasn't good for my baby, so I poured a glass of milk. I took a few swallows, but it wasn't what I wanted, so I dumped the milk and went back for the soda. It's not like I smoke, or use alcohol, or anything stupid like that, I told myself, trying not to feel guilty. But I couldn't really enjoy the soda, so I ended up dumping that, too.

I took a nap, watched Oprah Winfrey, and counted the minutes until Tammy would be home and I could call her—5:00 should do it, I thought. I made myself wait until 5:10.

"Is Tammy there?" I asked when Mrs. Preston answered.

"No, Honey. She called to say she was going to get a bite to eat with some of the girls from drill team. She'll probably be home around seven. Shall I have her call you?"

"Oh, it's okay. I'll try her again later."

"How are you feeling?"

"Pregnant," I sighed.

Mrs. Preston laughed. "Just wait until the ninth month if you think you feel pregnant now."

"Thanks a lot," I said, sarcastically.

"Sure. Any time you need a lift, call Mom Preston," she said, laughing again.

I *did* feel a little better after I hung up. Mrs. Preston was the only adult in my life who treated me the same now as she had before she knew I was pregnant. Pauline's parents didn't want Pauline hanging around with me anymore. And my own mom had been mad at me since the day I told her. "I can't take on the care and expense of another child," she kept telling me, as if she'd devoted her life to me and David. What a joke. As far as I was concerned, she'd never have to change one diaper or spend one penny on my baby.

The trouble was, I didn't know how I was going to get any pennies to spend on it either. My grandma had left $6,000 in a trust fund for me, but I couldn't get it until I was eighteen. David already got his. He spent it on a truck that wouldn't run, a great stereo, and I'm not sure what else.

In the circle at Teen Moms, several girls had talked about how their moms had taken them shopping for baby things, or were working to get a room put together for their babies. The only difference I could see in my mom since I'd told her I was pregnant was that she was staying out later than usual, and she was mad all the time instead of just most of the time.

A little after eight I was reaching for the phone to call Tammy when it rang. It was Tammy. That happened all the time.

"Hey, Mom," she said.

"I had my hand on the phone to call you."

"Weird," she said. "We've got those psychic waves."

Already I was in a better mood, talking to Tammy. I told her about Teen Moms, and having to ride in the disability bus. She told me about drill team, and lunch.

"I ate with Bobby today, so you know who else was there," she said, sounding apologetic.

"Art?"

"Yeah, Art. And Amy from hell."

I didn't say anything. It was bad enough that I was away from my old friends, and that I still had this Art-ache that ran through me, from gut to backbone, but now I had to hear about how Tammy had lunch with Art and Amy.

"I swear to God, Em, I hate that chick. Not just because she's with Art, and what an idiot Art's turned into, but just because she's an overall witch . . . Do you know what she did today?"

I should have changed the subject, but I couldn't help listening. It was like how you keep pressing a bruise, just to see if it still hurts. Anytime I heard anything about Art or Amy, I was all ears. And it always, without fail, hurt.

"Bobby and I were at a table in Senior Court, eating lunch and talking with Art. Well . . . Bobby was talking with Art. I was just sitting there. Anyway, the witch gives me this Lucretia look and says, 'Where's your friend today? You know, the one that used to be described as tall and thin? Did she go to the bad girl school?'"

"What did Art say?" I asked.

"He sat there, staring at his hamburger like he'd never seen one before . . . I felt like shoving her stupid smile clear down her throat, but I just got up and went to a different table. Bobby followed me.

"'I don't need that from her,' I told him. He doesn't like her either. He says Art's only with her for one reason."

"Like he was with me?"

"Bobby doesn't think that. He thinks Art still loves you, but he's using Amy to try to forget."

"He's got a nice way of showing his love," I said, absently rubbing my warm, protruding belly.

"Yeah, well, Bobby says Art's mom'd been raggin' him for months to break up with you—she wants him to only hang out with girls from Hamilton Estates."

"I wonder if that's why she invited me to go to the airport with them that time—just so she could check out where I live?"

"It wouldn't surprise me," Tammy said. "According to Bobby, Art's mom thinks she married beneath herself, marrying a gardener and all, and she doesn't want her precious baby to make the same mistake. Bobby says Art can't face telling his mom you're pregnant."

"So . . . he can pretend he had nothing to do with it?"

"Well, yeah, I guess. What can I say? His mom's really

crazy, and it runs in the family."

"I hope my baby doesn't take after them."

"Yeah, well, your mom's not exactly a model of sanity herself."

Tammy laughed and so did I, but I wondered, can babies inherit that stuff from grandparents?

"Hey, can you come over and stay tomorrow night? We haven't done a Tuesday night sleepover in a long time. Pizza?"

We hung up on that plan. It was after nine and, even though I'd had an afternoon nap, I was exhausted. That was just one of the joys of pregnancy. Besides being fat and awkward, I got to feel tired all the time. I went to bed, leaving the door unlocked so my mom wouldn't have to fumble with the key when she came in late and drunk.

I drifted off to sleep listening to street sounds, remembering the sound of Art's car as he turned the corner, and again as he turned into the driveway. I could pick the sound of his car out of hundreds. But no such sound cut through the darkness.

Was it possible Bobby was right? Did Art still love me? Was it only that his mom was in the way? I didn't think I loved him anymore—the things he'd said to me, acting as if I were a slut, how could I still love him? But then why was he always on my mind? Why did my heart quicken when Tammy said his name? Why, besides the obvious, couldn't I forget him?

14

At first I thought the school for Teen Mothers was way too easy. I was used to learning thirty vocabulary words a week—words like termagant and empiricism—learning definitions and spelling and how to use them in sentences. At Hamilton High School, between English, history, and science, I probably read about 300 pages a week, plus I learned new music and worked on lab assignments. I was still, officially, taking advanced courses in history, English, and Algebra II, but there was not nearly as much pressure as there had been at Hamilton.

I hate to admit it, but I think I kind of looked down on some of the other girls at Teen Moms in the beginning. Half of them were doing easy, easy work, like the math and English I'd had in the sixth grade. And at times it seemed like all they could talk about, besides babies and being pregnant, were boys, boys, boys.

One day in class meeting, after I'd listened to four girls in a row saying my boyfriend this and my boyfriend that, I'd had it.

"Can't we ever talk about anything besides boyfriends?" I shrieked. "Elections are coming up, homeless people are starving, our babies are going to have skin cancer by the time they're five because the world is losing its ozone layer, and we have to sit around like a bunch of airheads and talk about whose boyfriend bought a stupid teddy bear over the weekend!"

Everyone looked at me like I had turned into an extrater-restrial being. I sat staring at a space over Monique's head, feeling angry and trapped. The walls, the desks, the other girls, everything closed in on me in the silent, pulsating room.

I scraped my chair back from the circle and hurried to the restroom, slamming the door behind me. I hated those doors with no locks, this place with no privacy—this life with no privacy. Even my body was no longer my own. I was regularly being poked and prodded in my most private places by a doctor I hardly knew. Someone was inhabiting my innermost place, kicking out at me from time to time.

The Teen Moms nurse was constantly asking questions about food intake and sleeping habits. Did I drink? Smoke? Chew my nails? What had happened to my life? I leaned my head against the cool tile wall of the bathroom and images of Art, uncalled for, floated before me.

The door opened and Camille stood beside me, close enough that I could feel her breathing.

"Come on," she said. "Let's step outside and talk."

I shook my head no. I did *not* want to talk. I wanted to be left alone. But Camille took my arm and guided me back down the hall to the side door, across a little patch of lawn to a picnic table. We sat on the bench. I sensed Camille looking at me, looking through me, but I could not meet her gaze.

I looked at the white parking lines marked in the asphalt. How evenly drawn they were. How white and pure looking against their black background. Who put them there? Had the person used a brush with a well-worn giant stencil?

"Emily? Emily!"

Camille had a firm grip on my chin, turning my face, forcing me to look at her.

"You can't do this, Emily. You can't dump on the whole group and then run away."

"I wasn't dumping. I just think there's got to be more to talk about than stupid boyfriends. Why don't you give us different topics each day instead of letting everyone ramble on and on about the same old thing day after day?"

Camille pulled me closer to her and began rubbing my back. She had my grandmother's touch, firm, but gentle. When I was little and my grandmother would rub my back to help me go to sleep, I felt love radiating from her warm hands, through my skin and into my soul.

"I miss her so much," I said, choking back sobs.

"Who, Baby?"

"My grandmother. She loved me."

"Where is she?"

"Dead. She died when I was nine, an accident on the freeway. One day she was there, loving us and watching out for us, and the next day she was gone."

Then the Gramma dam broke. All the tears I wouldn't let my mother see or hear, the loneliness I'd tried not to feel, came pouring through. And there was the loneliness for David, locked away in some camp, and for the mother I thought I had long ago stopped wanting, and Art. Always Art.

Camille held me and rocked me in her arms while I sobbed. I held my breath, trying to stop, but there was no let-up.

"It's okay. Let yourself cry. You've been tied up in knots since you started here. Just let it out," Camille crooned softly.

I don't know how long we were out there. A long time, because I heard both recess bells for the elementary school down the street, and still I was crying. Then finally, like the winding down of a music box, the sobs subsided and my tears stopped.

"Stay here," Camille said, giving me a hug, then walking into the building. She was back immediately, carrying tissue, a damp washcloth, and a hand towel.

"Blow," she said, giving me a handful of tissue.

She took a wad of tissue and dabbed at her sweater, at the spot I'd been crying against.

"Girl, I'm glad I wasn't wearing silk today." Camille laughed and sat down beside me again. We talked for a very long time. She already knew a lot about me, from what I'd said in class meetings and all, and because she made it a point to get to know each of "her" girls. But now I told her about my grandmother, and David. She asked me questions about my mom and dad, and Art. But it didn't feel like she was being nosy, just like she cared.

"You've had some tough times in your short lifetime, girl," she said. "The trick is to stay strong. Give yourself all the love you deserve, even when it feels like no one else is loving you. And never give up. Every person is different and every story is special, but I've heard so many stories from so many girls, some with easy lives and some with lives as tough as yours, and a few who've lived through hells beyond what most of us care to imagine. And the amazing thing is, so many of you girls end up doing okay. Will you?"

"I think so."

"I think so, too. And you do have a lot of people who care about you, you know. It's not the same as having your grandma back, or having one of those moms like your friend Tammy has, but it's something. It's a great big something."

The sun was warm on my back. In the distance, I heard the far away sounds of little kids playing. I felt a gentle movement within me and pictured the tiny, curled-up almost-baby turn, and I was content.

"Just one more thing," Camille said.

"What?"

"You can't go dumping on the girls and then running out on them like you did."

"I wasn't dumping on anyone!"

"Maybe not, but I'll bet it felt that way to the ones who'd talked about their boyfriends."

"I didn't mean to hurt anyone's feelings."

"I know. Now we're going to go back and finish that meeting, so you'll get a chance to say that to everyone, not just me."

"But I don't want to go back. Maybe tomorrow?"

Camille just laughed. "Nope. We're like a family here, and if you want a family that works, you don't get to play dump and run. It ain't fair."

We went back into the classroom.

"I know this is your usual individual work time," Camille said, "but I think we've got some unfinished business here."

"Right," Stacy said, throwing a killer look at me.

We put the chairs in a circle again. I prayed for an earthquake but nothing happened, and I stayed on the spot.

Stacy started. "We're supposed to be able to say whatever we feel in class meetings without being put down by anyone else, and you were passing out some mean old putdowns, trying to make us feel like shit just because we've got boyfriends and yours ran out on you."

"I wasn't putting anyone down," I said.

"Oh, yeah? Well, I happen to think your remarks about boyfriends and stupid teddy bears was a putdown, since my boyfriend bought a teddy bear for our baby last night, and that's what I wanted to talk about."

It seemed then that everyone was talking at once. I was trying to explain that I hadn't meant it that way, Stacy was shouting over me, and Francine was trying to interrupt Stacy.

Camille used her school teacher voice to bring order back to the circle.

"One at a time," she said. "Let's go around the circle and say how we're feeling. Remember, just make "I" statements, and no putdowns. Francine, you start."

"Well . . . I felt put down at first, too, 'cause I'd just talked about my boyfriend. But then when I saw how upset Emily was, I knew it wasn't about me, and I didn't feel put down anymore."

Monique said, "Emily is my friend now, and I know she doesn't want to hurt anyone, so I just wondered what was wrong."

"It's no big deal," Karen said.

Then Veronica, one of the girls who was doing elementary math and reading the easiest stuff I'd seen since the
third grade, said, "I remembered how I felt at first, when
people would talk about their boyfriends doing nice things
for them, or being excited about their babies, and my
boyfriend had gone to Texas without even saying goodbye.
It made me feel hurt and worthless, knowing my boyfriend
would never be there for me.

"I would be angry just hearing about nice boyfriends. So
I didn't feel put down at all by what Emily said. I felt more
like we were sisters."

Veronica smiled shyly at me, and I smiled back. When it
was my turn, I told them I hadn't meant to offend anyone,
but sometimes I couldn't seem to think about anything but
my own problems. I guess they understood, because we all
did a group hug when we were through, and even Stacy
smiled at me.

When we were back at our tables for individual work, I
opened my English text to the assigned short story and
pretended to read, but I couldn't concentrate. I looked over
at Veronica. She was leaning on the table, reading from the
easy reader I had noticed my first day at Teen Moms. Her
shiny black hair fell forward, partly shielding her face. I
could see her lips moving as she silently labored over the
text.

I thought about how she had looked beneath my words
and known my feelings, and I realized that in some very
important ways, Veronica was a whole lot smarter than I
was. And I knew then that what I was learning at Teen
Moms was as important as anything I would have been
learning back at Hamilton High.

The next morning, just after juice and crackers, Candice
said, "I think it's starting."

"What's starting?" I asked. Was I dumb or what?

"Not her period," Monique said.

We all laughed. Mrs. Prim came over and put her hand on Candy's stomach.

"We'll see," she said, jotting 9:45 on the chalkboard.

Three pains and an hour later, Camille called the school nurse, Mrs. Fazio, and she came over from the junior high school where she worked every Wednesday.

"I wish you girls could arrange things so you'd always start labor on Thursdays," she said with a smile. She looked at the times on the board and went over to talk with Candy.

"When are you due?"

"Not for ten days."

"Well, it wouldn't be the first time a baby came ten days early."

"But I'm not quite ready," Candy whined.

Mrs. Fazio got a big laugh out of that.

We all gathered around Candy and Mrs. Fazio, listening, knowing that our time was coming—no escape.

Candy stiffened in her chair, grabbing the arms and thrusting her legs out in front of her. Mrs. Fazio spread her hand across Candy's abdomen and timed the pain with the second hand of her large-faced nurse's watch.

"How's it feel?"

"It hurts!"

"Where?"

"My back. My stomach. God!"

"High? Low?"

"All over ... or maybe low, I guess ... I'm scared," she said, her face pale and tight.

"Of course you're scared. You'd be a fool not to be. But you're quite healthy. You'll be okay. We all got through it." Mrs. Fazio waved her arm to indicate Camille, Mrs. Prim, and herself.

Mrs. Fazio helped Candy up when the next pain started.

"Come on. Let's take a walk across the room."

She held Candy's arm while Candy took a few steps forward, then stepped back, sinking into her chair, gripping her stomach.

"I can't do it," she said in a tight, breathless voice. "Too much pressure."

"High or low?"

"Low," she groaned, leaning forward, rocking.

"Ummm. I think this is the real thing, kiddo. Who shall we call to come get you?"

"My mom," Candy said, looking more relaxed now that the last pain had eased. "She's at work."

Camille handed Mrs. Fazio Candy's emergency card, and the nurse dialed the number. About fifteen minutes later, Candy's mom and boyfriend burst through the door.

"Are you okay? Are you okay?" the boyfriend kept asking over and over again, while the mom shouted orders.

"Take my arm. Walk slow. James—open the door!"

It was a moment of moving, hovering, pushing, ordering, and then they were gone. I was left with my own fears. The look of pain I'd seen on Candy's face, her grip on the arms of the chair—I'd not given much thought to pain until this very day. Discomfort, yes. Already my feet were so swollen that some days I didn't even tie my shoes. And I had to pee constantly. And my back hurt. But killer pain? I'd heard of the agony of childbirth, but somehow I'd not applied those stories to my own condition—until now. And another thing. When I started labor, who would come pick me up? Who would hover over me?

"David? It's been months!" I said, wanting both to laugh and cry as soon as I heard his voice.

"I know. I couldn't call for a while. I was in lock-up."

"What happened?"

"I was just in the wrong place at the wrong time. Really, Em, I've been trying so hard to stay out of trouble. I want out of here so bad . . ."

I heard him catch his breath and knew he was trying not to cry.

"But what do you mean—the wrong place at the wrong time?"

"There's this butthole who's my cell mate. What can I say? It's not like a day at Disneyland, you know. Anyway, they found a knife under my mattress when they did a surprise search. Something was supposed to be going down, and they searched everywhere. I swear, Em, I'd never seen that knife before, but I got lock-up for it anyway, and it probably means I won't get out on probation as soon as I thought."

"But can't you explain what happened?"

"C'mon, Em. It ain't like that."

"I wish you were here," I told him.

"Me, too . . . Hey, how's my little niecephew coming along?" he said, sounding less down. Once I'd referred to the baby as Rovid, telling him it would be Rose if it was a girl, and David if a boy. Ever since, he'd been calling the baby his niecephew. Things always seemed a little better when we used our own made-up terms—like something in the world was ours alone.

"Rovid's fine, I think. It's getting bigger and so am I."

"How much longer?"

"Only about nine weeks. I'm scared, but I really want to get it over with. I feel fat and ugly."

David laughed.

"It's not funny!"

"You know what they say . . . You made your bed—or was it my bed?"

"David. You're not being very nice."

He laughed again. "I've really missed talking to you," he said, and I could still hear a smile in his voice. "How's The Barb?"

"She's calmed down some."

"What about Art?"

"I don't know. I never see him. He's got a new girlfriend."

"Doesn't he ever even call to see how you're doing?"

"No. I haven't talked to him in months."

"That little weaselly bastard."

Why did I feel like defending Art? It didn't make sense, after the way Art had treated me, but I didn't like to hear David put him down. I changed the subject.

We talked about little stuff then. Safe stuff. Like what we'd do when he got out, how we'd order the biggest and best pizza in town, and we'd watch all the newly released videos.

"All we see in here is either animal stuff, like 'White Fang,' or religious stuff like that ancient 'Ten Commandments' thing. I guess they're okay, but I'd like more variety."

"Maybe they'll show one of my favorites, 'Keeping Baby Clean and Happy.' Take notes on the diaper changing section, would you?"

"Ugh! Do uncles *have* to change diapers?"

"Yep."

I heard some commotion in the background.

"Gotta go, Em. We've got four phones and about sixty

hoodlums wanting to use them. I wish I could see you. Are you taking pictures? Take care of yourself. Wuv you," and he was gone.

I got David's key from under the brick by the back door and went into his room. It was musty smelling. I opened the windows and stretched out on his bed. I tried to get a sense of my brother in this room, but mostly what came through was Art, lying with me on this bed, everything warm and secure.

I folded my hands across my raised belly. I couldn't see my feet, but I knew what they looked like—swollen, ankleless blobs. My breasts, my stomach, my feet—all were pulled tight, and I wasn't even in my ninth month yet.

With my eyes closed, I tried to picture my body the way it was before I got pregnant. My stomach was flat and my leg muscles were firm from soccer. My arms had been strong and firm, too. No more.

It wasn't just the part of me that had to do with Rovid that was all distorted. I never did anything physical any-more. My muscles were turning to flab. I hated the way I looked, and I hated that I couldn't even climb a flight of stairs without huffing and puffing and having to stop and rest midway.

I must have dozed off, because I dreamed that Pauline and I were running down the soccer field in a championship game. Pauline intercepted the ball and passed it to me. It was a perfect pass, and as I kicked it toward the goal, I knew it was in.

When I woke, I tried to feel the dream kick all over again. I took a few steps in the small room, turned my foot at an angle, and kicked toward the imaginary ball. I had to steady myself against the dresser. Would I do any of those things ever again? Would my body return to its normal state, or would I stay fat and awkward?

Why was Pauline in my dream? We weren't even friends anymore. It had taken me a while to realize she was avoiding me. When I called, her mom would always sound friendly and say she'd have Pauline call me back. But Pauline never called.

Once, when I dropped by Tammy's house on a Saturday, Pauline was there. I was really happy to see her, but she kept her distance and wouldn't even look at me. She said hi, but that was all—like I had some horrible disease or something.

I know we're not friends anymore, and it's weird, after all those years, to have someone just drop out of your life. I guess the dream-me still thinks Pauline's my friend.

Art is another one the dream-me hasn't caught up with yet. I dream about Art all the time, and in my dreams he always still loves me.

Mom's car lights flashed across the window. I dragged myself from David's bed and went back into the house.

"What were you doing in there?" she asked, opening the door and tossing a package toward me.

"I was thinking," I said.

She dropped her purse and jacket on the couch and sat down. "Well . . . see what it is," she said.

I looked inside the bag. There were three wrapping blankets and three sleeper sets, a pair of white booties, and a little fuzzy bear. At first I thought maybe Edie had sent some things to me, but my mom said, "I guess if I'm going to be a grandma, it's time I start acting like one."

I just looked at her, stunned.

"Well . . ."

"Thank you," I said, hardly believing my eyes. I mean, it wasn't the crib, stroller, high chair package that Monique's mom had given her, but it was a *very* unusual thing for my mom to do.

"Look," she said, unfolding one of the sleepers. "Isn't it cute? I got yellow and turquoise because that's good for a boy *or* a girl. And listen to this . . ." She picked up the teddy bear and wound a little key in its back. It played "Lullaby and Goodnight" with a sweet, tinkly, music-box sound.

"Thanks, Mom," I said again. I wished I could think of something else to say, but I couldn't.

"Some grandparents brought their new little grandson into the cafe today. It got me thinking. Don't get me wrong, I still think it's a terrible mistake for you to be having a baby, but there's nothing to do about that now. I might as well enjoy it."

That helped me get up my nerve to ask her if she'd go to the classes with me and be my coach during labor.

"I don't know, Emmy. I hate how they do things now. I liked the old way best, like when your grandma had me. They just knocked her out with anesthetic, and she woke up hours later after it was all over and I was squalling in the nursery. I begged the doctor to let me have you and David that way, but *NO*, all I could get was one of those saddleblock things."

"But you know, it's better for the baby without all that anesthetic. And mothers recover faster, too."

"I know. I watch T.V. I'm informed. But if there's a way to avoid the pain of labor, why not? I can't see that it hurt me any."

I wasn't so sure about that, but I didn't want to argue.

"Well, would you be my coach? Edie'd cover for you if it was during your work time, wouldn't she?"

"Sure," Mom said. "I'm sure she'd do that ... When do the classes start?"

"I think I'm supposed to start in a couple of weeks."

"Okay," she said, "Let me know what time they meet, and I'll rearrange my schedule."

She didn't seem enthused about the plan, but I was so relieved to have someone to help me, I hardly noticed. We talked for a while, about David and plans she and Edie had to remodel the cafe.

Before I went to bed, I stacked the baby's things neatly in a dresser drawer I had recently emptied. Those were the first things to go into it. Pretty soon I had to get some more things. I didn't know where I'd get the money.

My mom rearranged her schedule, and we started taking classes at the Red Cross eight weeks before the baby was due. Most of the others in the class were lots older than me, and they were there with doting husbands. I felt self-conscious at first, and I think my mom did, too. But then Veronica and her mom showed up so we weren't the only mother/daughter partners.

It was the first time ever that my mom and I had tried to work on anything as a team. I stretched out on my side on the carpeted floor, and Mom arranged the pillows we'd brought from home to support my back. She knelt down beside me, gingerly.

"Relax!" she ordered as she was trying to coach me through the beginning relaxation exercises. I immediately and involuntarily tensed.

"You're going to be in big trouble if you can't do any better than this!" she bellowed.

The instructor walked over and gently directed me first to contract, then to relax particular muscles, beginning with my left arm and ending with my right foot. It worked. I was relaxed.

"All right, try again," she said to my mother. We managed to get through the exercises, and the evening, but it was obvious we were both ill at ease. Veronica and her mother laughed and joked their way through it. During the instruction part, Veronica's mother sat smiling, absently rubbing her daughter's back as the teacher talked about breathing techniques. My mom sat on the floor beside me, out of arm's reach, repeatedly checking her watch.

In the car on the way home, she said, "I'm not very good at this stuff, you know."

"It was fine," I said, afraid she was going to try to get out of coaching me.

"No. It's not exactly my cup of tea."

I looked out the window at the headlights passing, steeling myself against what I expected her to say. But instead of backing out, she said, "I told you I'd take the class with you, and I will. I won't let you down."

It was a relief to hear her say it. From the times she didn't get around to picking me up someplace, or she came home a few days past the time she'd said she'd see me, I knew I couldn't totally depend on her, but I felt better knowing that she planned on being my coach. I really didn't want to go through it all alone.

I'd tossed out a coaching hint to Tammy several weeks back, but she had refused adamantly on the grounds that she was a coward. *She* was a coward? What about me? I was the one who would be giving birth. Tammy had just laughed and commented that she had a choice. I didn't. And her choice was to stay away from anything resembling a hospital. So, strange as it seemed, it would be Mom and me.

Dear Baby,

Today you got your picture taken for the very first time. Did you know that? I can't tell much about how you really look. The picture is dark and fuzzy. I want to be surprised, so I'm glad you hid your private parts from the camera. (It's not really a camera, but I'll tell you about that later.) Anyway, I'm saving the picture for your album.

In only about six weeks we'll meet each other face to face. I can hardly wait, but I'm scared, too. Are you? I'm learning to relax and breathe a special way, so it will make things easier when you're being born. Life is kind of hard for me right now. I'll tell you all about it when you get here. I already love you a lot. Camille (my teacher) says babies can feel love while they're still in the womb. I hope you can feel me loving you. Love, Your Mom

CHAPTER

16

I was getting ready for bed, checking out an ugly purplish-red stretch mark which had worked its way across my abdomen. Was it below the bikini line? I couldn't be sure. The house was so quiet I could hear myself breathing as I continued the stretch mark search. I nearly jumped out of my discolored skin when the phone rang.

"Emily?"

It was a guy, but not Art, the voice I most wanted to hear.

"This is Carl. Carl Saunders. From choir."

"Oh, Carl. Hi."

"What're you doin'?"

"Oh, nothing," I said. I didn't think he wanted to hear how I was examining my hideous stretch marks.

"So, I just wanted to tell you we'll miss you on tour."

Tour. May 21st to the 26th. I still had it marked on my calendar, as if I were going.

"Don't rub it in," I said, half pleased, half irritated.

"No. I'm not . . . I mean . . . I didn't mean that," he said. "I just . . . we just . . . miss you."

Poor Carl. He was more shy than I'd ever been.

"I'm not sure *everyone* misses me."

"I don't know about that. But a lot of people do. We don't sound as good as we did with you, I know that . . . Anyway, I thought, if you don't mind, I'd like to send you a postcard from New York."

I gave him my address, and it wasn't until after we hung

up that I thought about how rude I'd been not to even ask how he was, or what was going on with him. Camille says we have to be careful not to get so busy feeling sorry for ourselves we forget to care about anyone else. Carl was a really nice guy. Tammy still thought he bordered on nerdiness, but then Tammy had thought Art was Mr. Super Cool, so she may not be a great judge of people.

The day I would have been boarding United Airlines with the Hamilton Harmonics was the day I felt my first labor pain. I'd been home from school for an hour, and I was stretched out on the couch reading a mystery story. Just as the main character got shot in the gut, I felt a tinge of pain across my lower back.

At first I thought my pain was only in sympathy with Detective Stoneman, but then, about thirty minutes later, when Detective Stoneman was well and back on the street, I felt another pain. I was already two days overdue so labor pains should have been no surprise to me, but at first I didn't believe it anyway.

For one thing, the pains weren't very close, and they weren't very painful, either—nothing like when Candice had gone into labor at school that day. False labor?

My mom had been coming home right after work for the past two weeks, in case I needed her. Our childbirth preparation class had helped us both to understand each other a little better. I saw that she was trying.

I went to bed and tried to sleep, but instead I lay listening for my mom's car. I wavered between thinking I was for sure in labor or the whole thing was my imagination. When Mom still wasn't home by one in the morning, I began to worry. I called Barb and Edie's, but I only got the answering machine. At two, I called Edie's house. I was sure she'd be asleep, but I didn't know what else to do.

"Do you know where my mom is?"

"Who? Oh, Emmy . . . No, isn't she home? Wait, she said something about having a date with the new manager from the furniture outlet. Bob, or somebody . . . I thought she was going to call you before she left though. Are you okay?"

"I don't know. I've been having some pains."

"Labor?"

"Maybe . . ."

"Oh, God. I'd come over but my father's here with me. He just got out of the hospital from heart surgery, you know. Is there someone else you can call to come stay with you?"

"I'll be okay. I mean, it may not even be labor yet."

"Your mom will probably be home any minute. I've seen a big change in her since she decided to be a good grandmother. I notice she's really cut back on the partying. I bet she'll be driving in any minute. You try to get some rest."

I went back to bed and lay there, half-asleep, listening for Mom's car.

At 7:05 I was shocked into a state of anxiety by a warm wetness spreading from between by legs and onto the bed. I grabbed an old sweat shirt from the chair beside my bed and held it between my legs. Then I pulled my cow of a body out of bed and waddled down the hall to the kitchen. I called Dr. Kirkpatrick, who asked a few questions, then told me to come to the hospital. She'd see me there.

I dialed the number I had known by heart since I was seven years old and willed Tammy to answer. Please don't let her be gone for school yet. Please, please, please, I begged, as I felt the warmth of more water oozing into the sweat shirt still stuck awkwardly between my legs.

"Hello?"

"Tammy? Thank God."

"Emmy?"

"My water broke. I've been having pains. I've got to get to the hospital."

"Where's your mom?"

"She didn't come home last night. Oh, Tammy, I'm so scared!" I felt the catch in my throat and struggled to stay in control.

"Have you called the doctor?"

"Yes. She said to come straight to the hospital."

Suddenly there was a pain so swift and strong that our drab kitchen turned bright blue and sparkling. I clutched the table edge and gulped air. I tried to fill my lungs and then exhale slowly, the way I'd learned in childbirth class.

"Em? Emmy? Are you okay?"

"I guess so," I said, not believing it. "Please, can you take me to the hospital?"

Silence.

"Tammy, there's no one else. I know your mom's car is sitting in the garage right now. She and your dad are in Las Vegas, right?"

"Right. But what about Art?"

"Art!" I shrieked. "I'd die before I'd ask him to drive me around the block. Besides, he's on choir tour."

"Well, don't even talk about dying in childbirth, Em. You're so *dramatic*!"

"Easy for you to say," I sobbed. "You're not the one with water gushing out of her and pains that are getting worse and worse! . . . I'd do it for you, you know."

Tammy sighed. "Mom'll kill me if she finds out. I'll be grounded for life."

"Oh, thank you, Tammy," I gasped, tightening. Another pain. Too fast. They were coming too fast. I was scared. I wanted out. I wanted to be in New York, singing at St. Patrick's Cathedral. I wanted my life back.

"Wait for me out front," Tammy said. "I can't drive down your driveway because I still don't know how to get the car into reverse. I don't even have my license yet, you know."

"But you've been taking driver training, haven't you?"

"Yeah, but not on stick."

"Please, Tammy. Hurry."

"Okay. I'm leaving."

My book bag was already packed with a pair of jeans, big T-shirt, clean underwear, and a tiny sleeper and receiving blanket for the baby. Did they say to bring diapers? I was checking to be sure my toothbrush was tucked in the outer pocket when I was gripped by another pain, through my back and across my belly.

I sank to my bed, then forced myself up again. I had to get to the front curb. Then Tammy would help. I walked heavily, my stomach awkward in front of me as I turned to close the chipped and peeling front door. I walked past David's dismantled truck. If he were here, he'd help me.

I leaned against the fence that divided our property from Mrs. Dugan's. She was probably peering out her window at me, but I was past caring.

Another pain. Why wasn't I timing them? I was overcome by fear. What if the baby came now, right here in the driveway, with no one to help? Where was Tammy? Why did my mom always let me down? I sat on the curb crying, trying to breathe and rub my belly the way I'd learned in class.

Finally. The red Nissan made a wide turn at the corner. Tammy drove slowly down the half-block to where I waited at the curb, then stopped abruptly in the middle of the street. She reached over and opened the door for me.

"Buckle up," she said, as I sank into the passenger seat.

"Are you serious?" I asked, pointing to my protruding mid-section.

"If that belt will fit around my Aunt Mamie, it'll fit around you. The way I jumped this car over here, you'd better be tied in."

I stretched the belt across my stomach and fastened it.

"Are you okay?"

"I guess. I had two awful pains, close together, but they've let up now. I'm scared, though."

"I thought your mom was going to coach you."

"She was, but you know my mom. I was stupid to think I could depend on her. Something this important, you know, I thought maybe this time she'd be different."

"Maybe she can't help it. Maybe she was in an accident."

"I think she just got drunk and forgot. She'll turn up, just not in time." I stiffened, feeling the beginning of a pain.

"Oh, God. I've got to get you to the hospital . . ."

"Okay," she whispered to herself, "clutch in, shift to first, foot on gas." She was frowning the way she used to during math tests. Suddenly, she released the clutch, floored the gas pedal, and the Nissan jumped forward with a screech.

"Clutch, second, gas," she said, and the car lurched forward again.

"Tammy!" I yelled, just as she almost ran into the curb.

She slammed on the brakes, and the car died. "Okay. Okay. Don't worry. I forgot to steer because I was concentrating on the clutch. I wish they'd taken this car to Vegas and left the automatic in the garage. Okay. Here goes."

Tammy put in the clutch, started the engine, and started the "clutch first, gas" chant again. We jumped forward. Neither of us spoke. Tammy's eyes were on the road ahead, both hands gripping the wheel of the forbidden car. Her face tightened into a math test frown each time she had to shift.

As we turned onto the street in front of the hospital, I directed her to the emergency entrance.

"Can you make it inside? I can't park. Oh, Em, I'm sorry I can't stay with you," Tammy said, looking as if she'd cry.

I was already out of the car. "Thanks, Tammy," I said, fighting tears.

"Well. Good luck. I'll come back after school."

"Call my mom, will you? She never misses work. She'll be there by three or so. And tell Bobby, too, just in case he talks to Art in New York."

I hated that it still mattered to me about Art, but after all, he was about to be a father, whether or not he believed it.

I walked through the big doors at the emergency entrance. I'd been here before, on a field trip with Teen Moms, so I pretty much knew where to go.

Often, in my sixteen years of life, I'd felt alone and neglected. Like when I'd see how Tammy's and Pauline's parents treated them, that would make me miss what I didn't have. But I'd never felt so alone as I did that day, bending double in pain, trying to control my breathing, waiting. And waiting.

I was a tiny, fear-filled speck, tumbling through a vast, uncaring universe. And what of my baby? I stood waiting at the counter, crying, wondering if the receptionist would ever look up.

17

After I signed about twenty papers, an orderly helped me into a wheelchair and wheeled me back to the maternity ward. There my clothes were replaced with a hospital gown, then I was helped into a bed. A doctor, not mine, came in, glanced at my chart, and said, "Feet in the stirrups, Emily. I need to examine you, see how this baby is doing."

He smiled, but I didn't see anything to smile about, especially when he started poking around in my private space.

To the nurse he said, "3.2 centimeters."

Then I was hooked up to this thing that kept track of the baby's heartbeat.

"Okay, Emily, it will be a while yet. Dr. Kirkpatrick will be here in another hour or so," he said, then patted me on the leg and left the room.

The nurse handed me a switch thing which was attached to a long cord. She cranked my bed up so I was almost in a sitting position.

"Turn on your light if you need anything," she said. "Jot down the time of your contractions, if you can. I'll be back to check on you shortly."

I picked up the notepad and pencil that were sitting on my bedside table, and waited. I'd only had two pains since I got to the hospital. At 7:40 or so, I'd thought I would deliver my baby in my own driveway. But here it was already 10:00 and I was beginning to wonder about false labor. Just when

I was thinking I might as well get dressed and go back home, a pain started, easy, then harder and harder. I watched the big clock on the wall, counting seconds, but then I closed my eyes, trying to shut out the pain, the overwhelming pain, and I lost count. I was all clammy and shaky. I pressed the button for the nurse.

"Can you give me something? This really hurts," I said.

She came over and laid her hand on my stomach.

"Are you having a pain now?"

"No, but I just did. It hurt a lot."

"Your doctor should be here pretty soon. We'll talk to her about something for pain."

The nurse sat beside me, and when the next pain started, she placed her hand on my stomach and watched the second hand on the clock.

I guess I was kind of out of my head with pain because I barely remember all that went on. It seemed like people were busy around me, but I'm not sure what they were doing. They were all strangers. No one who loved me was there.

"Can't you give me something?" I begged as soon as I saw Dr. Kirkpatrick enter my room.

"Let's check," she said, lowering my bed and putting my feet in the stirrups.

"Looks to me like you're going to have a baby," she said.

What a time for humor. I gave a little laugh, and then another pain attacked.

"Don't hold your breath. Breathe, remember?" the nurse said, wiping my forehead with a damp cloth while my doctor felt the contraction from the outside. That's how *I* wanted to be feeling the pain, from the outside, not from the inside. I tried breathing slow and deep, then fast and shallow as the pain increased. I tried to remember what I'd learned at the class, but it wasn't working.

It's embarrassing to remember now, but in the middle of my pain, I threw up in my bed. I didn't even know it was coming, or if I did, I didn't care.

"I don't think I can take this," I said, crying, longing for the pain to lessen.

"I don't want to give you anything that will slow the process, or make your baby sluggish. Remember, we talked about that? You said you wanted a drug-free birth."

"But I didn't know it would be like this!" I cried.

"Well, I'll set you up with something that will ease things a bit for you, okay? It won't take away all of your pain, but it will help some."

Soon after the doctor left, the nurse brought in an I.V. unit, secured the needle into my arm, and started a solution dripping into me. I still felt the pains, but it seemed like I fell sound asleep between them, even though they were only a few minutes apart. A nurse brought me some ice to suck on and explained that I couldn't have anything to eat until after I'd had the baby. Who was hungry, anyway?

About seven that evening, the pains changed. They kept coming, almost no time in between. Right then I learned the meaning of excruciating. I felt like someone else was in control of my body and I *had* to push. It sounds gross, but it was like I was working on having the world's biggest B.M.

Dr. Kirkpatrick was back, checking me again.

"Okay," she said, "let's get this baby born—not much longer, Emily. You're fully dilated."

Another pain. And another. Faces floated over me.

"PUSH . . . PUSH . . . PUSH . . . BREATHE . . . BREATHE . . . BREATHE . . . "

The words hovered, mixed with each intake of air, reaching for my brain. A scream. A moan. Mine? I was drenched in sweat. Sounds, high-pitched, then guttural, rushed past my throat and into the room. God! My back! My gut! Something was tightening, pushing, propelling my very insides out.

"Help! Please! Somebody!" I cried, but knew my words were jumbled, lost in the depths of a groan.

Gramma. Art. David. Momma. Someone, I called within myself, feeling the hurt intensify.

"PUSH! You're getting close. PUSH!"

Someone was leaning/pushing heavily against my mid-section. Every cell of my body, from the tip of my head to the ends of my toes, was concentrated on the gripping pain, the demand to push. Nothing mattered but to push.

"Okay. You're doing okay. Everything's fine."

I heard her first. The catlike cry. Then saw my bloody/mucousy baby.

"She's a beauty," the nurse said. "Tiny, but beautiful."

I couldn't take my eyes off her. The nurse was cleaning the baby off while the doctor cut and clamped the cord. She *was* beautiful. The nurse placed her in the crook of my arm.

"Here you are, Mama. She's all yours."

Then she turned and said to the doctor, as if I were not there, "Only a child herself, and no one here with her or even in the waiting room. What's wrong with these kids?"

I looked at the perfect little being lying next to me. She was looking back, checking me out.

"I'll do the best I can, Rosemary. You're my little Rose-mary, and I won't ever let anyone hurt you," I promised, holding her close. "We're going to have fun together. Disneyland. Magic Mountain. The beach. I'll be your Brownie leader, and you'll never have to wait for me to pick you up. I'll be there for you, Baby."

"Here, we'll give her a bath now, and get you cleaned up a bit, too," the nurse said, taking the baby from me.

"Is there anyone you want us to call for you?"

"You can try my mom's work," I said, and gave her the number.

I felt the pressure of the doctor's needle, stitch by stitch, closing up the incision at the edge of my vagina.

"You'll be fine in no time," the doctor told me as she tied off the last stitch. "Pretty short labor for a first baby—piece of cake," she laughed.

I laughed, too. It hadn't felt like a piece of cake a few minutes ago.

I must have sunk into a deep sleep then, because the next

thing I knew, I was in a room with three women, all lots older than me. I thought maybe I remembered Tammy's voice straining to reach me through a muffled haze, but I wasn't sure if she'd really been there, or if it was only a dream.

A nurse brought the baby to me about 10:00 that night. Rosemary was only three hours old. They gave me a bottle of some watery solution, saying it would help clear the mucus from her throat.

I loved her little lips, the way they groped for the nipple, and how her tiny tongue moved in and out. It reminded me of a lizard, and I laughed, but it was a laugh filled with love, not ridicule.

My doctor had encouraged me to nurse the baby. She said it was the healthiest diet a baby could have. But the idea grossed me out. I wouldn't want anyone to see me. I know it's natural and all, but, to me, it was too disgusting. Besides, almost all the Teen Moms who'd already had their babies were giving them formula, and their babies seemed healthy enough.

Rosemary didn't take much of her bottle. I held her, feeling the warmth of her body against my own. I ran my finger lightly over her smooth cheek. She was a miracle. I know it sounds corny to say that, but she was an honest to goodness miracle. Everything on her—her feet, her hands, her little eyelids, all were perfect.

"You're my miracle," I whispered to her. "I love you. You're going to love me too. I know it." I sat crooning to her, loving her, while she slept an even, easy sleep. I wasn't alone anymore.

After the nurse took the baby back, I got scared. She was so little. What if I couldn't take care of her when I got her home? What if I dropped her? What if I fed her the wrong stuff? What if I made some awful mistake with her and she died? It could happen. But no, I wouldn't let it happen. Monique's baby was doing fine. I could be as good a mom as Monique, couldn't I? But Monique's mom helped her.

A nurse came in with some milk of magnesia and a sleeping pill, and that put an end to my worries for a while.

In the morning I was awakened by my mother's familiar, raspy voice.

"I came last night as soon as I heard, but you were already sleeping. I stopped and saw the baby. She's adorable, Em."

I looked at her, still groggy. "What time is it?"

"It's only 6:30, but I had to come see you. I feel bad about missing the major event."

I rubbed my eyes, "Yeah, well . . ."

"What a rotten time to pick for a twenty-four hour party, huh?" she said, laughing.

"I needed you, Mom. You promised you'd coach me, and I needed your help and you weren't there." I felt tears gathering, and I turned away from her. I'd learned years ago not to cry over being disappointed in my mom. What good did it ever do? I hated that I was crying now.

She took my hand. I pulled it away.

"I'm sorry, Emmy. I really am. It was just a spur of the moment thing. This guy, Bob, keeps asking me out, and I keep saying sure, but we never go. So he came in the other night with plane tickets to Las Vegas and show tickets to see Johnny Mathis. You know how I love Johnny Mathis."

"More than any promise you made to me, I guess."

"No, come on. I didn't know. I didn't want to wake you up—it was nearly midnight when we decided to go."

"And then there were no phones in Las Vegas?"

"Don't be sarcastic. Of course there are phones in Las Vegas. I called about 8:00 yesterday morning, but no one answered. I thought maybe you'd left a little early for school. But when I called Edie around 4:00 in the afternoon, she told me Tammy had called, and you were in the hospital. I came back as soon as I could. I didn't even stay to see Johnny."

"What a mom," I said.

"I talked to the doctor, and she said you did great. You had plenty of help here anyway, doctors and nurses and all."

What could I say to her? I had let myself need her for the first time since I was about nine years old. It was my mistake. Not hers. Nothing would ever change her. David and I had figured that out years ago. I just forgot.

"Anyway, you got a great baby. Have you named her?"

"Rosemary," I said.

"Rosemary? After Grandma?"

"Yes."

"Isn't that kind of old-fashioned?"

"Maybe, but that's her name. She likes it."

I suppose we could have gone on for hours, talking without communicating, but a nurse came in and pulled a curtain around my bed.

"Time to check you out," she said to me. To my mother she said, "Visiting hours don't start until 11:00."

"I'll check back this evening," Mom said.

She leaned over and gave me a peck on the forehead, and then she was gone. All the time she'd been sitting by my bed, I wanted to be left alone. Then when she was gone, I wanted her back.

CHAPTER

18

Tammy, still in her red and white drill team outfit, and I in my robe and slippers, stood with our faces pressed against the nursery window, peering in at Baby Rosemary.

"She's so little," Tammy said.

"Exactly five pounds when she was born. But the doctor says she's strong and healthy. Look. She's stretching."

"Her legs are about as big around as my finger. Aren't you afraid you'll break her?"

"Well . . . I was a little bit afraid last night—not when I was holding her, but after, when they took her back to the nursery. But really, I don't think I can hurt her, because I love her so much."

I remembered how I had been filled with love for her, from the moment I first held her—how I'd willed my love to surround my helpless, innocent baby. I was a transmitter of love. I wanted to tell Tammy how that felt, but I couldn't find the words.

"You know how your friend Becky, from choir, always acts like she hates Richard?" Tammy was giving me the latest school gossip. "Well, now they're going to the prom together. And Julie and Angel have supposedly broken up, except . . ."

As Tammy talked on, I found myself drawn closer to the baby, as if I could float through the glass to the side of Rosemary's bassinet, hear her soft breathing, and see the dark newborn fuzz on the back of her neck.

Back in my room, when the baby was brought in for her afternoon feeding, Tammy watched while I tried to get her to drink from the bottle.

"She takes a long time, doesn't she?"

"The nurse said that's 'cause she's so new, and so little. I have to be patient and not rush her."

"It'll get kind of boring, don't you think? I mean, she's cute and all, but this is taking forever."

Tammy watched for a while longer. I moved the bottle a bit whenever Rosemary stopped sucking. She'd take another swallow or two and then stop. After a while, it seemed like neither Tammy or I could think of anything to say. I held the baby against my shoulder and rubbed her back, trying to coax a burp from her. Tammy got up to leave.

"I'll stop by your house tomorrow. You'll be home then, right?"

"Maybe. Better call first."

Secretly, I wished Rosemary and I could stay in the clean, well-ordered hospital, but the doctor said she was sure I could go home the next day. I thought about trying to fake a massive headache or something, so they'd keep us here, safe, another day. But I'm not a very good faker, so I didn't even try. I had to face going home and taking full responsibility for Baby Rosemary. Really, Rosemary Dee Morrison. The Dee was for David.

After the evening feeding, about 9:00, the nurse left the babies in our room for a long time. One of the babies, a boy I think, and about twice the size of Rosemary, cried for a long time. But Rosemary was peaceful, looking into my eyes, then drifting off to sleep, then opening her eyes again and looking. I rubbed my cheek gently, back and forth, against the fuzzy head.

"We'll be okay," I told her. "We'll be okay," as if saying the words might make it so.

That night I dreamed of writhing snakes covering the floor of my bedroom at home. The baby was crying, but I couldn't get past the snakes to reach her. I felt a long, slick reptile wrap itself slowly, tightly, around my neck. My arms wouldn't move. I was paralyzed—defenseless. Rosie's cries turned to screams. The whole room undulated, snake-like.

"Emily? Emily!"

The woman from the next bed was shaking me awake.

"What's wrong? Are you sick? You were gasping like you couldn't breathe. Are you okay?"

I looked around, not knowing where I was—the little room with four beds, a dim light shining through the partially opened door, the woman, none of it was familiar. The snakes. Were they there?

"Oh. A nightmare!" I said, rubbing my neck and looking anxiously at the floor, half expecting to see snakes.

The woman, fortyish and in with her third baby, sat beside me on the bed. She put her arms around me and rocked back and forth.

"Okay, Sweetheart," she said. "My Linda, she's about your age, and she has bad dreams sometimes, too. I'll sit with you for a while. That always calms Linda. Just think, in a few years you'll be holding your little girl like this when she wakes up with a nightmare . . ."

The woman talked on and on, softly, almost singing her words, until I was soothed and sleepy.

"Okay now, Honey?" she asked as I slid down on my bed.

"Yes. Thank you," I said. I sank back into sleep, wondering why I didn't have a mother like that.

In the morning, at 10:00, my mom came to get us. She was on time for a change. I was sitting in a wheelchair in the hospital hallway, with my backpack and a bag of hospital-provided baby supplies piled on the floor next to me. I was in the wheelchair because of some stupid hospital rule. Like having a baby means you can't walk anymore or something.

"I stopped by the nursery to see our little Rosebud," Mom said. "Don't worry. I'll be a good grandma. Well . . . I don't want her to *call* me Grandma. She can call me Auntie Barb if she wants to but . . ."

"Mother, have you been drinking already today?"

"No, I haven't been drinking, Miss Goody-Goody. And so what if I have? I'm over twenty-one, you know."

I got a whiff of stale beer. I definitely did not want the baby riding in a car with my mother if she'd been drinking. On the other hand, how else would we get home?

"Come on, worrier, let's go get that cute little baby. I think she looks exactly like my baby pictures. Don't you?"

"Maybe," I said, secretly hoping she was wrong.

A nurse brought the baby out, wrapped tightly in a light-weight blanket, and handed her carefully to me. She told us that babies like to be wrapped tight because they're used to living in such a small space. I thought about where my baby had been just two short days ago. Unbelievable!

The nurse then pushed my wheelchair down the long antiseptic-smelling corridor and through the automatic doors to the broad sidewalk.

"If you want to bring your car around, we'll wait here for you, Grandmother," the nurse said with a smile.

"We can walk from here," Mom said, reaching for the baby. "It's not far."

"But I have to be sure the baby is safely secured in her car seat. Hospital regulations, you know."

"Car seat? Where'll we get a car seat?" Mom asked.

"The hospital's loaning us one. It's taken care of, Mom."

"Why doesn't anyone ever tell *me* anything?"

Mom turned and walked toward the parking lot. I watched her clickety-clacking down the sidewalk in her high-heeled shoes and her too-short skirt. I looked at the nurse in her crisp white uniform and thick-soled shoes. Maybe I'll be a nurse. Can you be a mother and a nurse both? You sure can't be a mother and a bar queen—at least not much of a mother.

On the way home, Mom started out being super nice.

"Wait 'til you see," she said. "I got this really nice little sleeper set and a cute little rabbit, real soft, that plays 'Rockabye, Baby.'"

"Thanks, Mom," I said, not taking my eyes off the baby. Was her head secure? She looked so tiny in the car seat. The nurse said the safest place for the car seat was strapped in with the middle strap in the back seat. I sat next to her, leaving the passenger seat in front empty.

"I'm sorry I wasn't with you when she was born. I know I let you down."

Just when I was ready to accept her apology, she reached for her purse, pulled out a cigarette, and put it in her mouth. She took her lighter from the little compartment between the front seats.

"Mom, please don't smoke in the car with the baby. It's really not good for her."

"My God, Emily, relax. A little smoke isn't going to hurt her," she said, lighting the cigarette. "It didn't hurt you."

I lunged forward, grabbed the cigarette and threw it out the window. The car screeched to a halt in the middle of the street.

"That was uncalled for, Emily. This is *my* car and I'll damn well smoke in it if I want to!"

"Not with the baby in the car! It can damage her lungs!"

"That school gives you such high and mighty ideas. Don't smoke. Don't drink. Well, don't think you're going to start telling *me* what to do just because you were stupid enough to have a baby!"

I heard squealing tires skid to a stop behind us.

"Out of the middle of the street, you dumb broad," a man yelled out his car window as he pulled around us on the right.

"Could we just go home now?" I asked.

Mom took another cigarette from her purse and put it in her mouth. I felt the heat of anger rising within me. How could she be so selfish, to endanger the health of her innocent granddaughter? I waited for her to light the cigarette, ready to throw that one out, too. But she drove on, unspeaking, leaving the cigarette unlit.

From the back seat, I saw the tightness in my mother's jaw, the rhythmic clenching and unclenching. I remembered the sense of comfort and warmth from the woman who sat on my bed the night before. Looking at Rosemary's tiny, sleeping face, seeing the steady rise and fall of the blanketed, breathing bundle, I made a silent pledge to do better than *my* mother had. At least I knew I could do that.

I got out of the car and opened the gate so my mother could drive back to our carport. I went to get Rosemary from the car. It took both me and my mom a long time to figure out how to undo the straps and get the baby out of her seat.

"Why do they make these damned carseat laws, anyway? I never used one for you or your brother, and you both lived through it."

"Things are different now, Mom," I said, laying the baby gently on the bed. "You're home now, Baby Rosemary," I whispered, then stretched out beside her.

My mother looked down at us.

"I don't know why you had to name this baby after my mother. Why not something modern and cute, like Courtney, or Brittainy. Peg's daughter named her baby Brittainy. It has a romantic ring, not like old, plain, Rosemary."

"I like the name, Mom. And I loved Grandma."

"More than me, I suppose. Well, that's the kind of thanks parents get, anyway. You work your tail off, trying to support your kids, but it's never enough. You'll see that for yourself soon enough, when little *Rosemary* gets bigger."

I sighed. I was suddenly very tired and wanted only to fall asleep on my bed, next to my baby. I hoped my mom would go away and leave us alone.

Around 2:00 the baby started to stir. I warmed a bottle and got ready to change her. I spread a diaper under her and then undid the soiled one, the way they'd shown me in Teen Moms. I took a damp, warm washcloth and began wiping her tiny butt. That's when I saw it for the first time. The triangular-shaped mole, on her lower left cheek, exactly like Art's. That should be proof enough even for him. But I wasn't sure whether I would ever show him. Maybe I wanted her all to myself. Maybe he didn't deserve her. Maybe I'd get a little triangle tattooed on my butt, so she'd think she got it from me.

19

I hadn't expected things to be easy, but it turned out that taking care of Rosemary was harder than I had ever imagined. Sometimes she woke up crying in the middle of the night, after she'd been asleep just a short time. I would change her and feed her, always wondering if there was something else she needed, something I didn't know about.

She would suck and rest, suck and rest, often for an hour or more. My arm got tired, cradling her, keeping her at the right feeding angle. My stitches still hurt, and it was hard to sit comfortably. When Rosemary would finally fall asleep, I, too, would fall into an exhausted, dreamless sleep. And then, such a short time later, maybe only an hour, I'd hear the light whimper which soon turned into a full cry. And sometimes I would cry, too, as the cycle began again—change, feed, sleep; change, feed, sleep.

At other times, usually in the daytime, the baby would sleep so long that I'd worry about her. Maybe she was sick. Maybe she was dying. But, in spite of worries and exhaustion, there was the warmth of love that would come unexpectedly, a mysterious gift that momentarily made the thankless cycle seem insignificant.

One day, when the baby was about two weeks old and into her sixth straight hour of sleep, I asked my mom, "Did I sleep this much when I was a baby?"

"God, Em, I don't remember. I wasn't around that much, you know. Jack was working the rodeo circuit, and I always followed along, trying to keep him out of trouble. I couldn't be bothered with how much a baby was sleeping."

"Well, what about David? Do you remember with him?"

"Same thing. He was with Grandma most of the time, too, when he was a baby."

I watched as my mom put a final coat of bright pink polish on her nails, then spread her fingers wide in front of her to admire the result.

"Why even have us if you weren't going to take care of us?"

"For the same reason you've got this one," she said, gesturing with a freshly-manicured hand toward the sleeping baby. "I spread my legs when I should have kept them closed."

I felt a rush of anger. Why did she always have to be so crude? I picked Rosemary up and carried her back to the room we shared, closing the door behind me.

"You don't have to get uppity with me, Miss Purity," my mom screamed. "You're no better than me. At least your father married me when I got pregnant with David. That's more than your little school-boy Art did for you!"

Tears ran hot on my cheeks. I wished I could take Rosemary and go live somewhere by ourselves, in the mountains, maybe. Some place peaceful and quiet. I wished I could talk to my grandmother about the baby—how much she slept, and how little she ate.

I wished my mother had been the one to die instead of my grandmother. I pictured me and Gram taking care of Baby Rosemary together, in her little house with the vegetable garden out back. We'd feed the baby homegrown food, and the house would never smell of smoke.

Rosemary began fussing, bringing me out of my fantasy, back to the reality of my life with The Barb. Who was I trying to kid? There was no way the baby and I could live anywhere but here. And honestly, we were lucky to have this place. At least my mom hadn't kicked me out.

Two girls from Teen Moms were sharing a trashed apartment—the cheapest they could find. Their folks had kicked them out when it became obvious they were pregnant. They were trying to live on welfare and food stamps, and it was awful. Sometimes they didn't even have enough for diapers. They couldn't afford to buy a supply of cloth diapers. Toward the end of the month they'd be trying to cut down to three diapers a day. Gross!

When I first found out that I would be eligible for welfare, I wanted to sign up. I didn't want my mom supporting my baby, and I knew I couldn't work for a while. But Mom wouldn't hear of it. "No daughter of mine's going on the dole," she said. She told me that if we ever got started on welfare, neither of us would have any privacy at all. And we'd be ashamed, besides.

I don't know. Some of my friends, Monique for instance, couldn't get along without it. I didn't think that made her a bad person. But my mom was right about the privacy thing—and waiting forever in lines, and being treated with no respect at all. I knew that was true from hearing some of the others talk.

I got special food stamps for important things like milk and baby food, that stuff. At least I didn't have to listen to The Barb complain about buying food for the baby. That would have been unbearable. I had a lot of pride, it's just that I didn't have anything to back it up. I was too dependent. I hated that part.

One evening, just before school was out for the summer, Art called.

"Emmy?"

"Yes," I said, feeling all stiff and choked-up the minute I heard his voice.

"How are you?"

"What do *you* care?"

Silence. Breathing. "Look, Em, I'm sorry things turned out this way. I've been thinking. I want to be friends—not be mad at each other forever."

I wanted to hang up, but my hand wouldn't move.

"Hey, I called as soon as I heard you'd had your baby. A little girl?"

"I had *my* baby three weeks ago, Art."

"Yeah, I know. But I was on choir tour. And then as soon as we got back, my folks and I went up to Stanford for orientation. You know how that goes."

"No. I used to know how that stuff went. I don't anymore."

"Want to tell me about it? How were things in the hospital? How's the baby?"

He was being his nicest self, but I kept hearing the words from months ago: "How do I know it's mine?" "Have it if you want. That's your business. Just don't expect anything from me." I got angry all over again, only this time I didn't keep it inside.

"No! I *don't* want to tell you about it. You should have been there, Art. You were as much to blame as I was, and then you left everything on me. You're nothing but a selfish coward, Art, an irresponsible, selfish coward. You're so worried about what your mommie thinks that you can't ever grow up!" I slammed the phone down hard on the receiver and sat on the bed, sobbing.

I hated him. He wasn't worth Rosemary's little finger. But the sound of his voice, the way he'd said my name. The images—Art in his tuxedo at the Harvest Ball. His thick, black, curly hair. The smell of his cologne, the warmth of his hand against my back as we'd slow-danced to "Unchained Melody." Why couldn't I wipe out those memories?

Summer was slow. Two years ago I'd been going to the beach with Tammy and Pauline almost every day, and poring over *The Joy of Sex* and giggling constantly. And last summer I'd worked at the cafe and gone to parties and the beach with Art (the beach—don't remind me), and I'd been part of Project Hope—I was alive.

And now, sometimes I felt half dead. Tied down, trapped. Sometimes I wondered if I'd made a big mistake by not having an abortion. I would imagine my life going on in a normal, high school sort of way. Then I would look at my innocent baby and feel so guilty, so ashamed for wishing her life away—what kind of mother was I anyway?

Not that I didn't love Rosie. I did—with all my heart. But all I did was feed, bathe, change. I tried to read to her, but she wasn't really interested yet. She'd started to smile—I loved that. But I was used to being active. I wanted to get back some of the muscle I'd lost during my pregnancy.

I'd tried playing softball one evening at the park, but it made me nervous when I was up at bat, knowing I wasn't paying attention to Rosemary who was sleeping in her stroller right behind the dugout. Tammy was kind of halfway watching, but not the way she needed to be watched. So I quit after the second inning.

I hung around with Rosemary for a while, watching the game, but I wanted to be *doing* it, not just hanging around the sidelines. So I gave that up. Besides, it's not like I fit in with my old softball group anymore.

I complained so about being flabby, my mom bought me one of those aerobic work-out tapes. I used it now and then, but it wasn't fun, like soccer or softball—it was work.

One thing I did that summer was read *Anne Frank: The Diary of a Young Girl* about eight times. I practically memorized it. It was overly dramatic of me to compare my life to hers—they were really nothing alike on the outside. She and her family lived in a kind of attic for over two years, hiding from the Nazis. She ended up dying in a concentration camp just a few months before she would have been liberated. It was *so* sad. My life was *so* easy in comparison to Anne Frank's. But in some ways, we had a lot in common. I was sort of confined, too. I couldn't come and go as I pleased. I felt crowded. I longed for a girlfriend I could talk with and know we would understand each other.

Well, Tammy and I were still good friends. But there were a lot of things I couldn't tell her. For instance, one day I told Tammy how I thought Rosemary still carried some secrets from her life before birth. She had such a wide-eyed look of pure trust, and her eyes were . . . deep. I didn't know how to explain it, but the depth of her eyes pulled me beyond myself in a way that made me feel calm and peaceful.

When I tried to talk with Tammy about any of this, she got a strange look on her face, as if I'd told her I'd developed a taste for worms, or something. And then she'd change the subject. And truthfully, some of the stuff Tammy talked about didn't interest me much anymore, either.

Veronica and I got together sometimes. Our babies were almost exactly the same age, and it was nice to have someone to talk with about all the little baby things. But there was a lot I *couldn't* talk to Veronica about. Like school stuff, or my hopes for college. So I could understand how Anne Frank would long for a special friend, because I wanted someone I could share everything with, too.

When I went in for my six week check-up, Dr. Kirkpatrick told me everything looked fine. "Do you want a prescription for birth control pills? Or shall I fit you with a diaphragm?"

"No way. I'm through with sex."

She laughed. "I doubt that."

"Well . . . until I'm at least thirty."

"Right. But just in case?"

"Nope. I'm celibate."

"Okay. Anything else I can do for you? You look as good as new. How do you feel?"

"I have no energy."

"Sleeping a lot?"

"Whenever the baby sleeps, so do I."

"Like about sixteen hours a day?"

I nodded.

"Ever feel like you'd like to get violent with the baby? Hit her because she's crying, anything like that?"

"No!" I was shocked.

"Just checking. Some mothers do. It's very common for new mothers to get depressed. Your whole life has changed, so of course it takes some getting used to. And as you've recently found out, being a mother is a very difficult task."

She advised me to walk three miles a day, with Rosemary in her stroller, being careful that neither of us gets too much sun. She suggested that I get out without the baby at least once a week. How could I do that? There was absolutely no one to baby-sit. I guessed I could take the baby on walks, though, if I had the energy.

I was counting the days until school would start. Rosemary could stay at the Infant Center while I was in class. In the meantime, we had to get through the long, slow, smoggy, hot, boring summer.

One night—I hadn't even gotten dressed the whole day—why bother getting dressed 'cause I wasn't going to do anything, anyway. So I was lying around, feeling sorry for myself, reading, but only half paying attention. And I got to the part in Anne's diary where she wrote about what to do when one feels melancholy. She was annoyed by her mother's idea, which was to look at all the misery in the world and be glad not to be sharing in it. Anne had a different attitude. She said:

> *Go outside, to the fields, enjoy nature and the sunshine, go out and try to recapture happiness in yourself and in God. Think of all the beauty that's still left in and around you and be happy! . . . I've found that there is always some beauty left—in nature, sunshine, freedom, in yourself; these can all help you. Look at these things, then you find yourself again, and God, and then you regain your balance. And whoever is happy will make others happy too. He who has courage and faith will never perish in misery.* (1972: Pocket Books, page 154)

That really got to me. Here I was, feeling all down because I couldn't do everything I'd always done, and Anne was locked up in the secret annex, seeing the beauty of life. I promised myself that I would start noticing the beauty around me. I could start by taking walks, like the doctor told me to do. I'd look for beauty then. I didn't have to lie around all day like some big blob.

I didn't know where the God part applied to me. I wasn't religious, like a church person, but having Rosemary and watching her grow made me lean in the God direction.

Walking turned out to be a good idea. We'd leave the house about 8:30 in the morning, after I'd fed and bathed Rosemary. We'd walk for about an hour (well, I walked. Rosemary rode.) and get home before it got too hot. Then we'd go out again in the evening after Rosie's dinner.

She liked the walks. She looked at everything, as if she were memorizing trees and flowers. Or she'd sleep, but with the sweetest kind of half-smile, calm and contented.

I noticed details which had once been a blur to me. Like the deep purple petunias that lined Mrs. Dugan's front curb. They were just plain old petunias, but when I really looked at them, I knew exactly what Anne Frank had been saying. The vivid color of the flowers, contrasting with the deep-green leaves, amazed me. And then there was this other tiny flower. I didn't know its name, but it was common, too. It had five teeny-tiny petals that went from white at the edges, to deep purple, to a bright pink in the middle. Those little, so-beautiful things, Anne Frank helped me see. I wanted to thank her. I hoped Anne was right about there being a God, and that she was in heaven looking down on me and knowing how she'd helped me out.

Often on our walks people would stop and admire Rosemary and talk silly baby talk to her. She would smile and show her dimples, Art's dimples, and then they'd go nuts. How sweet. How precious. A lot of corny stuff, but I liked hearing it, and I guess Rosie did, too, 'cause she sure turned on the charm.

I couldn't believe it. Just past two months old, and she already knew how to be charming. She was a cutie. I know you're not supposed to say that about your own kid, but there was no denying how cute she was. She was even charming The Barb.

CHAPTER

20

Tammy and I were drinking iced tea under the walnut tree in my front yard, with the baby on a blanket next to us. Rosie was moving her arms and legs around, watching her hands.

"C'mon, Em, it'll be fun. You've been living in Dull City," Tammy said.

"I can't. Who would take care of Rosemary?"

"She can stay with your mom. We're not leaving until around midnight, anyway. Your mom could be home by then, and the baby'd just sleep."

I was tempted. Tammy's cousin, Brad, was visiting from Oregon, and she wanted to set me up with him for a double date. I'd met him once a long time ago, when he was about ten. He was kind of cute then, in an Oregon sort of way.

"I don't know. What if my mom comes home drunk?"

"Oh, so what? You got through it when you were a kid. It's time to start living again. This'll be so cool. A Rave! Rave 'til you drop. They don't have anything close to Raves where Brad's from. It's the first thing he asked me about when he got to our house. Bobby's parents probably wouldn't let him stay out so late, but they're out of town. The timing is totally perfect. How long has it been since you went anywhere for fun?"

"Before Art and I broke up, I guess. About five months before I had the baby."

"And how old is she now, two months?"

"Almost three."

"Oh, wow! What are you trying to do, hit the one-year mark? C'mon, you and me. I *miss* the old fun-loving Emmy."

"Well . . . I don't even know what I'd wear."

"Black. Everyone wears black. And big, dangly earrings, you know, like those silver ones you got at the swap meet. I *love* those earrings. C'mon, let's go see what you've got."

Tammy jumped up and ran into the house. I picked Rosemary up and carried her in with me. Tammy was already pulling stuff out of my closet.

"God, you looked so great in this dress," she said, running her hand lightly over the silky dark green dress I'd worn to the Harvest Ball . . . "Here, check this out," she said, pulling a long black T-shirt from the far, scrunched-up end of my closet.

"Tammy! That was my pregnant T-shirt! I'm not wearing a leftover pregnancy shirt on my once-a-year date!"

"No, really. I've got the perfect belt for it. Trust me."

We figured it out, down to the last detail, what I would wear. "And look," she said, running her fingers through my hair and making it stick out all over. "This is great. This is the look Bradley will go nuts for. If only you had MTV, Em, then you'd know how cool this is."

I called my mom at work and told her I wanted to go out with Tammy and her cousin, and asked if she could be home by midnight to baby-sit.

"Sure, Em. You need a break."

"That was easy," Tammy said. "It took me and Bradley about two hours to get my mom to say we could stay out until 5:00. She'd *never* let just me and Bobby go to a Rave, but she thinks her nephew Bradley is super clean."

"Is he?"

"I don't know. I guess you'll find out tonight," Tammy said.

I kept Rosie up later than usual, playing with her. She was getting to be a real person, watching and smiling, reaching for me. She even had thighs and calves, not just those little stick legs she'd started out with.

I held her stretched out on my legs, facing me. She smiled the smile she always had for me. I leaned over and pulled up her little undershirt and gave her a tickly kiss on her soft sweet belly. She smiled wider, gurgled, kicked, and waved her arms all at once. She hadn't laughed yet, but I thought she would soon.

"Rosie, I'm going out for a while tonight, after you're asleep."

She watched, moving her arms around, then sticking a fist in her mouth.

"See, sometimes I want to be with my friends—you'll understand this later. I love you best of all, Baby, and I'll get you all settled in before Grandma even gets home."

My mom said I was wasting my breath, talking so much to the baby, but I didn't think so. The way she watched me, I thought she knew a lot of what I was saying. And even if she didn't totally get it, for sure she already knew I cared about her opinion.

I warmed a bottle, changed Rosie's diaper, and put her down on the bed. I lay beside her, holding her bottle and rubbing her back. I sang a song to her that my grandmother had taught me. She'd had it on a record that my grandfather bought for her a long time ago. I thought it was very romantic. I couldn't remember all the words, but the first few lines went, "Rosemary, I love you. I'm always thinking of you . . . " It had an old-fashioned melody, too.

When Rosie'd finished her milk and fallen asleep, I piled pillows around the edge of the bed and tiptoed out. I couldn't afford a crib, so when I wasn't in bed with her, guarding her, I used pillows. She couldn't roll over yet, anyway. I didn't know what I'd do when she started rolling over, or crawling. I'd worry about that later.

I felt guilty leaving her. She wasn't like Monique's baby, who cried constantly no matter what she did for him. That would have driven me nuts. I didn't know how Monique could stand it. Her mom and her boyfriend both helped take care of her son, but even so, it was crazymaking. Lucky for me, Rosie was easy. She hardly ever cried unless she was hungry or had poopie pants.

The most I'd ever left her was for half an hour or so when Mom would watch her while I ran up to the little corner store. In spite of Mom's earlier insistence that I have an abortion, and that she wouldn't take responsibility for my baby, I could see that Rosemary was winning her over. Mom would usually play with her for a while in the afternoon, just before she went off to work. I don't know what I was worried about. Rosie would be fine with Mom, unless Mom came home drunk. Then I just wouldn't go.

I pressed my clothes, bloused my old T-shirt over Tammy's heavy, silver belt, roughed up my hair the way she'd showed me, and put on my big silver earrings. I added lipstick and blush, eye shadow and liner. I checked myself out in the full-length mirror in my mom's room. It had been so long since I'd tried to look good, I was surprised to see that I still could. I was a little heavier than I had been before I got pregnant, but probably only about five pounds now. My pants fit. Really, maybe I even looked better this way—a little older.

What if I liked Bradley, and he liked me? What if we ran into Art and Amy? I hoped we would, unless Brad turned out to be a nerd. But Tammy would have told me, wouldn't she?

My mom got home about 11:30, clear eyed, without a trace of alcohol on her breath.

"I think she's down for the night," I said.

"Don't worry. Have fun. You look great."

"Thanks, Mom." I felt like hugging her, but we don't do that.

It was slightly past midnight when Tammy gave a light knock and opened our front door.

"Brad's embarrassed to come in, so the guys are waiting in the car." She walked over to me and fussed with my hair. "Groovy," she said. Sometimes Tammy talked like a hippy.

Brad was standing beside the car, waiting for us. He was tall, with short blond hair and light skin.

"Long time no see," he said, smiling.

"Right." I tried to think of something more to say, but no luck. He held the door open for me, and I slid across the back seat and buckled up. Brad got in beside me, leaving his seat belt unused.

"Pretty careful, huh?" he said, nodding at my fastened strap.

"Oh, I'm just used to it. I buckle my baby in, then me— setting a good example, you know."

"How old is your baby?"

"Almost three months."

"And you're setting an example? . . . Weird."

I could tell it was going to be a long evening.

"You should see Em's baby. She's really cute," Tammy said.

"I'm not into babies."

"What are you into?" I asked.

"Football and partying, that's my life."

"Bobby was captain of the J.V. team last year, huh, Bobby?" Tammy said.

Before Bobby even had a chance to answer, Brad said, "I guess that's okay if you're little. Me, I wouldn't bother playing if I couldn't be on the varsity team. What's the point?"

Bobby just kept driving, as if he hadn't even heard Brad's remarks. Tammy turned to face Brad with a look that could kill.

"Well?" he said.

She turned around and faced front, and from then on, the only conversation in the car consisted of where we should turn and where we should park.

When we got there, a giant of a guy at the door motioned us in. It was a big warehouse, bare except for tables that were set up with drinks and, up front, tons of sound equipment. The music was about 8.2 on the Richter scale—

heavy, pulsating, jarring the room and everyone in it. There was a huge wall of speakers. Heavy-duty cords were strung all over the place. Projectors flashed strange, psychedelic images on the walls. Brad went straight for the drinks and brought four big paper cups filled with punch back to us.

He handed us each a drink, then pulled a flat kind of bottle from his jeans pocket, opened it, and poured something from it into each of our drinks. I took one taste of it and almost gagged. I didn't know what was in it, but something alcoholic and burning.

"No thanks," I said, handing my drink back to him.

He shrugged. "All the more for me, then."

We had to yell to make ourselves heard.

Bobby and Tammy took a few sips of theirs, then they went back to the drink table.

"I guess I offended Tammy's boyfriend with my varsity football talk. That's just the way I feel, but I wasn't trying to put anyone down."

"Maybe it just came out wrong," I yelled, feeling a little sorry for him.

"Yeah. I'm always putting my big foot in my mouth."

Tammy and Bobby came back with fresh drinks. "Non-spiked," Bobby said, handing one to me.

We stood around for a while, watching. The room was dark, lit only by strobe lights and colored lights that illuminated the area where people were dancing. Most of the guys were wearing hightop work boots. Everything was black. Jeans, shirts, baseball caps, boots, and clunky shoes. I guess we sort of fit in. We were all in black and the guys were wearing caps. As long as no one looked at our shoes . . . I think I was probably the only one in sandals. Bobby and Brad were wearing athletic shoes. There weren't many of those around, either. Tammy was the only one whose feet fit the style of the evening. She was wearing her Doc Martins. But Tammy had shoes for every occasion. Tammy got more money for shoes than I did for food for the baby.

"Wow! I can't believe I'm really at a Rave," Brad screamed

over the sounds. "We hear about this stuff up where I live, but the closest place to find one would probably be Seattle. This is *awesome!*"

When we finished our drinks, we made our way toward the center of the room where people were dancing. Brad and I faced front, not touching. The music was loud and pounding and harsh—the kind of sound that Mr. Michaels used to describe as an affront to the aural sensibilities. At first it seemed to surround me, then grow within me, moving my body until I was lost in the hammering rhythm. Brad moved in a strobe-distorted haze before me, insignificant. All was insignificant but the noise, the deafening, insistent beat, absorbing me and moving me, pounding through me, overcoming all else.

Minutes or hours later, I had lost all sense of time, Brad took me by the hand and led me out to a porch area where Tammy and Bobby were standing. It was crowded, but it was cooler than inside. I was damp with perspiration, and my legs and arms were tingling from the exertion.

"I guess you like to dance, huh?" Brad said.

I nodded my head. How free I'd felt on the dance floor! And how long it had been since I'd had that feeling! I hadn't even thought of Rosemary once while I was dancing.

"Give me a sip," I said, reaching for Tammy's punch.

I took a long swallow.

"Some sip . . . Why don't you buy your date a drink, Cousin?"

"Okay. I'm a little dry myself," Brad said. He and I went for drinks. He poured whiskey from his flask into his drink. We walked back to the edge of the room where Tammy and Bobby were sitting. There was room for one more, next to Tammy, and Brad sat down. Bobby stood up and offered me his seat.

"At least there's *one* gentleman in the crowd," Tammy said.

"I never claimed to be a gentleman. Just a *man*," Brad said. He stood, striking a body-builder pose, and flexed his well-developed muscles.

"Here—sorry," he said to me, indicating his spot on the bench. I sat down, and we all scrunched over, making room for about half of Brad. He sat, smiling.

"Cheek to cheek," he said to me. "I like it."

When he finished his drink, Brad said, "I have to step outside for a few minutes. I'll be right back. Okay?"

"Sure."

"He likes you," Tammy said. "I can tell."

I didn't say anything. I didn't want to hurt Tammy's feelings about her cousin, but he seemed like kind of a jerk to me. I mean, he was sort of nice, but sort of not.

When Brad came back inside, he took four tiny squares of aluminum foil from his pocket and held them out in front of us.

"How about it?" he said.

I had no idea what he was talking about until Bobby said, "Nah, Man. I'm afraid of that acid stuff."

Brad offered a little square to me, then to Tammy. We both shook our heads. I guess I was kind of shocked. Of course I knew a lot of kids did drugs, and that all kinds of things were available. We were constantly hearing about it in school, either through some anti-drug program, or from friends talking about who had been stoned on what. But I'd never seen anything at parties or dances except beer, and once a friend of Art's had a joint, but no one had seemed interested.

"I thought I was out for a wild, party-hearty time in L.A.," he said. "My friends in Oregon would already be feeling no pain."

"We're not in pain," Tammy said.

He gave her a sideways look. "Well, you're not exactly a party girl, either." He gazed fondly at his four foil-wrapped prizes. "I'll just take my little tabs back to Oregon with me. Man, they *know* how to party up there."

The music had started again. Blasting. Causing the whole building to vibrate.

"Come on, let's dance," he said, taking my arm and

leading me back inside. "I like to see that dance action of yours."

I didn't care what kind of remarks he made about my "dance action." It was my dance. Me. Free.

The next time we went outside, Tammy and Bobby were leaning against a corner rail, arms wrapped around each other, kissing in a way that made me feel like an intruder.

"It looks like those two are enjoying themselves. Let's try it." Brad pulled me close and leaned his head down over mine.

"Your hair smells good," he whispered. "I could really learn to like you." Then he sort of nibbled at my ear. It was weird. I'd never even really had a date with anyone but Art, and Brad didn't *feel* right to me.

For one thing, he was too tall. For another, he was trying to give me disgusting, sloppy-wet kisses. And he was holding me so close that I was kind of bent backward. I managed to slide through his arms and take a few steps away. I didn't want to be rude, but he was too much. He reached for me again, just as Tammy and Bobby broke for air.

"Isn't this cool?" Tammy said, looking flushed and dreamy.

"Yeah, it's okay," I said.

"Oh, admit it. You've been having a great time dancing. Anyone can see that."

Brad left and came back with drinks, spiked for him and regular for the rest of us. I hadn't been counting, but I thought he'd probably had at least five drinks so far. If he got drunk enough, I wouldn't have to worry about kissing him goodnight.

Suddenly, we heard screams and shouting from inside and rushed in to see what was happening. Two guys, big guys with shaved heads, were fighting near the drinks place. They were serious. One knocked the other down and started kicking him with loud, sickening blows. Another guy was trying to pull the kicker back. People were gathered around, forming a wide, loose circle, watching. Two bouncers came running in from the parking lot.

"Hey, c'mon," Brad said, "Let's get some action." He had

Bobby by the arm, pulling him toward the fight. His eyes were bright with excitement. Bobby jerked away.

"What, are you crazy? People get killed doing that. We're not in the apple orchard here, you know."

Brad went running over to the edge of the circle. Bobby and Tammy ran after him, pulling him back. The bouncers had each of the guys from behind, dragging them away from each other. The bouncers were giants, but so were the two fighters, and one of them, the one that had been down on the floor, got away and ran over to the guy who was being held and kicked him really hard where I'm told it hurts. He crumpled onto the floor, and the bouncer got hold of the slippery one again.

"Did you see that? Right in the family jewels," Brad said, laughing like it was the funniest thing he'd ever seen, poking Bobby in the arm. "Man, did you see that?"

"Yeah, I saw it," Bobby said. "Let's get out of here."

Half the people were headed for the doors.

"Aw, just when it was getting to be fun," Brad said, still laughing, wiping his eyes.

We walked to the car. We were inching out of the crowded parking lot when Brad tapped Bobby on the shoulder.

"Hey man, I've got to leak my lizard. I'll catch up."

He got out of the car and walked over by a telephone pole.

"Leak his *lizard*?" I said.

We looked over at him. Right there, in front of hundreds of people in cars, he was peeing. I couldn't believe my eyes.

"Gross. He's really gross," I said, scooting over against the door so I would be as far away from him as possible.

"Well, don't blame me," Tammy said. "I haven't seen him in seven years. He used to be cute. Remember?"

He came running back to the car and slid in close to me.

"Better," he said.

21

I was surprised to see Bobby turning down his street. Not just his, but Art's. I could see Art's car parked out front. Of course it would be. Art's mom would never let him be out this late.

We turned into Bobby's driveway.

"Tammy and I have to go in and check on some stuff. We'll be back in half an hour or so. She doesn't have to be home until five o'clock anyway."

Tammy got out of the car with a quick, sheepish glance in my direction. I checked my watch. 3:45. Why hadn't they taken me home first? But it was too late to ask. They were already inside.

"Convenient, huh?" Brad said, pulling me toward him.

I could see Art's bedroom window from where I was sitting. All the lights were out in his house. Was he dreaming? Did he ever dream of me?

"Hey, c'mere. Don't be so stiff," Brad said. "Let's get better acquainted."

I dodged his kisses, ducking and turning my head.

"Look. I'm a regular guy," he said. "Half the girls in my school would love to be where you are right now. Loosen up and we'll have a little fun."

I let him kiss me, but I didn't like it. There was nothing gentle or affectionate about it, and his breath was heavy with alcohol.

"I'm sorry," I said. "I'm just not interested."

"I can help you get interested," he said, slurring his words slightly. "Just give me a chance." He tried to kiss me again, but I turned away.

"No. C'mon. I mean it," he said, trying again to find my lips. "You want it. I could tell as soon as I saw you dancing." He was breathing harder. "You can pretend you don't like it, but I know better." He grabbed my breast—rough and mean. With his other hand, he caught my chin, held it firmly, and kissed me on the lips, forcing my head back against the seat. He thrust his tongue between my tight lips, pushing against my clenched teeth. I pushed him away. He pulled me closer. His hands were all over me.

"C'mon. C'mon. Don't give me this hard-to-get routine."

I pushed at him again. He had his hands under my shirt, groping.

"STOP!" I demanded.

"It's not like you're a virgin," he hissed, grabbing under my skirt, ripping at my underpants.

"It's not like I want your grubby hands on me, either!"

"I'll show you something besides hands," he said, undoing his jeans in one quick move and throwing himself on top of me.

"GOD! STOP!" I shoved at him with all my strength. It didn't faze him. I could feel him hard against me, pushing. I squeezed my legs together, tight.

"TAMMY! BOBBY!" I screamed, even knowing they probably couldn't hear me.

Brad shoved his knee between my thighs, forcing them open. I grabbed him by the nose and scratched at his eye. I felt skin give way beneath my fingernails.

"SHIT!" he screamed.

I went for his eye again, this time going deeper, gouging. He covered his face with his free hand. I scooted out from under him and grasped the door handle. He grabbed at me.

"SLUT!"

I bit his hand with all the strength in my jaws. He jerked away. I lunged out the door and and fell to the ground. He threw himself on top of me, covered my face with his hand, forced my head backward so I could hardly breathe. "I'll teach you! I'll teach you!" he hissed, jabbing my head back.

I struggled for air, for strength. My God, he was killing me! The eye. The eye. I went for the eye again, with all my strength, gouging deeper, deeper, grasping at the firmness of the eyeball in the slippery ooze of blood.

He reared back with a cry that sounded more animal than human. I squirmed away, struggled to my feet, and started running.

"BITCH!" he screamed after me, a scream turned cry. I heard no following footsteps. I ran faster than I knew I could, tasting his blood, opening my mouth to the dark morning air, wiping my blood-wet hand on my skirt as I ran. Heart pounding, lungs burning, I ran. Home. Home. Home was the hope I ran to with each slap of my foot against pavement as I closed the gap between me and safety.

I heard a car slowing behind me. Oh, God! Had he come after me? I jumped from the street to the sidewalk and found a new burst of speed. If I could just get home. Suddenly I was surrounded by light. A voice over a bullhorn said, "This is the police. Stop. Put your hands in the air. This is the police. Stop. Put your hands in the air."

I stopped and turned toward the light. I was blinded.

"Hands up!"

I put my hands up.

A policeman grabbed me and roughly pulled me toward the car where he told me to stand, spread-eagled. His partner, a woman, searched me.

"What's your hurry?" the man asked.

"Going home," I panted.

The woman shone her flashlight on my face, then looked me up and down.

"What happened to you?"

"I got in an argument with my date."

They put me in the car and drove me home, then followed me inside.

"Get your parents out here," the gruff one demanded. I went to my mom's room and called her. Then I went to my room, weak and trembling, to check on Rosie. She was sound asleep. I picked her up and held her close. Who would love her if Brad had killed me? Who would take care of her the way I did? It wasn't just me anymore. It wasn't just *my* life anymore. I held her close, shaking.

My mom came to my room in her beat-up chenille robe. "They want you out here, Emily, and I want to know what's going on!"

I put Rosie back down on the bed and went out to the living room. I kept my arms wrapped tightly around me, trying to control my shaking body.

"My God! What happened to you?" my mom gasped.

"That's what we'd like to know, too, Mrs. Morrison," the gruff cop said. "We found your daughter running down the street like a bat out of hell. Four a.m. is not an appropriate time for a sixteen-year-old girl to be out training for the Olympics."

My mom was still staring at me, her mouth half open. I looked down at my legs. They were all scratched up. One knee was bleeding, I guess from when I jumped out of the car. My skirt was torn, and my T-shirt was ripped half-way down the middle. Tammy's belt was gone, I had no idea where. The fingernails of my right hand were caked with blood.

I ran to the bathroom and threw up. The woman cop, Sergeant Powers, was right behind me, watching. I splashed cold water on my face and was shocked by what I saw in the mirror. My right cheek was bloody. My neck showed clear finger and thumb marks where Brad had gripped the breath from me. I threw up again. Sergeant Powers rinsed a washcloth in cool water, dabbed it on my face, and led me back to the living room.

"So tell us about your date," she said. "What happened?"

"Nothing much. I got mad at him and fell getting out of the car."

"Running or parked?"

"Parked."

"And these bruises at your neck?"

I shrugged.

"Did he rape you?"

"No."

"Did he try?"

I shrugged again.

"Someone's running around out there who we should put under arrest. How about giving us a little information?"

I shook my head no.

"Let's go, Powers, we're wasting our time here," the partner said, standing up to leave. "We can't do anything without cooperation." Then he lectured my mom on curfew laws and parental responsibility, and left. The sun was up by that time.

My mother took me by the hand and led me to the living room. She got an ice pack from the kitchen and had me hold it against my bloodied, swollen cheek. She fixed a cup of tea for us both and sat on the couch beside me.

"Tell me," she said. So I did.

She sat quietly, listening as the words poured from me. When I finished, she said, "You should have told the police. I'll call them back."

"I can't. I mean, it's Tammy's cousin, you know."

"But Em. He practically killed you. He'll do it again to someone else if he gets away with this."

"I don't think he exactly got away," I said, remembering the feel of flesh, blood, and eyeball beneath my grasping nails. "I think I may really have hurt him."

"You hurt *him*? Look at *you*!"

"Please, Mom. I'm so tired."

"Okay, okay. We'll talk more later."

I showered, scrubbing every part of me, head to toe. I scrubbed my nails hard with a brush. I threw my clothes in the wastebasket and sprayed some antiseptic stuff on every place where the skin was broken.

I pulled on a pair of sweats and my Hamilton Harmonics long-sleeved shirt. By that time the baby was fussing. I changed her and fed her, gave her a bath in the sink, and lay down beside her, hoping she would go back to sleep. I ached all over. My legs were tense and cramped from all the running. My right arm had a nasty bruise, and my left hip, around to where my pelvic bone stuck out, was all red and scraped from where Brad had been holding me down.

I felt Rosie's little body next to mine. It scared me all over again, thinking how alone she would be without me. That was my first thought—not how awful it would be to die, how much I would miss, but how awful it would be for Rosie to be without me. When I realized that I cared more for Rosie than for myself, I knew I didn't need to worry anymore about what kind of mother I was turning out to be.

It wasn't fair to Rosie that I was the only one she could depend on, though. She was a part of Art, too. The longer I lay there watching her untroubled, guiltless sleep, the angrier I got. She deserved more. Was it asking too much for a baby to have a dad who cared? I didn't think so. Just because Art didn't want to see his mom upset, he refused to think Rosie was his. Well, I had something to show him!

Tammy and Bobby stopped by about eight in the morning, still in the same clothes they'd worn to the Rave. I walked outside to talk with them 'cause I didn't want to wake my mom or the baby.

"What happened last night?" Tammy asked. She was standing, arms folded in front of her, looking very angry.

"Your precious cousin tried to rape me, that's what happened. And when I didn't give in, he practically killed me. Look," I said, pointing to the bruise marks around my throat. "How could you have set me up with such a jerk, and then left me alone with him?"

"I didn't know he was a jerk."

"You knew he was a jerk by the time you left me alone with him."

"Not exactly," she said.

"Oh, you did too. Bobby?"

Bobby was just standing there, a little behind Tammy, looking like he'd rather be in a chicken-feet-eating contest or something. He nodded. "She's right about that, Babe. He'd been acting like a jerk all night."

Tammy's face softened a bit. "Well, you didn't have to practically blind him, though." She started to cry. "God, we had to rush him to the emergency hospital. He was holding his hand over his eye. Blood was oozing out. He was crying like a baby. My mom went nuts when she saw him at the hospital. He had to have stitches all around his eye, and he's got a big patch over it. He's going to have to have surgery. He may even be blinded in that eye. I don't get it. How could you have done such a thing?"

"TAMMY! HE TRIED TO RAPE ME!"

"That's not what he said."

Just then Rosie started crying.

"I'll get her," Bobby said, looking relieved to have an excuse to leave.

"Bring her out here, okay? Grab a diaper from my dresser, too, would you?". . . I turned back to Tammy. "So what *did* your cousin say, anyway?"

"He said you got really angry with him because he was tired and didn't want to give you any. He said you're sex crazed and anyone who saw you dancing knew that much."

"Tammy, we've been best friends forever. Who do you know best, me or Brad, who you've only seen about three times in your whole life? Look at these bruises." I showed her my arm. "And there's more," I said, pointing to the injured area which was covered by my sweats. "He tried to rape me. Your cousin tried to rape me, and I really think he could have killed me. Get it straight."

I remembered the awful struggle in the car—how it felt like I couldn't get out from under him. I remembered the feel of tiny pieces of flesh under my fingernails. I began shaking again, choking back sobs.

"Look," I said, pulling my sweats down so she could see the scratched and bruised area around my pelvic bone. "And look at this—he could have killed me, Tammy. I could be dead this morning, and Rosie would be an orphan."

"God," she said, finally looking at me, really looking at me for the first time that morning. "Oh, God. I'm so sorry."

We hugged each other, both of us crying. "It's just that it's so awful at my house. I don't think my mom will ever let me go out again. And my Uncle Jerry hates me now 'cause he thinks it's my fault Brad got hurt. And he's kind of mad at my mom, too. And my dad says she should never have let us go to one of those things in the first place."

"My mom wants me to press charges against him."

"He's already at the airport. His parents wanted him out on the first available flight. I think it leaves in about fifteen minutes. They want him to see a specialist up there, and they want him out of California. Now!"

All the time Tammy and I were standing there talking, Bobby was taking care of Rosie. He'd put her on the old comforter under the tree. He had baby wipes and a diaper in his hand, but he wasn't using them. Not that he didn't know how. He had two little sisters who he'd taken care of as babies. He'd often held Rosie and given her a bottle, but this was the first time he'd changed her. He was kneeling there beside her, staring at her bare butt. I walked over and wiped her off and put a fresh diaper on.

Bobby pushed the diaper far up on her leg, so he could look at the mole again. Tammy came and sat beside him.

"What's wrong?" she said.

Bobby just sat there, staring.

"It's just a mole," Tammy said. "It won't hurt her. It's not even ugly. Really, it's kind of cute, don't you think? Almost heart shaped."

"It's not just any old mole, Tammy, it's a mole exactly like Art's. Same shape, same place."

"How do you know Art's got a mole there?"

"Years of skinny-dipping in my pool."

I scooted Rosie's diaper back and covered her with a light blanket. The sun was out, but I felt cold. I wondered if I would ever stop trembling.

"Whose did you think she was anyway, Bobby? God, sometimes I feel like nobody in the world cares about me, or believes me!" I was shaking so hard my teeth were chattering, and crying so hard I could barely talk.

"Art thinks Rosie's not his. Tammy sticks up for her cousin when he tries to rape me. And you, Bobby, you act like Rosie's mole is the strangest thing you've ever seen. Don't tell me you didn't know Rosie was Art's. Look at her —you don't need a mole to tell you whose baby she is. And look at me. All I ever did was love him, and look at me now. And my friends act like I'm a liar and a slut!" I hid my face in the darkness of my hands and wept great heaving sobs, unrestrained.

"No, Em. It's not like that. I never thought you were with anyone else. It's just that Art ... he's like my brother. I didn't want to believe he was lying. I mean, I knew, but . . ."

Tammy put her arms around me but I pushed her away.

"I'm really sorry, Em. God, if you hadn't got away from Brad . . . I shouldn't have left you alone with him. I just wanted some time with Bobby . . . I mean, his folks were away, and we hardly ever have a private place," she blushed. "I guess I wasn't much of a friend right then. But I've always believed you about the baby. You know that. I've always been on your side." Now Tammy was crying, too. Bobby put an arm around each of us and drew us close to him. "Forgive me, Emmy? I'm a really nice guy," he said, smiling.

I nodded. We sat there, worn out, until Rosie let a little baby fart. We laughed hysterically. As soon as one of us stopped, the others would get us going again. I couldn't catch my breath. My stomach ached with laughter. It really wasn't that funny, but we laughed for the longest time.

Later, after they'd gone and I was trying to sort things through in my mind, I wondered if Anne Frank had ever laughed in the concentration camp.

22

The first time I called, Mrs. Rodriguez answered. Two o'clock on a Sunday afternoon. I'd wait until three-thirty before I called again. Then she'd be busy in the kitchen. Sweet, chocolaty chicken mole, fresh jalapeños and sliced tomatoes from Mr. Rodriguez's garden, steaming hot flour tortillas, a pot of simmering red beans. I could see it, smell it, almost taste it. My mouth watered at the thought.

I opened a bag of corn chips and a can of Dr. Pepper. Not the same.

"I'm going to introduce you to your daddy," I told Rosie as I held her in my arms on the couch. I was watching Shirley Temple in "The Little Princess," choking up over a little girl who was searching for her soldier dad.

"You've got a right to know who he is. And it's important for people to know their genetic background."

We'd talked about that a lot in Teen Moms. How even if we didn't like our baby's dad anymore, we should keep track of him for the sake of our baby. We should know if there was any diabetes or cancer in the family.

"I can't make him love you, or take care of you. Maybe you just have to be satisfied with me. But I'm not going to let him keep pretending you're not half his. I've been stupid to let it go on this long, but for sure he's not getting away to Stanford without proof positive. I'm going to see to that!"

"Ghaaaa," she said, giving me her wise old look.

 A t exactly three o'clock, I dialed Art's number. My heart was pounding hard, the way it had when he first started talking to me at Hamilton High. That had been almost two years ago. It seemed like ten.

I hadn't talked to Art for at least two months, when he called that time and I hung up on him. When I heard his voice this time, I almost hung up again. But I didn't.

"Art? This is Emily." My voice was all hoarse and shaky.

"Emily?"

"Emily Morrison. Remember me?"

"Don't be sarcastic, Em. I'm glad you called."

"You are?"

"Well, yeah. I've always told you I wanted to stay friends. You're the one who hangs up on me. Right?"

"Right."

Long pause.

"So . . . how've you been?" Art said.

"Okay."

Another pause.

"Art, I was just wondering . . . I mean . . . I'd kind of like to see you before you leave for college. Maybe you could drop by some time?"

Pause.

"But if you don't want to . . ."

"No. No. I want to. I'd like to see you before I leave. I meant it when I told you I wanted to be friends. You know I'm with Amy now, but—friends—that'd be great."

"I wasn't asking you to marry me," I said.

"Well . . . how about tomorrow after work? I could drop by about 5:30. I leave for school a week from today, so it has to be pretty soon."

 M y stomach turned flip-flops all day Monday. What should I wear? And the baby? She looked cute in anything, but this was a special day. I cleaned the house and straightened everything up. I put all the old newspapers and magazines out back in our recycling bin. I cut two long-stemmed white roses from a bush out back and put them in a pretty bud vase that had belonged to my grandmother. When I was finished working around the house, I took a shower and washed my hair with the vanilla-scented shampoo.

On our afternoon walk, Rosie and I stopped at the baby shop, and I bought her a ruffled pink elastic headband and some lacy pink socks. That would dress up the little shorts and top set that Monique had given her.

Back home, I decided the house looked too nice. I didn't want Art to think his visit was some kind of a big deal, even if it was. So I put the flowers in David's room where Art wouldn't see them. Then I retrieved some of the newspapers and dumped them around on the couch and the kitchen table.

When I heard the distinct and familiar sound of Art's car in the driveway, my heart started pounding again. I checked myself in the mirror one final time. I adjusted Rosie's headband. Her hair was dark and starting to get curly, like Art's. We met him at the door.

"Hi, Em," he said, smiling, showing his dimples.

"Hi," I said, searching his face for a sign of love. "Want a soda?"

"Yeah. Great. It's hot out there."

He followed me into the kitchen.

"Want ice?"

"Yeah. Please."

"This is Rosie," I said, turning so she was facing him.

"She's cute," he said, barely looking at her.

"Here, hold her while I get the ice." I handed her toward him. Instead of taking her, he reached for the refrigerator.

"I'll get the ice. I'm not too good with babies."

We took a blanket outside and sat under the tree where there was a cool breeze.

After what seemed like a long time before either of us could think of anything to say, Art said, "It's finally here, Em. I'm off to Stanford six days from now. Can you believe it? I've never even been away from my parents for more than a week. Just choir tours, really. And once they went to Mexico for my aunt's funeral. But that's it. And now I'm going to be living three hundred miles away. It's so beautiful. You should see it. I've already been accepted for the choir. How about you? Are you singing with the Harmonics this year?"

"I don't know. I hope so. If the Infant Care Center opens early enough, I will—otherwise I'll just sing in the chorus."

"What about soccer? Will you be on the team again?"

"Well . . . I want to. But that depends on the Infant Center hours, too. I'm not sure yet how late they stay open . . . Sit with her for just a minute, would you? I've got to get a fresh diaper for her."

I went inside and got a Pampers from the box. My hands were shaking. I took three deep breaths, then went back outside. Rosie was kicking and smiling and Art was smiling back.

"Time for a change, Rosie Dee," I said, positioning her so that Art would have a clear view of the left side of her butt. I took the still clean diaper off and slipped a new one under her.

"Look," I said, touching her look-alike mole. "What do you think this is?" I held my breath.

At first it was as if he couldn't focus his eyes. Then he got up closer. He ran his finger lightly over the tiny mark. He touched the back of his jeans at the spot I knew his own mole to be.

"What do you think it is?" I asked again.

"I know what it is," he whispered. "I know what it is."

I fastened the diaper and handed the baby to him. He held her in his arms, looking down at her face. She looked back, the way she always did—checking everything out.

"Am I holding her right?" he asked. His eyes were teary, and I could feel that mine were, too.

"She's fine," I said.

"I'm going to Stanford," he said, as much to himself as to me. He rubbed his hand across the top of her head.

"Her hair is so soft," he said. "She's so little."

"If you think she's little now, you should have seen her when she was born."

He nodded. "I should have. I know I should have. I know I've made a mess of things," he said softly, not looking away from the baby.

We sat under the tree talking and playing with Rosie until it was almost dark.

"I've got to go home," Art said. "After dinner my folks are taking me to buy stuff I need for school. Sheets, towels, that kind of stuff. But can I come back tomorrow? If I call, will you not hang up on me?"

"I won't hang up."

I left Rosemary on the blanket and walked with him to the car. He put his arms around me and held me tight. "I'm sorry. I'm sorry," he whispered.

Lots of times I had thought I hated him. I had wanted to hurt him the way I'd been hurt. But it felt good, and warm, and right, to be in Art's arms again. He kissed the top of my head and got into his car. I watched him back out of the driveway, and then I picked up the baby and took her inside.

"He knows he's your daddy," I said. "You've got a daddy now."

From the moment I woke up, I began reliving my time with Art the day before. How good it had felt to have his arms around me. Did he still love me? Would he love Rosie? What did his kiss mean? Was it only a friendly kiss, or was it more? What about Amy? I tried not to expect anything. It seemed to me that whenever I expected anything good from life, I got a big disappointment. But I couldn't help listening for his car—hoping for a phone call. I didn't even take Rosie for a walk that morning, in case he would call while we were gone. It was a long, dreamy day of waiting and wondering. Then, late in the afternoon, the phone rang.

"I get off work in about twenty minutes. Your mom's home today, isn't she?"

"No. Usually she is on Tuesdays, but this week she's covering for one of the waitresses who's sick."

"Do you have any sodas?"

"Yes."

"I'll see you in a few minutes, then."

I was giving the baby her bottle when he arrived carrying a big pizza—my favorite kind. I could see there was still a lot he remembered, like my mother's day off, and my taste for black olive and mushroom pizza.

"Thanks," I said, eyeing the pizza hungrily. I handed Rosie to him.

"Finish feeding her, would you?"

He held her stiffly, but she didn't seem to mind.

"You just have to be sure to support her head and neck. She's still kind of wobbly sometimes."

He readjusted her head against his arm while she went on sucking at her bottle. I got paper plates and napkins, sodas, and the jar of crushed peppers. Whatever kind of pizza Art ate, he liked to smother it in dried red pepper flakes.

"You remembered." He smiled at me as I placed the jar in front of him.

"You, too," I said, pointing to the pizza.

"I remember everything," he said.

"Me, too."

I took Rosie from him and held her against me in the standard burping position. I rubbed her back. She let out a loud, deep burp. We laughed.

"She burps like my Uncle Manny," Art said. We laughed even harder. Then Art got all serious. "I've missed you, Em."

"I've been right here."

After we ate, I filled the sink with warm water and gave Rosie her bath.

"In the sink?" Art said.

"She's too little for the bathtub. Besides, I scour it out."

"But don't you have one of those little plastic bathtub things? My cousin had one of those."

"Yeah, well, I barely have enough money for diapers and food. This works."

Art watched in silence as I washed Rosie's little body. He held the washcloth over her eyes while I rinsed the shampoo out of her hair. I dried her and rubbed baby powder on her chest and belly and butt. He traced her mole with his index finger. I carried her, wrapped in a towel, into my room. An undershirt and diaper, that's all she needed. It was too hot to put her in a sleeper.

"Okay to use your phone?" Art asked, walking back to the kitchen.

While I was dressing Rosie, I heard Art explaining to his mom that he would be late. He had some last minute things to do to get ready for school. "Oh, you know, Mom," I heard him say. "Assignment calendar, notebook organizer, toothbrush, deodorant, all that stuff. And maybe I'll stop by Bobby's work for a while." Had he told her about Rosie? It didn't sound like it.

Later, after Rosie had dropped off to sleep, Art and I went out in the back yard where there was a light, cool breeze. We spread the old comforter out and sat down on it. The sounds of "Wheel of Fortune" came blasting from our back neighbor's T.V. We sat close enough that I caught a whiff of Art's fresh, clean, soapy scent—close enough to touch, but we didn't.

"Emmy?"

"What?"

"I want us to try again."

"What do you mean?"

"You know. Be together again. You and me. Like before."

"What about Amy?"

"She's not important. You're important. Your baby is important."

"*Our* baby, Art. She's *our* baby."

"I know. I know. I'm just not used to it. But I want to try. Please try." He moved closer to me, facing me. "I love you," he said. "I've never stopped loving you. I wanted to, but I couldn't."

The warm breath of his words reached my lips. We kissed, and I felt the tension, the emptiness, the hurt, release in a flood of tears. He stroked my hair, rubbed my back.

"Shhh. Shhh. It's okay. Everything's going to be okay." He leaned back on the comforter, pulling me down next to him, whispering reassurances until I stopped crying.

"Amy was important enough that she'd met Mr. Mole," I said, remembering the conversation I'd overheard months ago.

"Listen," he said, leaning over me, smoothing back my hair, kissing my forehead. "I don't want to lie to you. I like sex. You know that. And Amy was available. But I never loved her. I didn't even ever *tell* her I loved her. I don't think she cared all that much about me, either."

"Does she know you're here?"

"*I* barely know I'm here . . . Besides, she left for Santa Barbara this afternoon. We said we wouldn't be exclusive, anyway. You know, we'll both be meeting new people. We already said we wouldn't be tied down. I'm telling you, Em, you're my only love."

He kissed me—a long, gentle kiss.

I clung to him. "I want to believe you."

"Then do. You'll see. Give me a chance."

I moved my lips to meet his, then kissed his neck, behind his ear, the palm of his hand, the places I knew to kiss. I felt the dampness of tears on his cheeks as he nestled his head between my neck and shoulder. How good it was to feel him next to me, breathe in rhythm to his breathing. He slipped his warm hand under my shirt and undid my bra. I fumbled at his shirt, wanting to get closer, feel skin against skin.

The baby cried. I froze.

"She'll be okay," Art said, kissing the hollow spot at the base of my neck.

She cried louder. I sat up. Art held onto my hand.

"Let her be," he said, pulling me down.

"No. I need to check on her." I got back up and ran toward the house. As soon as I opened the door, I could smell her problem.

"You didn't choose a very good time, Rosie," I told her. Art came in just as I undid her diaper. He walked back out to the living room.

"How can you stand it? That makes me want to puke!"

"You get used to it," I called back to him.

"Yuck. Not me. I'd never get used to that. When will she learn to use a toilet?"

"Probably when she's two or so."

"Two? You mean she's going to be doing ca-ca in her pants until she's two? Disgusting!"

When she was clean again, I took her out to the living room and rocked her for a while.

"Will she go back to sleep?" Art asked.

"Probably. Do you want to hold her?"

"No. It's okay. I've got to run a few errands. But I'll come back in half an hour or so. Will she be asleep then?"

"I think so. I can't exactly predict, you know."

"Well, I'll stop back by, anyway. I love you," he said, leaning over to kiss me. He kissed Rosemary, too, on the forehead, and ran the back of his fingers across her cheek.

"She's got such soft skin. Is that normal?"

"Of course it's normal. She's totally normal, except that she may be a bit advanced."

"Probably gets that from her dad," he said, then walked out the door. He was back twenty minutes later with a package from the drugstore.

"Is she asleep?"

"Yes."

"Come on. Let's see if everything's okay in David's room," he grinned. I followed him around to David's door. He took the key from its hiding place in the geranium plant, and we entered the musty, unused room. Art took foam and condoms from the drugstore bag, and we did what I had told the doctor I didn't plan on doing again until I was thirty.

Just like in the old days, Art eased his way out of bed at 9:40 and began dressing. I watched dreamily as he pulled on his boxers, then his jeans and shirt, which he didn't bother to button. He looked at his watch, then sat on the bed beside me.

"I can't believe it. Next week at this time I can stay out as late as I want—no one to answer to. Cool, huh?"

"Cool," I said, pulling him down for one last kiss. We said our goodbyes. I dressed and straightened David's bed, put our "protection" away in the bathroom drawer, then went back to my own bed, next to Rosie. I tried to read for a while but my mind kept wandering. Finally I turned off my booklight and lay in the dark, listening to Rosie breathe, trying to sort out my feelings.

Two phrases kept running through my mind—Art loves me, and Rosie has a daddy. But did he *really* love me the way I once believed he did? He must have told me so at least twenty times. I felt tingly all over just remembering those words. But I couldn't say them back to him. I didn't know why. Maybe it was because I didn't feel safe with him yet. It was not that I didn't love him. I just couldn't say it.

As for Rosie having a daddy, it bothered me that he was disgusted by her dirty diapers. I'd never been disgusted by anything that came from her—I loved her too much to be disgusted. Tammy would hold her nose and leave the room when I changed Rosie, but that was different. And I wished he had wanted to hold her more. I talked to Monique about it the next day.

"Give him a chance. He hasn't known her from the beginning like you have."

"That's not her fault," I said.

When Art came over that evening, he brought a plastic bathtub with him, and a big, stuffed dog, yellow, with black floppy ears. He helped me bathe Rosie.

"Usually after her bath I take her for a walk. Do you want to go?"

"Let's just stay here."

"Let's go for a short walk. It won't take long. She likes it."

"No. You go ahead if you want to. I'll come back later."

"It's okay. I guess we don't have to, but she really likes it. She's really cute the way she gets all excited when she sees a dog or cat. She starts jerking her arms and legs around, smiling her big, dimply, Art-kind of smile."

"See, that's just it. Maybe I'm not used to the idea of being a father yet. If someone saw us, and told my mom . . . I guess I'm just not ready to deal with all of that yet."

We saw each other every night the last week that Art was home. We stayed at my place and played with Rosie and watched T.V. until it was her bedtime. Then we made love. Once, when we were lying together, still sticky from lovemaking, Art said, "Tell me you love me, Em. You used to tell me all the time. What's wrong?"

"I don't know. I guess I'm just scared. Like you're going to leave, and I'm going to be hurt all over again."

"Trust me, Em. I'm not leaving. Well . . . I'm leaving, but I'm not leaving you. I love *you*. Can't you get that through your thick red head?" he smiled, ruffling my hair.

I laughed and kissed him.

"You do love me. I know you do. I can see it and feel it," he said.

I nodded, smiling. He was right. I just couldn't say the words.

Saturday night he brought over a sunsuit for Rosie and a silver chain with a heart pendant for me.

"So you both will remember me while I'm gone," he said.

"Thanks. I've got something for you to remember us with, too." I gave him a pocket-sized picture album which started with our Harvest Ball picture and then jumped ahead to Rosie's first picture from the hospital. Then there were some from a picnic at the park with me and Tammy and Bobby. He glanced through the pictures and gave me a quick kiss.

"Will there be room on your dresser for us?"

"I'll make room."

"How do you feel about it all? Stanford—that's going to be hard work, isn't it?"

"I'm jazzed, Emmy. I'll miss you so much, now that I just got you back—that part's going to be hell. But it's like I'm finally starting a real life—all this preparation and planning, and now it's really going to happen. I'll write every day, I swear. And you'd better write me, too. And you too, you little poop-head," he said, lifting Rosie's shirt and buzzing her on the stomach.

"What time does your plane leave tomorrow?"

"Ten."

"In the morning?"

"No. At night."

"So will we see you tomorrow evening?"

"No," he said, looking down. "I've been meaning to tell you. My mom and dad are throwing this big going-away party for me tomorrow afternoon. You know, barbecue, tamales, the whole works—all the family."

"Great! Wouldn't that be a perfect time to introduce Rosemary to everyone? I can't wait for your dad to see her. He'll be a great grampa. Do you think that's what he'll want to be called, or should it be Grandad?"

"No. Wait. We can't do this yet. I've been thinking about when would be best. Right now would be too much of a shock to my mom—you know, losing me to college and then having this bombshell dropped on her."

"I'm not sure I like the bombshell label."

"No. Come on. Give me time. I'll be back home for Thanksgiving. Things will be easier then. I'll write to my folks and drop some hints about us getting back and all—do a little preparation. She doesn't even know Amy and I aren't still together. She just thinks Amy's away at school. She really likes Amy."

"Figures," I said. "What about your dad?"

"You know my dad. He likes everybody. But he did tell me

once that he thought Amy was kind of stuck up. And whenever Tammy and Bobby stop by, he always asks Tammy
how her friend 'Roja' is doing."

"And what does Tammy say—fine—Roja is busy taking
care of your granddaughter?" I picked Rosie up from the
couch and put her in her stroller. I knew I was going to cry,
and I didn't want to do it in front of Art. I pushed the stroller
toward the door, but Art blocked it.

"Where are you going?"

"Out. What do you care?"

"I care, damn it. I just need to work some things out. But
I care. I love you. I want Rosie to know me. I know I can't be
much of a dad to her right now, but I'll do the best I can."

"Then don't be ashamed of her!" Tears came running
down my cheeks. Art put his arms around me. Then he
reached for Rosie and held her in his arms, looking into
those seemingly all-knowing eyes.

"I'm not ashamed," he said. "I just need time."

We made up. After Rosie went to sleep we made up again,
in David's room. Art stayed until after eleven. We vowed to
write and send pictures.

"Rosie will be a lot bigger the next time you see her."

"Yeah, but I'll still recognize her."

"'Cause it's like looking in the mirror for you."

We held each other close for a long time.

"I'd better go before we get something started again," he
said, giving me a long, tender kiss. "Bye, Em. I love you. I
hope you can say that to me by Thanksgiving."

I listened to the sound of his car, the sound I knew I would
not be hearing again for months. Back in the house I turned
on David Letterman. There, on top of the T.V., was the
picture album I'd made for Art.

23

It had been four long, slow months since I'd been in school—over seven months since I'd been on the Hamilton High School campus. The minute I walked on campus and spotted Tammy and Pauline by the flag pole, I felt free. No diapers to change, no bottles to fix, no baby demands to be met. Free!

As the day wore on, my sense of freedom dwindled. Chemistry, second period, 9:30—Rosie's fussy time. Would someone hold her when she cried? Was she missing me? At 11:00 I wondered if she were being given her juice bottle.

I met Tammy outside the girl's gym at lunch time.

"I've got the car today. Let's go up to Benny's Burgers."

I sat in front, and Becky, from choir, and Pauline climbed in the back. I felt really strange with Pauline.

"Order a cheeseburger and coke for me, would you?" I handed Tammy three dollars, ran back to the pay phone, and called the Infant Center. Mrs. Bergstrom, the woman in charge, assured me that Rosie was fine.

"What a sweetheart she is. Don't worry about a thing except paying attention in your classes. We'll see you at three."

I cut through a crowd of loud, laughing, vaguely familiar kids and joined Tammy and the others at a table near the door.

"Can you believe how little the freshmen are? I know we weren't that little," Becky was saying.

"The boys especially. They look like they're about ten."

Tammy, Pauline, and Becky talked on while I lost myself in the buzz of life around me. Going to a hamburger place was no big deal, but except for that awful Rave night with Tammy's cousin, I hadn't been out among my peers since Rosie was born.

"Earth to Emily. Earth to Emily," Tammy was saying. "Becky's talking to you. Join the crowd."

"Oh, sorry," I said, giving Becky my attention.

"How old is your baby?"

"She'll be four months next week."

"I'd have an abortion if that happened to me," Tammy said. "You wouldn't believe it. Emmy doesn't do anything anymore but take care of Rosie. Do you, Emmy?"

"Well . . . it's going to be different now that school's started and Rosie's at the Infant Care Center part of the time."

"I have a friend who had an abortion," Pauline said.

"Did you think about getting an abortion?" Becky asked.

"I thought about it. My mom wanted me to, and so did my boyfriend. I guess I just started loving the baby too soon, like when I felt those tiny movements and I thought about a little person inside me, trying to live."

Pauline got up, leaving her untouched french fries on the table, and walked out into the parking lot.

"I don't think it was her friend," Tammy said.

"What do you mean?"

"Who had the abortion—I think it was Pauline."

"Pauline? Miss Goody-Goody? An abortion?" I said.

"Shhh!" Tammy said. "Don't spread it around."

"She never even dates, does she?" Becky asked.

"Well . . . it's just a feeling," Tammy said. "I don't know anything for sure."

I looked out the window at Pauline. She was sitting on the bumper of Tammy's car, staring off into space.

"I think that's gross, to have an abortion. It's like murder," Becky said.

"That's stupid!" Tammy said. "It's just a mass of cells, it's not like there's a brain or anything. I'm talking about the first three months or so—be honest, Emmy, don't you ever wish you'd had an abortion? Like when she cries for a long, long time, or when you think about all the things you're missing because you always have to take care of the baby?"

"No. I do feel trapped sometimes, and I know there's a whole lot I'll probably never do because of Rosie—things I'm pretty sure I'd have done without her."

"So you do wish you'd had an abortion?" Becky asked.

"No. I would never wish Rosie's life away. But I know now that I had her for selfish reasons—for someone to love me, to give something to me. But babies have to be given to, all day, every day, instead of the other way around. My whole life has changed, that's all. But Rosie's a great kid."

We dumped our trash and went back to the car.

"Would you hate me if I ever got an abortion?" Tammy asked while we were sitting in the school parking lot waiting for the first bell to ring.

"No. I'd think you were really stupid, though, if you got pregnant."

On the way to class Pauline walked alongside me.

"You don't think it's a sin to have an abortion?"

"No. It just wouldn't have been right for me, that's all."

"I had an abortion," she said, her voice so low I could barely hear her. "I just didn't think I could handle it."

"Yeah. It's really hard," I admitted.

"Sometimes I feel bad, that I had an abortion," she said.

"Sometimes I feel bad, too, that I had Rosie before I was really ready to be a mom . . . I think once you let yourself get pregnant, you have a lot to feel bad about, whether you keep the baby, or have an abortion, or put it up for adoption—any way you turn, you're left with some bad feelings. I guess if you're older and married, maybe things are different . . ."

Pauline stopped at B-13. "This is my class—you won't tell anyone, will you? About my abortion?"

I shook my head no, and walked on to English, thinking about how complicated life could be. Maybe that's why

Pauline wouldn't have anything to do with me when I was pregnant—maybe it was a reminder that she'd ended a pregnancy, and maybe she felt guilty.

Whatever, I would never feel really close to her again because of the way she'd ignored me when I needed her. But maybe her abortion explained some things.

It was good to be back in a school routine, but it was more work and less fun than it had been before Rosie. For one thing, the Infant Care hours weren't long enough for me to get to school in time for the Harmonics, or to stay long enough for soccer practice. I sang with the big chorus, third period, but not the special group. And I played soccer during P.E. sometimes, but it wasn't the same as being on the team.

At the end of the first week of school, Mr. Michaels called me aside after chorus and asked me, "Isn't there any way you can arrange to get here in time for Harmonics practice? We sure could use another strong soprano like you."

"I really want to, but I don't have anyone to take care of my baby that early in the morning."

"Too bad. We need you. You need the musical challenge."

I stayed up late that night to talk with my mom. As soon as she got home, she went straight to the refrigerator for a beer, then flopped down on the couch with her feet up on the coffee table. She leaned over and rubbed the calves of her legs.

"I'm beat. I'm getting too old for this kind of work. I'm telling you, Em, aim for a good desk job, none of this waitressing, hair stylist stuff where you're always on your feet . . . Why are you still up, anyway?"

"I wanted to talk to you."

"God, now what?" she groaned.

"No, nothing bad. It's just . . . Mr. Michaels wants me to come back to the Harmonics, and I really, really want to."

"So do it. You don't need my permission for that, do you?"

"No. That's not it. They meet at 7:00 in the morning, and I can't take Rosie to the Infant Center until 7:30. So I was wondering, if I got her all fed and ready, could you drop her off in the mornings at 7:30?"

She looked at me like I'd just asked her to swallow arsenic.

"Every day???"

"Well, yeah, every *school* day."

"Look at me, Em. I'm practically forty. I'm always tired as it is, and you're asking me to get up, sometimes after only four or five hours of sleep, and drive *your* baby to day care?"

"Well, you could go to sleep again when you got back, couldn't you? You'd have all the rest of the morning."

She looked at me for a long time, then said, "No. And don't give me that you're-not-a-good-mother look, either. I warned you having a baby was not like having a toy, and you just went right ahead. I admit I love her now. But she's your responsibility. It's not up to me to juggle my life around for your convenience."

"Just thought I'd ask, even if I knew you wouldn't help," I said, stomping past her and into my room, closing the door behind me. I wanted to slam the door. HARD! I hated that I couldn't even slam the door anymore, but as angry as I was, I knew I didn't want to wake Rosie.

"Listen here, Em," my mom said, opening the door. "I do plenty to help you, even though I said I wouldn't. Who pays the rent? Who buys the food? Where would you be without that?"

"Welfare, I guess."

"And where would your pride be? I'll tell you, it would be in the gutter, that's where."

"Where do you think my pride is now, Mom, with you always throwing up to me that I can't even support my own baby?"

"Dealing with me is *nothing* in comparison to dealing with the government!"

Rosie started to stir.

"Could we just drop this, before we wake the baby?"

"I'm not through talking. Come back out here if you're

worried about waking Rosie."

I followed her back to the living room, again feeling trapped because I couldn't slam the door in her face.

"Now. Here's an idea for you to get to sing in that group."

"What?"

"Rosie has more than one grandmother. Ask *her*. She doesn't work or anything anyway, and her son's done nothing but visit you in private and buy a few token gifts from Thrifty. It's time a Rodriguez pitched in."

"MOM! Mrs. Rodriguez doesn't even know yet."

"I repeat. It's time."

"We're going to talk to her at Thanksgiving," I said.

"Yeah, well, that's my idea. Take it or leave it."

So I didn't sing in the Harmonics first semester. I might have felt more a part of things if I could have done that. As it was, I felt like an outsider. The friends I'd hung out with before the baby had been mostly seniors, Art's friends, and they were gone. I'd have been totally lost without Tammy. Veronica and I were pretty good friends, but she'd gone to the continuation high school after Teen Moms so she could get more individual help. And I liked Becky, but we weren't really good friends. And Pauline? I still didn't feel like I could trust her, even though she had trusted me with her abortion secret.

As far as my classes went, it was hard to get my home-work done sometimes. I was taking all college prep courses. It wasn't that I didn't understand the work, it was just that I usually couldn't get started on it until after I got Rosie fed, bathed, and down for the night. And another thing—she was always picking up a cold or something from the other babies at the Infant Center. Then I'd have to keep her home with me until she was well, and I'd get behind in my classes. I always turned in the work I'd missed, but it was a constant fight to keep up.

In October there was a meeting for the "Project Hope" kids and their parents. I heard about it from a girl in my

Honors English class. No one had even bothered to send me a notice. I went marching down to the office.

"I want to see Mrs. Werly," I told the secretary.

"Do you have an appointment?"

"No."

"Well, I can schedule you to see her a week from Monday."

"I need to see her today."

"That's not possible. She's busy until 3:15, and then she has to leave immediately after that."

I sat down on the bench outside Mrs. Werly's office and began reading the assigned section of *The Scarlet Letter*.

"Perhaps you misunderstood," the secretary said, getting up from her desk and walking over to where I was sitting. "Mrs. Werly can't see you today."

"I'll wait."

"No. Go back to class. Leave your name, and if Mrs. Werly gets a chance to see you, I'll have her call you out of class."

I sat there, pretending to read.

"You're wasting your time here."

I kept my eyes on the book.

The secretary shrugged and went back to her desk.

The room was crowded with kids sitting on benches outside their counselors' offices. Why could they get in and I couldn't? Two of the guys I knew for sure were in a gang. One of the girls, Eva, I'd known from Palm, and she'd always been in trouble there—cutting class, mouthing off to teachers. I guessed that's how you got to see your counselor, by getting in trouble. I walked over to the Palm Avenue alum.

"Could I bum a cigarette?" I asked.

She looked at me very strangely, then fished around in her purse and took out a cigarette, being careful to do so in a way that the secretary would not notice.

"Thanks. A match?"

She handed me a lighter. I lit the cigarette, coughing a little, and gave the lighter back. I returned to my place on the bench and took a puff on the cigarette. I hated the taste in my mouth. It made me want to barf. I took another puff.

The secretary paused in her typing, lifting her nose to the air, sniffing. She looked around the room.

"You! What on earth do you think you're doing?"

She marched over and grabbed the cigarette from my hand and crushed it out on the floor.

"Don't you dare leave this room!" she said.

I sat there. She went back to her desk and picked up the phone. I couldn't hear what she was saying, but she looked at me all the time she was talking. In less than a minute, Mrs. Werly's door opened and she motioned me in.

"Sit down, Emily," she said, closing the door behind me. "You certainly know you can get suspended for smoking on campus. Is that what you want?"

"I want my invitation to the Project Hope meeting."

"Smoking in the office is not exactly Project Hope behavior, is it?"

"How else could I get to see you before the meeting? Your secretary said I couldn't see you until a week from Monday."

"I am quite busy, Emily," she said, gesturing toward stacks of papers on her desk and file cabinet. "I'm in the middle of preparing this year's Project Hope grant request. If I don't get this done, we'll lose our funding and the whole program will fold. I'm sorry about not sending you an invitation. Officially, I suppose you're still part of the program. I simply assumed you wouldn't be interested, what with the baby and all."

"Well, I am. I told you before, I'm still going to college. Why can't you believe me?"

She looked at me for a long time. "Here," she said, handing me a notice about the meeting. "Come out, bring your mom. I'll be sure you get informed of other activities. And you missed the spring battery of tests. Stop by the testing center and make arrangements to take the tests."

"Am I suspended?"

"No. But you'd better apologize to Mrs. Bunker on the way out. Now go on, and let me get back to this grant proposal."

As I stood to leave, she said, "By the way, how's your baby?"

"She's fine," I said, as I went out to talk to the secretary.

Mom changed her work schedule to go to the meeting with me. We sat with the baby in the back of the room while Mrs. Werly talked of college opportunities and the importance of solidifying our goals this semester. Next semester, representatives from colleges all over the nation would be coming to talk with our group and interested seniors. In December, each of us would have an individual consultation with Mrs. Werly, and we would modify our portfolios at that time.

The baby started crying toward the end of the meeting, so we had to leave a little early.

"I don't see how you can do this Project Hope business, Em," my mom said to me on the way home. "How in the world do you think you can go away to college now that you've got Rosie?"

No answer came to me, but I wasn't ready to give up, either.

24

"**D**avid!" I screamed when I saw him sitting on the bumper of his truck, fiddling with some engine part. He jumped up and came running to us.

"Is this my niece?" he said, enclosing us both in a clumsy embrace, holding his greasy hands away from us. He stepped back, smiling, his eyes on Rosie.

"She's beautiful," he said. "How old now? Six months?"

"In another week."

"Can she do any tricks yet?"

I laughed. "She can sort of sit up. And feel," I said, running my finger across her lower gum. "I think she's getting a tooth."

"I'll take your word for it," he said, showing me his dirty hands. "I've been working on this junk heap. I thought you'd have it running for me by now."

"Right. You're just lucky mom hasn't had it towed away."

"So how is The Barb, anyway?"

"She's okay. She thinks I'm stupid for taking Art back, and she tells me so pretty often. And sometimes she tries to tell me what to do with the baby. She doesn't think I should give Rosie any table foods yet. Like I'm going to see *our* mom as an expert on child care? But she does help me sometimes, too . . . My life is really different now."

David followed me inside to the kitchen where I put Rosie in her high chair, fastened the safety strap, and peeled and cut a quarter of an apple into little pieces for her. David and

I sat watching her eat, talking.

"Why didn't you tell me you were getting home today?"

"I didn't know until yesterday morning. They called me into the warden's office. It scared me. I hadn't done anything to get in trouble for but so much can go wrong. They gave me a bus pass, a hundred dollars, and the clothes I'd had when I came in. I got the standard issue pants and shirt and that was it. Man, was I glad to walk out those gates!"

So much had happened in our lives since I'd last seen him. "You look different," I said.

"You too. Motherhood becomes you. You're prettier—older—grown-up. When I left, you were still a little girl."

"You look older, too."

"Yeah, well, nothing like being locked up for a year to age a guy. I don't ever, ever want that again. God, Em . . ." he looked at me and shook his head, like maybe there was so much to tell he couldn't even start.

Rosie squealed and pounded on the high chair tray. I took her out and put her on my lap, with her back to me, and got her to laugh by playing the patty-cake game. She had a funny little chuckle of a laugh that always made me laugh, too. I guess David thought it was pretty funny himself, because the three of us sat there doing patty-cake and laughing for a long time.

Then I lay her down on her stomach on a blanket on the floor with the big floppy dog Art had given her, and we went on trying to catch up. We'd talked on the phone almost every week since he'd left, but it wasn't the same as face to face.

"How are things with Art?"

"We got back together for a week, and then he went to Stanford."

"Are you still together?"

"I think so."

"What does that mean?"

"We write. We started out writing every day, but now it's more like once or twice a week. It's hard to tell from letters," I said. "But we're going to tell his parents about Rosie when he gets home next week for Thanksgiving."

"Wow! Thanksgiving. I hope this one is better than the last," he said.

"Me, too." I knew he was thinking about being taken to jail. I was remembering that, too. But I was also remembering that awful phone call from Art, when he'd turned his back on me.

"Have you called mom?"

"Yep. She's coming home early. And she's bringing some surprise dinner. Can you believe it?"

"She's mellowed out some. Partly because of the baby, I think. She stays home more on her days off, and sometimes she'll hold Rosie and rock her for a long time."

"Still drinking?"

"Well, yeah. She's still Mom."

"It really burned me when I heard how she wouldn't help out so you could sing in the Harmonics."

"It did me, too. But if you think about it, she was right. Rosie's my responsibility, and I needed Mom at a time when she's always asleep. So, I could kind of see her point, even if I didn't admit it."

"Maybe I can help out," David said. "I've never changed a diaper, but how hard can that be?"

Mom came breezing in with a dozen tamales and enchiladas. I made a salad and we opened sodas.

"Aren't these great? Fran's mom makes them."

"Fran?" David asked.

"One of the waitresses at the cafe."

"Yeah. They are great—this is great," he said, smiling a gentle smile and looking from one to the other of us. It gave me a strong feeling, for a moment, that we were all connected by some tough, invisible cord.

Mom rocked Rosie and gave her a bottle while David and I cleaned up the dishes.

"What are your plans now, David?" Mom asked. I tensed, thinking this could be the start of a fight—maybe he'd say none of her business, or maybe she'd say don't think you can stay here and freeload off me.

"I'm not sure," he said. "I just know I'm really tired of wasting my life. I finished my G.E.D. at camp. I've been thinking maybe I'd like to learn carpentry, or electrical stuff. I don't think I can work nine to five cooped up. I've been cooped up long enough," he laughed.

"There's a bunch of regulars who stop for breakfast every morning at the cafe—they do remodels mostly. Two of them do carpentry work, one's an electrician, one guy does dry wall. Sometimes there's a roofer with them. I could introduce you if you want to come in some morning. They might be able to tell you how to get started in one of those trades."

"Are you sure they'd want to talk to me?"

"Those guys'll talk to walls if there's no one else listening. They'll talk to you, but you'll have to cut through the B.S."

"I'm used to that. When should I come in?"

"Whenever you want. Just warn me the day before, so I'll know to get to bed at a decent hour."

"How about tomorrow morning then?"

"Sure," she said. She looked down at the baby. "I think this kid's ready for bed," she said, rising gently and carrying her back to my bedroom. Soon we heard her singing softly, "I'm a rovin' gambler, I gamble all around. Whenever I meet with a deck of cards, I lay my money down. Lay my money down, boys . . ."

It was no lullaby, but she often put Rosie to sleep with it.

"The Barb *has* changed," David said. "I think you're right about the baby mellowing her out."

"I guess. She's already paid more attention to Rosie than she ever did to either one of us."

"Maybe it's kind of a second chance for her."

"Yeah. Well, she's still not exactly June Cleaver."

"No. And we're not Wally and Beaver, either."

We laughed. He put his arm around my shoulder.

"I've missed you, Little Sister."

We stayed up until two in the morning, telling each other

all the things that had been too awkward to talk about during our limited weekly phone calls when guys were waiting
in line behind David, demanding their turns.

When Rosie and I got back the next afternoon, David was
working on his truck. Greasy parts were spread out in the
driveway, on top of old newspapers.

"How's it going?" I asked.

He backed out from under the raised hood and stood up.
"Great!" he said, wiping his hands on a rag. "I think I've got
a job lined up."

"From the guys at the cafe?"

"Yeah. This one guy, a roofer, needs a helper—you know,
run out for materials, clean up, haul trash. Ten bucks an
hour."

"When do you start?"

"Next week—after Thanksgiving, if I can get this thing
running by then. I've got to have transportation for the job."

He worked on the truck for hours every day. Mom even
loaned him $400 for a rebuilt carburetor and new tires. The
truck had been sitting in the same place for so long, the tires
were all rotted away.

Tammy and Bobby stopped by Saturday for a while.

"Want help?" Bobby asked.

"Sure."

Bobby walked over and looked under the hood. "Do you
know what's wrong?"

"No—I thought the carburetor might do it, but it hasn't."

Bobby fiddled around, twisting, turning, adjusting.

"Come on, Bobby, we were going to take Bonnie to see
'Pinnochio,' remember?"

"We've got plenty of time," he said.

"Come inside with me while I check on Rosie," I said to
Tammy. "It's about time for her to wake up."

She followed me in, reluctantly. "I'll never get Bobby out
of here now. He works on cars all week at his dad's shop,
and it's still his idea of how to have fun on the weekend."

"Look." I held up the new outfit I'd bought for Rosie. Mostly she wore hand-me-downs. There was a special shelf at the Infant Center where girls put the clothes their babies had outgrown—that way we kept recycling baby clothes, and it saved us all money.

"That's darling," Tammy said, holding the little jersey print top next to the sleeping Rosie. "Those are her colors, all right. She's an autumn—earth colors, you know. Let's dress her up as soon as she wakes up."

"No. I'm saving it for Thanksgiving, when she gets to meet her grandma and grandpa Rodriguez."

"Are you sure that's going to happen?"

"Why wouldn't it?"

"Don't you think Art's being weird about all this?"

"No. He only learned for sure that Rosie was his the week before he went away. He was still getting used to the idea."

Tammy sat there, checking out the ruffled panties that went with the little jersey top.

"Really, Tammy, you don't know Art the way I do. He cried the night we got back together, saying how sorry he was, and how he was going to make everything up to us."

"Okay, okay. I hope you're right."

"I am. I know I am," I said, fingering the heart pendant I'd worn around my neck since the day Art gave it to me.

After Tammy and Bobby left, I took the package of Art's letters from the corner of my sweater drawer where I kept them safe and secret. There was a big stack for September, even though he'd been home the first week of that month. The stack for October was about half as high. There were only two letters for November, but maybe that was because he knew he'd be seeing me soon, and he could tell me everything in person.

I reread them all, starting with the first in September.

Dear Em and Rosie, I already miss you a lot, and I've only been gone for two days. My roommate is a guy from Texas who's an engineering major. He plays country music all night long. I hate it, but I can't help almost crying sometimes, hearing such sad, lonesome lyrics and missing you so.

It's beautiful up here—lots of trees and green rolling lawns. The campus is over one hundred years old. How I wish we could be sharing this, Emmy. Hurry up and finish high school. The married housing section looks great. There's even a little playground for the rug rat.

I'm going to bed now, to dream of you. I love you, love you, love you. Write. And send those pictures, please. Love always, Art.

The September letters were filled with love and longing. By October there was more talk of new friends and parties. For the first time in his life, Art could stay out as late as he wanted without fear of worrying his mother, and he was apparently enjoying his new freedom.

Toward the end of October his letters were starting with apologies—"sorry not to have written sooner, but I had this big test to study for"—or "a bunch of us went to San Francisco for the weekend. What a city!—sorry I didn't get around to writing." They were signed simply, "Love, Art." By the end of October, the only mention of love in his letters was in the closing.

The last letter, dated November 15, wasn't even a letter. It was a postcard, with a picture of the Fine Arts building on the front. It said, "See you Wednesday night, late. Get David's bed warmed up for me. I'll tap at the window. Can't wait to get my hands on you. Love, Art." How embarrassing. Luckily it arrived on a Saturday when I happened to pick up the mail. So at least my mom didn't read it. But I bet the mail carrier did!

I couldn't wait to see Art so I would know for sure everything was okay. He probably just wasn't into writing letters once his classes started taking up more of his time. A lot of guys didn't like to write letters. I knew that.

The night before Thanksgiving I sat watching an old movie on T.V., listening for the sound of Art's car. I had to catch him before he went tapping on David's window, suggesting love games. David didn't like Art because he hadn't stood by me and Rosie. No matter how many times I explained to David that Art had changed, he couldn't seem to forgive the past.

I was dozing on the couch when I heard the old distinctive rumble. I ran out the door to meet Art.

"Hey, Babe," he said, jumping from the car and throwing his arms around me. He kissed me and held me back and kissed me again. I *knew* everything would be okay. How could I have let Tammy and David and my mom cause me to doubt Art?

"Come see the baby," I said. We went inside and stood over the bed, watching her sleep.

"She's bigger, isn't she?" Art whispered.

"Two months makes a big difference in a baby's life. You should hear her laugh. And she's got two teeth."

He ran the back of his finger across her cheek. She didn't stir. "Still so soft," he whispered. We stood for a long time, watching the rise and fall of her breathing.

"Come on," Art said, leading me back outside. "I want to greet the mama properly." We kissed long and hard, and then he led me toward David's room. I held back.

"What?"

"The room is occupied. No vacancy," I said.

"Your brother's back?"

"He got back a week ago."

"What rotten timing. When does your mom get home?"

"Usually after midnight, but I'm not sure about tonight."

He looked at his watch. "Eleven. We've got an hour. Plenty of time, right?"

"I guess."

"Well, come on. Let's take our favorite old comforter out back and just see how far we can get." He laughed. "It's been a long time. You've missed me," he whispered, nuzzling my neck. "Come on, the truth now, or the torture of a thousand kisses."

"I've missed you. I've missed you," I said, leaning into him. We got what we needed from the house and went outside to our dark, secluded corner. We spread the comforter on the grass and lay side by side, then wrapped it around us. It was cold out.

"Wait until you see Rosie awake. She's changed *so* much!" I tried to tell him of her latest achievements, but he covered my mouth with his and began fondling me in the old familiar way.

He drew back for an instant, looking into my eyes.

"Let's save the talking for tomorrow. I've wanted this so long, missed you so much." He was breathing hard, rushing. It was over in no time. Art buttoned his pants and tucked in his shirt. He kissed me on the cheek.

"I better go. Your mom will be home soon, and my mom and dad are waiting up for me."

"Do they know you're here?"

"No. I didn't want to take time to explain anything. I just wanted to get over here to you. I needed some nooky," he said, smiling.

"Nooky?"

Art laughed. "Yeah, you know. Lovin'. Sex. Nooky. It's a new word on the college man's vocabulary list."

He stood up, reached his hand out to me and pulled me

up. He began folding the comforter.

"I got Rosie a new outfit for tomorrow. I want her to make a good impression on her Rodriguez family."

Art's face clouded over. "I'm not sure that's possible."

"How could anyone not love Rosie? They need to get used to the idea. If *my* mom could come around, anyone could."

"I suppose. But *my* mom is so nervous all the time. She's super proud that I'm at Stanford—the first in the family ever to go to college, and then to Stanford no less. It is kind of a big deal. But then she cries all the time, too—'I miss my babies'—'My life is nothing without my babies'—you know."

"Well, now there's another baby for her to love."

I walked with Art to his car.

"Hey. What happened to the junk heap?" he asked, pointing to the vacant place David's truck had occupied.

"He and Bobby towed it to Bobby's dad's shop this evening."

"Bobby? Reyes? My friend? I didn't even think he knew your brother."

"Well, you know. Tammy and Bobby come over sometimes, and Bobby saw that David needed help with his truck. And the shop is closed until Monday. Bobby said they could use his dad's tools and diagnostic equipment. They just have to get it out of there by 6:00 Monday morning. Bobby's cool."

"Cool but stupid."

"Why do you say that? I thought you were best friends."

"We are. But he could do a lot. He could have gone to Stanford too, with Project Hope, but all he's interested in is working on cars. There's no future."

"His dad will make him a partner later," I said.

"So? He's still going to be a grease monkey. He's a nice guy, but that doesn't make for success." Art looked at his watch.

"Well—gotta go."

"What time will you come get us tomorrow?"

"I'll give you a call in the morning."

"Shall I bring a salad or something?"

"No, I don't think so. But we'll figure that out tomorrow."

I was up early in the morning, showered, shampooed my hair, fed Rosie, and played with her for a while.

"Rosie, Baby," I whispered, holding her on my lap and jostling her on my knees, "today's the day you meet your Rodriguez family." I ran my hand across her thick, soft black hair. "They're going to love you. You look like your daddy, and you've got these cute little dimples. And you're smart. And today you can try mashed potatoes and gravy."

Mom came in and held her arms out to Rosie, who leaned toward her, smiling.

"What a kid," my mom laughed. "I love this kid." She took Rosie and walked outside with her.

Sometimes I felt funny, watching my mom with Rosie. I can't remember her ever telling me she loved me except that one time, back when she was upset over David's arrest. But she told Rosie all the time. I hated to admit it, even to myself, but I guess I was kind of jealous. I *wanted* my mom to love Rosie. I wanted Rosie to get all the love she could. Still . . . what about me?

The phone rang around eleven, and I jumped for it. It turned out to be Bobby calling to see what time David wanted to meet him at the shop.

"When're we going to dinner, Mom?" David asked.

"5:00. And I don't want anything messing up this one," she called back.

"How about if I meet you there in an hour?" David said. They talked back and forth, figuring out how to cover the family dinners and squeeze in some time to work on the truck.

Art didn't call until after 2:00. "Things are all messed up over here," he said. "My Uncle Manny's drunk. My mom's crying about Joey. My aunts are upset because each one thought the other was supposed to make the tamales. Why don't I just come see you for a while instead of you coming over here?"

"But Art!"

"I know. I know. I said Thanksgiving. But tomorrow really will be better, when there aren't all these people around. What difference can one more day make? . . . Is your mom home?"

"Yes."

"David?"

"Yes."

"Are they going to be there all day?"

"Well, they're going to dinner around 5:00."

"Why don't I drop by around 5:30 then?"

"Why? Are you afraid to see my family?"

"No. It's just a little embarrassing. Besides, I'd rather see you alone."

"Okay, I guess," I said.

It wasn't until after we'd hung up that I realized he hadn't even asked about Rosie.

"**G**o to dinner with us," my mom said as she and David were getting ready to leave.

"No. Thanks anyway. I need to see Art."

"Don't sit around waiting for some guy who only wants to see you on the sly. Where's your pride?"

"Come on, Barb," David said. "A girl's got to do what a girl's got to do."

At six I called Art.

"I thought you were coming over."

"I was, but dinner's later than I thought it would be. You wouldn't believe the chaos. My cousin Danny was running out back and tripped over my Dad's hoe. He cut his chin really bad. They had to take him to the hospital for stitches. My mom is yelling at my dad about leaving his tools laying around . . . I think maybe we'd better just see each other tomorrow. How about if I come get you around ten?"

I went to bed early, with Rosie, before David and my mom got home. I didn't want to answer any questions. I tried to ignore the hollow, sinking feeling that was growing within me.

When Art didn't show up the next day, I called his house again. His mom answered the phone. I heard muttering in the background, and then his mom told me that Art wasn't home. I slammed down the receiver and went storming outside. How could he? How *could* he? Was this how he loved me? Was this how he was making it all up to me? And what about Rosie? What kind of guy was ashamed of his own baby? And why didn't he have the guts to come right out and say he would never admit to his precious mother that Rosie was his?

I paced up and down the driveway, letting myself feel what I had been denying all along. What we'd done Wednesday night, in the back yard, hadn't felt like love to me. Art hadn't even bothered to notice whether or not I enjoyed it. He was selfish, and he didn't care about me—maybe he cared a little, but he was so wrapped up in himself he couldn't even love his baby. I'd been counting the days until he got home, wanting to love him, and all he wanted was sex.

When we first started out together, when I was a freshman, he had seemed so mature—so cool. And now he seemed like some emotionally underdeveloped Bart Simpson type. Well, okay. I could deal with that. I could live without Mr.-I-can't-be-seen-with-you-yet Art Rodriguez. But he wasn't going to get away with that stuff with Rosie. She was going to grow up knowing who her father was, for better or worse. And she would know who her grandparents were, too.

I marched back into the house and called David at the shop where he and Bobby were working on the truck.

"I need your help," I said, as soon as he answered.

"Is everyone okay? What's up?"

I spewed out my anger, and then asked if he would drive me to Art's house.

"I don't have my license yet," I explained, "or I'd borrow Mom's car."

"Let me see if I can borrow Bobby's car."

I heard him yelling back and forth to Bobby, then, "I'll be there in fifteen minutes."

I changed Rosie's diaper and put her new outfit on her. "We're going to see your dad, and your other grandma, and I hope your grandpa will be there, too. Just remember, I love you, and your Uncle David loves you, and Grandma Barb loves you. It's not that you have to have those other people love you, but you need to at least know they exist. And *they* need to know *you* exist, too."

I took her into the bathroom and washed her face. I brushed her hair with the soft baby brush. I held her up over my head, jiggling her, making her laugh. The sweet, chuckling sounds, the feel of her little body, drained my anger, but strengthened my resolve. It was the right thing to do—no doubt.

Bobby and David came driving up the driveway in Bobby's car. I got the car seat from the porch, fastened it into Bobby's back seat, and strapped Rosie in securely. I climbed in beside her.

"Boy, I'm ready for this," David said. "I've hated that little weasel since you first started hanging out with him."

"No, David. This isn't about you and Art. This is about Rosie and Art and his family. Don't even *think* about letting loose with your notorious temper."

"I like how she talks when she's mad," Bobby said.

"I'm serious. Either be civil or wait in the car."

"Yeah, okay. If I have to see Art I'll do it on my own time. This is your time right now."

"David. Forget the tough guy noises, okay?"

"I hate that guy—what he's done to you," David mumbled.

Bobby said, "I'm going in with you."

"Why?"

"Because I've known Art's family since I was about Rosie's age. His mom listens to me."

"His mom doesn't listen to anyone," I said.

Mr. Rodriguez was planting bulbs out front when we drove up. He waved to Bobby and went back to his work. There was a whole gunnysack of bulbs setting beside him. By spring, bright-colored flowers of all sizes and heights would blanket the front flower beds. Rosie will like them, I thought.

When Mr. R. saw me get out of the car, he brushed the dirt from his hands and walked over to meet me.

"Aye, Roja. Why do you stay gone so long? Because my foolish boy let you slip away, must I lose you, too?" he said, grinning his big, friendly grin.

"Hi, Mr. Rodriguez," I said, kissing his cheek. "I've missed you . . . This is my brother, David."

Mr. Rodriguez wiped his hand on his pants leg and shook hands with David. Bobby had unstrapped Rosie and taken her from the car. He handed her to me.

"And who is this? Are you baby-sitting today?"

"This is Rosie," I said. "My baby. Your granddaughter."

Mr. Rodriguez' dark face turned pale. He stood, looking closely at Rosie, saying nothing.

"Your granddaughter," I repeated. "My baby. Art's baby."

Art came running from the house and grabbed me by the arm.

"What are you doing here? I *told* you, *not yet!*"

"No. It's way past time."

"Arturo. Arturo," his father said, gently drawing Art's arm from mine and turning him so they were face to face. "What is this all about? You tell me."

"It's nothing, Dad. Don't worry about it."

Art stepped in front of me again, turning his back on his father. "Now go home, Emily. Please. I need to do this my way," he hissed.

Mr. Rodriguez stepped between us—face to face with Art. "I want the truth, Mijo. Is this your baby?"

Art stood silent.

"YOU COWARDLY PIECE OF SHIT! STAND UP FOR MY SISTER! STAND UP FOR YOUR BABY!" David yelled, lunging for Art. Bobby jumped between them, holding David back.

"Cool it, Man," Bobby said, blocking David's would-be blows while Art backed out of reach.

"DAVID!" I screamed. "Don't do this!"

Rosie started crying. Mrs. Rodriguez came running out of the house, shouting something in Spanish. David stood stiff, fists clenched, red-faced, staring daggers at Art, who was urging his mother to go back inside. Mr. Rodriguez eased Rosie from my arms and began soothing her, walking her back and forth and talking to her in his soft, easy way.

"Calm down, David," I pleaded.

"I'd like to beat that little weasel until he's nothin' but a spot of grease on the sidewalk," he said menacingly, but he turned and walked away. He sat on the bumper of Bobby's car. I could tell by his heavy, even breathing that he was struggling for control. Bobby walked over and sat beside him. Art and Mrs. Rodriguez were already back in the house, with the door closed behind them. Mr. Rodriguez stood beside me, jostling my now smiling baby.

"I believe this is my granddaughter. I believe you, Emily."

"Thank you," I said, turning from him, trying to hide my sudden rush of tears.

"We'll go inside now," he said. I took Rosie from his arms. He turned to David and Bobby, "Come inside. All of the family must be inside. No more outdoor shows, please."

We all walked together to the house. The door was locked. Mr. Rodriguez went to the garage and got the spare key. He unlocked the door and we went in.

Art's mother was half sitting, half lying on their couch. Art was sitting on the edge, handing her the "heart" pills I had so often seen her take.

"Call your grandmother out here, Art," Mr. Rodriguez said.

"She's taking a nap."

"I said call her. This is family business. She has a right. Sit," he said, gesturing to the rest of us.

I sat in the rocker with Rosie. Bobby sat on the floor, leaning back against the couch at the opposite end from where Art had been perched. David pulled a chair out from the kitchen. He placed it as near the door as possible, turning it backwards, and straddling it.

Art's grandmother's face lit up when she saw me. "Roja!" she said, hobbling over to me with her little short steps, touching my hair and laughing as she'd always done. Then she noticed Rosie. She reached down for her, taking her and holding her close, smiling and laughing. She handed her back to me, then started a careful inspection, running the back of her finger across each of Rosie's dimples, feeling the curly black hair, looking long into the fascinated baby's eyes.

"Aye, Art—like you," she laughed. "Like you." When grandma Rodriguez laughed, so did Rosie. The two of them laughed and laughed, while the rest of us sat silent.

I started with Mr. Rodriguez. The easy one.

"I wanted you to know Rosie exists, and that she's part of your family, too . . ."

"You get out of my house," Mrs. Rodriguez said, standing. "From the beginning you've been trying to use any trick you can to get my Arturo to marry you. He's with a nice girl now, high class. Nice family. He won't marry down. This is not Art's baby," she said, crying.

"Oh, man," David moaned. "You people are crazy!"

Bobby stood and put his arm around Mrs. Rodriguez. "Look, Mama R., I want you to see something."

Bobby took Rosie from me and carried her to the couch. Art's mom backed away, as if my baby carried some horrible disease. Bobby pulled Rosie's new little panties and diaper away from her fat little leg.

"See?" Bobby said, pointing to Rosie's telltale mole.

Mr. Rodriguez and his mother came over to the couch. Mrs. Rodriguez kept her back to the baby. Art sat in a chair, staring at his shoes.

The old grandmother laughed again when she saw the mole. She went to Art and began kissing his cheeks and forehead, over and over again, carrying on in Spanish— bueno, bueno, and a lot more I couldn't understand. Art just sat there, not responding.

"Look at this," Mr. Rodriguez said, turning his wife gently so she was facing the baby. He leaned over and touched the mole. "You see, Emily is telling us true."

"She's a liar. Why should I believe her? She's had her baby tattooed. It's all a trick!"

"Tell your mother, Mijo."

Art remained silent, eyes down. Rosie was making cooing noises at the ceiling fan. In that one instant, all I'd ever felt for Art went dry. That he wouldn't stand proudly for me and Rosie. That he would sit there looking at the floor as if we didn't exist.

Mrs. Rodriguez leaned into her husband, crying. He pushed her away so he could look her in the face again.

"You shame me, Karlita," he said. "You and Arturo, with your high ideas. I am ashamed of my son, who turns his back on his own baby. Even a gardener, no school, does better than that. I do better than that."

"Oh, shush, shush, shush," she screamed, running from the room. "I can't take this!"

Art looked up at me. "Happy now?" he asked, his tone nasty and sarcastic.

"I'm glad everyone knows, if that's what you mean," I said. I straightened Rosie's diaper and picked her up. She nestled her head against my shoulder. "Can you take us home now, Bobby?"

"Sure. Just give me a minute, okay?"

David and I walked out to Bobby's car, with Art's dad and grandmother following.

"Let me hold her," Mr. Rodriguez said. He sang a little song as he rocked back and forth with her, "Rosie, Rosie, pretty as a posy, I kiss her on the nosy, she's my baby, Rosie."

I laughed. Even David laughed. Art's grandmother put her little short arms around her great-granddaughter and her son and gave them both a big hug.

"Come tomorrow, Roja and Rosie?" Mr. Rodriguez asked, smiling at me.

"No. I won't come over here again. You can come visit Rosie at my house if you want," I said, taking the baby and strapping her into the car seat. He stood watching us.

"I am sorry, Roja. My son must marry you. I will see to that."

"No, Mr. Rodriguez. I don't want to marry your son."

"But he is the father. And he must take care of his familia. It is right."

"I don't love him anymore. I don't respect him. I got through the hardest part on my own. I'll do the rest."

Bobby came out. He shook Mr. Rodriguez' hand, kissed Art's grandmother, and we all drove away.

"What a couple of loonies your boyfriend and his mother are," David said.

"He's not my boyfriend," I said. But for the first time, I didn't feel the old sadness or emptiness at the thought of not being with Art. I felt strong, and free. It sounds crazy, that a sixteen-year-old mother of a six-month-old baby would feel free. But, right then, I did.

"They're okay," Bobby said. "They've had some hard times that keep dragging them down."

"Yeah, yeah. Em told me about the brother and all, but give me a break—a tattooed mole? And Art? What a mama's boy. I'm surprised he *could* get anyone pregnant. Did his mama have to come show him where to put it, Em?"

"Not funny, David."

"God, I wanted to smash him into little pieces," David said. I didn't respond to that remark. I hated when David talked like he was Mr. Rambo.

"I probably would have been doing the world a favor— sneaky little wussy. And it sounds like maybe his mom wasn't exactly Miss High Class when she was young. Like she was already pregnant when the old man married her. Why else would anyone marry that witch?" David laughed a mean laugh.

"Come on, David. Those people are like family to me," Bobby said. "I don't like you making fun of them behind their backs."

"Oh, aren't we just too good," David said sarcastically.

"I mean it. I've known them my whole life, and they've helped me out a lot. And I've helped them some, too. I know they've got their faults, but just let it go."

I sat in the back seat with the baby, only half hearing the
words between David and Bobby. Three blocks away, and
Rosie was already asleep. Good. It would make her nap-time
easy. Sometimes she fought sleep and got really grouchy,
but a car ride was like a magic sleeping pill.

Once home, I eased her out of her seat and carried her in
to bed. David and Bobby came inside for a quick sandwich,
then headed back to the shop. I stretched out on the bed
beside Rosie.

Art called around eleven.

"We finally got my mom calmed down. She's taken two
Valiums and probably won't wake up until morning. I think
I can get away. How about if I come over for a while?"

"As if nothing happened?"

"Well, yeah. I mean, I was real mad at first, that you just
barged in like that. But I'm over it now. My dad had a long
talk with me, and it's probably good that everyone knows.
I still don't think it needed to be so soon, but I'm not mad."

"Art. Listen. I'm the one who should be mad. Not you.
You've let me down for the last time."

"What do you mean?"

"I mean you're never going to get the chance to hurt me
again."

"What? No, Emmy. Everything's going to be fine. You'll
see."

"Everything's already fine with me. Couldn't be finer," I
said, and hung up. Minutes later I heard Art's car in the
driveway and walked out to meet him. He cried and said he
needed me. I felt sorry for him, but it was as if he were some
distant, detached acquaintance, not the Art who had once
been the center of my life.

"What can I do?" he asked, cheeks wet with tears.

"Nothing," I said. "You broke something that can never
be fixed."

Rosie was fussing, and I went in to check on her. A few
minutes later I heard Art leave.

Early the next afternoon, Mr. Rodriguez and his mother came to the door. My mother was just leaving for work.

"I am José Rodriguez, Rosie's grandfather," he said. "And this is her great-grandmother. Emily said we could come visit."

"Well, come in," she said. "Company!" she called to me, as she walked out the door. I was in the kitchen cleaning up after lunch. Rosie was still in her high chair, but facing the living room so she could see "Sesame Street" on T.V. She probably didn't understand anything that was going on, but she would sway her whole body back and forth to the beat of the music.

"We've come. Okay?" Mr. Rodriguez said.

"Sure," I said, drying my hands and walking into the living room.

Mr. Rodriguez took Rosie from her high chair and held her, talking to her in a mixture of English and Spanish. The grandmother stood patting the baby's back, smiling. They hardly noticed me, so I went on with the dishes. When I came back out, they were showing her a rattle they'd brought. She was coordinated enough to reach for things, and grab, so the rattle went quickly to her mouth.

They stayed for over an hour, playing with Rosie. I wasn't worried about them spoiling her. That's something I learned in my parenting class. You can't spoil a baby with love.

"Tomorrow?" Mr. Rodriguez said.

"Sure. Anytime."

After his mother was in the car, Mr. Rodriguez walked me back to my front door.

"Here, Mija," he said, pressing a hundred-dollar bill into the palm of my hand. I tried to give it back to him, but he said, "No. Take it. Do it for me. It will help my shame. Por favor."

So I kept it. Mr. Rodriguez and his mother visited at least twice a week. And on the first visit of every month, he pressed a fresh one-hundred-dollar bill in my hand. It helped. I was always careful to spend it on Rosie, not on myself. Well . . . once David and I sent out for pizza. But the rest of it went to diapers and baby food, and clothes for Rosie.

Several months after Mr. Rodriguez started giving us those one-hundred-dollar bills, Bobby told me that Mr. R. had taken on another gardening job.

I thought of the dirt-ingrained, calloused hands, scrubbed pink on the days he visited his granddaughter, and of the gentle way he lifted her overhead and made her laugh, and I loved him more than I had ever loved his son. Not sex, I don't mean that kind of love. It's hard to explain. I guess because we both loved Rosie so much, that made us love each other.

27

My life had been tied up with Art's, one way or another, for almost three years. First came the joy and excitement of new love, and the times we shared together. Then there was the emptiness, the grief over his desertion of me when I was pregnant, and then, for a while, I hated him. When he came to me again, in September, there had been a rush of happiness and new hope. Always, within me, there was Art.

He *had* been my hero. He had opened new worlds to me—the in-world of Hamilton High, the Project Hope world, the world of romance and sex and love. But finally, that Thanksgiving weekend, I realized that somewhere along the way, probably through the trials and responsibilities of motherhood, I had outgrown him. His love wasn't strong enough to meet life's tests. I didn't need him. I no longer respected him. I was free of Art.

Early Christmas morning, Mr. R. called. "Could I come get little Rosie and bring her to the house for a while, so she can be with her dad and grandmother, too?"

"I don't know, Mr. R. I'm afraid she wouldn't be welcome at your house, with your wife."

"Aye, Roja, she's changed. She is too stubborn to say so, but I can see it in her face when I tell her of the little one."

I heard him call to her—"Karlita, come talk to Emily—por favor."

I waited.

"She is not feeling well right now, but she wants to see the baby. I know she does."

I never wanted to hurt Mr. Rodriguez. He was so good to Rosie, and to me, too. But I just couldn't bring myself to let Rosie go anywhere that she might not be wanted.

"Well . . . let's wait until your wife's feeling well enough to at least talk to me before Rosie goes to visit."

"Aye, Mija," he sighed sadly.

In the afternoon, Mr. Rodriguez and his mother came loaded with gifts. Art was with them. When David saw Art, he got up and went outside.

Art stood looking at me for a full minute, then said, "Hi, Em. How's it going?"

"Okay," I answered. My heart was not pounding. I wondered if his was, but I couldn't tell.

Mr. Rodriguez had already taken Rosie from where she'd been sitting propped with pillows, looking at the lights on the Christmas tree. "My wife is home resting. She is not well," he explained to my mother.

"Yeah. Right," my mom said.

I got the grandparents' gifts from under the tree.

"Here's for Great-grandmother Rodriguez." I handed her a package with a card that was signed, "Love, Rosie," and was covered with Rosie's little baby handprints. Veronica and I got together the week before Christmas and made fingerpaint with liquid starch and green food coloring. We let the babies mush their hands all around in it. Then they "signed" cards with their handprints.

The cards turned out really cute—more personal than Hallmark and not nearly as expensive. We got the fingerpaint recipe from Mrs. Bergstrom at the Infant Care Center. She had a card file with all kinds of ideas like that.

When old Mrs. Rodriguez unwrapped her package, she smiled with delight. It was a picture of Rosie in a heart-shaped frame.

"Gracias, Mija," she said, coming over and kissing me on

the cheek. "And Baby Mija, too," she said, kissing Rosie. "Feliz Navidad."

I gave the grandpa package to Mr. Rodriguez.

"Here, I need both hands," he said, handing Rosie to Art.

Mr. R's gift was a small snapshot album with pictures of him and Rosie together. Each time he and his mother came to visit, I took three or four pictures, so by the week before Christmas there were plenty to choose from. Art seemed surprised to see the pictures. Maybe he hadn't known that his dad and grandmother visited us regularly.

"Eggnog? Beer? Coffee? Soda?" my mother asked. I could hardly believe how she had warmed to the two Rodriguezes since they'd been coming around to see Rosie. She'd always looked down on Mexicans, no matter how many times I'd pointed out to her that they were here first. Art's reaction to my pregnancy made things even worse. But after the first two visits, she couldn't say enough nice things about Mr. R. and old Mrs. R.

Mom brought the drinks out on a tray, complete with little Christmas napkins. My grandmother had always been the one to organize Christmas for us. This was the first year we'd even had a tree since she died. But my mom had gone all out. I guessed it had to do with Rosie, and with David being home.

"Okay, okay," Mr. R. said. "Now it's Rosie's turn. Look, Rosie-posy." He moved closer to where Art sat with Rosie and handed her a small, wrapped package, which she immediately put in her mouth. We all laughed. Even Art.

I took the package from her and helped her unwrap it. It was a cardboard book with brightly colored pictures of flowers on each page, and the name of the flower printed in bold letters below it. There was a rose and a lily, petunias and mums.

"Look," Art said, slowly turning the pages and saying the names. Then Mr. Rodriguez went outside and came back with a little rocking horse on springs, with a big red bow tied around its neck. We put Rosie on it and fastened the straps, then bounced her gently up and down. She laughed and laughed, and so did we. Finally, David came in from outside and sat down on the opposite side of the room from Art. His angry face relaxed as he watched Rosie bouncing and laughing.

There were other things, too. Necessities. Nine-month-size sleepers and a hooded sweat shirt and a red knit cap.

After a long time of bouncing, Rosie began nodding off to sleep. I took her from her new rocking horse to put her down for a nap. Art's dad and grandma stood and kissed her on the forehead before I took her into the bedroom. Art kissed her, too, then me, on the cheek. The three of them were still standing when I came out. We said our goodbyes. Art walked over to David and extended his hand. David hesitated, but finally reached out and shook hands with Art.

After they left, my mother and David started in on me about how stupid I would be to take Art back.

"Don't worry," I said. "That's over."

"Then why does he have to come around here?" David asked.

"He *is* Rosie's father. He has a right to see her."

"He has no rights at all," my mother said. "What's he done to deserve any rights? He's nothing more than a sperm donor."

"Well, I won't keep him from seeing Rosie, if he wants to."

"He only came because his dad wanted him to."

"Well, okay. If it makes Mr. R. happy, why not? It's not like Art's dangerous or anything."

Later, David went to KFC and brought back extra crispy chicken with mashed potatoes, cole slaw, and biscuits. My mom had gone all out, compared to what she usually did, but she hadn't gone as far as preparing a Christmas dinner. She offered to pay, but David said, "This is on me. Just let me take your car." She tossed him the keys, laughing. It had become a joke, how since David got his truck reupholstered, he wouldn't bring take-out food home in it.

"No way," he'd say when I'd ask him to pick up pizza on his way home from work. "My truck is pure. I don't want it to start smelling like a roach coach."

I couldn't believe the change in David's truck in just one month's time. It was a minor miracle. David and Bobby barely got the truck running during the long Thanksgiving weekend, but it was enough to get David to the roofing jobs and to run a few errands that first day.

Then, at night and on Sundays, he and Bobby worked on the engine. It took them two weeks to get it running really well.

"Good as new," Bobby had said.

"Purrs like a kitten," David said.

By that time David had a full paycheck, and they started on making it look good. I think Tammy was jealous of the time Bobby was spending with David, helping him with the truck. But I was relieved. David was constantly busy, and he seemed happy. But more than that, Bobby was the first decent friend David had hung out with since Grandma died.

Besides, I liked when they worked late on Saturday nights because then Tammy and I would take Rosie and go to the drive-in. Tammy always made Bobby feel so guilty about working on "their" time that he'd let us borrow his car.

That Christmas evening, when David got back with the chicken, he and my mom and I munched out while we watched "A Christmas Carol." I thought of my own ghosts of Christmases past, how bright and festive my grandmother's house had been at Christmas time, with all her German nutcrackers and special ornaments, and with sugared walnuts and hot apple cider. How she had loved Christmas carols. She would play the piano, and she and David and I would sing. I wiped tears from my eyes, hoping no one had noticed.

Last Christmas David was gone, and my mom and I were barely speaking because I hadn't given in to her demands that I get an abortion. We hadn't exchanged gifts or had any kind of celebration at all.

But now there was more of a family feeling, what with Rosie, and David home, and Mr. R. and his mother being such a part of Rosie's life. I thought back to summer, how lonely and depressed I had been—how I'd been caught up in the loss of Art. And then there was that terrible, frightening time with Tammy's cousin. It all seemed a long way away now. Slowly, I was getting a life back. But this time it was a life that didn't depend on Art for happiness.

New Year's Eve The Barb was out at some big party and David and I were home watching the Times Square ball.

"Next year I'm going to have a date and do something exciting for New Year's Eve," David said.

"This isn't exciting?"

"Well, nothing against you and Rosie, but no, I can't say this is an evening I'll be bragging about to my fellow roofers."

"Yeah, well, I suppose it beats last New Year's Eve, watching T.V. with a bunch of convicts."

"You got that right," he laughed, then turned serious. "I think things are going to be okay for me now. I don't need to prove anything anymore, or be a troublemaker. Twenty years old—I guess it's time, huh?"

We heard a funny little cry from the bedroom, and I went to check on Rosie. She was hacking and gasping for air. I grabbed her from the bed and went running to David.

"What's wrong?" He jumped up.

Rosie coughed an awful, barking cough. Her chest heaved, trying to get a breath. Her face was pale. She looked at me with wide, pleading eyes.

"Oh, God, David," I cried, "Call the doctor! Call the doctor!"

"Where's the number?"

"Right there. On the wall. By the phone!"

I held the baby upright, over my shoulder, thinking

maybe she could breathe better in that position. I felt her little body struggling for air.

"Hurry, David . . ."

"What do you mean, he'll call back? We need a doctor now! This is an emergency!"

Rosie shook with a series of coughs that sounded more like a barking dog than a baby.

"SHIT!" David screamed, and slammed down the phone. "I'm calling 911."

"My niece! She can't breathe!" he yelled in the phone. I was crying, holding my helpless baby. Why couldn't I help? What could I do? In the background, David was answering a bunch of questions.

"Seven months. Yes. Hacking. Can't breathe." He turned to me. "They're on their way . . . Take her outside for fresh cold air for about a minute."

I rushed out the front door, counting one-thousand-one, one-thousand-two . . . to sixty. It made no sense to me to take a coughing baby out in the cold, but I was desperate.

David was gripping the phone, jotting down notes, when I took her back inside. She was still hacking and gasping, though maybe not as much as before.

"Take her into the bathroom and turn on all the hot water. Close the windows and the door so the room will steam up."

I rushed to the bathroom and did as David told me to do. In a short time, the little room was filled with steam, and Rosie was breathing somewhat easier. David came in and closed the door behind him.

"How's she doing?"

"A little better, I think."

"The paramedics are on their way. I'm going to stand out front and watch for them. You're supposed to stay in here until there's no more steam." He left, closing the door quickly behind him.

I looked down at my baby, laboring for breath. Please, God. Please, God, don't take her away. I know sometimes I wish I could come and go whenever I want, but please, please, don't let that wish come true.

By the time the paramedics arrived, Rosie was breathing a little more easily, but her chest was still doing a scary, heaving thing. They checked everything out and asked a lot of questions. While they were there, my doctor called. In the background I heard the sounds of clinking glasses and laughter and realized he must be calling from a party. First he talked with me, then the paramedics, then with me again.

"Because it's New Year's Eve, and because you'll have to use a Medicare hospital, you could wait hours in the emergency room before anyone can see you. Do you have access to a car?"

"Yes."

"Okay. This is just a judgment call, and if you want to get her to the hospital, that's exactly what we'll do. But the paramedics seem to think the crisis is past. If you decide to keep her home, I want you to send someone to the all-night pharmacy—you know where I mean?"

"On Sunset?"

"That's the one. I'll call in a prescription for you to get started on right away, and I want you to buy a vaporizer and set it up right next to where she sleeps. Just follow the instructions—it's all written on the box. Then bring the baby in to my office at eight in the morning. Okay? Bring her to the door just west of the parking lot. I'll meet you there."

"Just a minute," I said, covering the mouthpiece with my hand. "Do you have any money, David?"

"About twenty bucks."

"How much will all this cost?" I asked the doctor.

He sighed. "I don't know. I'll tell them to put it on my account and you can work out the details with my book-keeper later."

I sat with Rosie all night, keeping the vaporizer going and giving her some kind of pink medicine every three hours.

David stayed with us for a while, until her breathing was less labored.

"Call me if you need me, Em," he said, then went off to his room. My mother came home, in a taxi, about 6:00.

"Where's the car, Mom?" I said, meeting her in the hallway.

"I don't know," she said, her words slightly slurred. "Edie's maybe? Or that place where we were dancing?"

I didn't even tell her about Rosie then. I'd wait until she'd slept it off.

It turned out that Rosie had some sort of virus that led to a condition called croup. She got better fast, but it sure had been scary. There was so much that could go wrong with babies, sometimes I thought I couldn't handle it. But I had to. So I just did my best. What else could I do?

CHAPTER

28

In February I managed to work out a schedule with Mrs. Bergstrom that made it possible for me to sing with the Harmonics. It meant Rosie and I had to get to the Infant Care Center on our own, at seven in the morning. David always had to be at work by 7:30, so he agreed to drop us off every morning.

Everything worked out well if David's job was nearby, but when they were roofing a condominium complex over in Century City, it meant Rosie and I had to be dropped off by 6:30. We'd wait, half-asleep and all bundled up, under the lunch awning until Bergie arrived.

Here was my schedule for a 6:30 morning: Up at 5:00 and in the shower, wash and blow-dry my hair, dress for the day; 5:45, warm Rosie's bottle and take it in to her; let her start on it, still mostly asleep, while I sponge her nighttime-wet bottom, put a fresh diaper on her, and dress her in clean clothes; 6:00, strap Rosie in her high chair, with a bib, and give her zwieback and slices of banana; pour a glass of orange juice for myself to drink while I pack the diaper bag; check my own backpack to be sure I have the books I need; grab towels, Rosie's clothes from the day before, and yesterday's underwear, throw them in the washing machine; wash Rosie's face and banana-sticky hands, put her hooded sweat shirt on her; 6:15, grab diaper bag, backpack, and Rosie, and meet David in the driveway.

In spite of the early morning rush, though, I loved being

back in the Harmonics. It was different without last year's seniors, and with a new group of sophomores. But Carl was still there, and Becky, and, of course, Mr. Michaels.

We were working on a piece with complicated harmonies and rhythms, and at first no one liked it much.

"Give it a chance, singers," Mr. Michaels said.

The group groaned in unison and started over. He stopped us. "Tenors, pay attention—Carl, sing it for your section. Tenors, listen. Watch your music."

"Now, sopranos—Emily, sing it for them."

It scared me to be called on like that, after being away from the group for so long. But it thrilled me, too, to know that Mr. Michaels still thought I was good enough to be a leader. I sang the part.

"Nice, Emily—great to have you back. All right now, singers, let's put it together. Watch me for entrances. Pay attention!" He gave the pitch and downbeat and every one of us gave it our all. I could hear it. I could feel it.

"Wonderful! One more time!"

We did it again, strong, full, clear.

"Glorious. What a group!"

I left the music room feeling fresh and lighthearted. I realized that all the time we were working on that one piece, there was nothing else on my mind. I was totally involved. That didn't happen to me much anymore.

Often in my classes I was distracted, wondering how I could find a way to pay my mom for Rosie's new shoes, or who would take care of her on Saturday so I could go to a Project Hope meeting, or was her cold getting worse, or how could I arrange for a make-up test in chemistry from the time last week I had to leave school early because of Rosie's cough.

Juggling. Always juggling. But to have a whole hour singing and working on music, and to think of nothing but that? I loved it. I needed it. It was worth being jarred awake at five in the morning by my obnoxious alarm clock.

Valentine's Day, there was a card in the mailbox from Palo Alto. Art. I put Rosie on her rocking horse and bounced her with my foot while I read the card. It had a big red heart on the outside, and inside it said, "To one who is always in my heart, no matter far or near. Happy Valentine's Day, Dear." I was relieved to notice that my heart was not racing as I unfolded the letter which was included in the card.

> *Dear Em, Remember our first Valentine's Day together? I'll always think of you on Valentine's Day. So much has happened since then. It's amazing to me that I'm here at this place, hangin' with the rich kids—me, Art Rodriguez.*
>
> *I've been doing a lot of thinking lately, Emmy, about us and all. You were right to be upset with me when you brought the baby to my house that time. I can't stand to see my mom upset, so I was scared of any confrontation. But I know I didn't handle things very well. I guess girls are stronger than guys. I was really hurt when you broke up with me, but I know now it's the right thing. I just wasn't ready to be tied down to a baby. I know you understand. I've got college, and plans, and a baby just didn't fit. She's cute, and I love her, but honestly, Em, I can't hang with that baby stuff. Anyway, I want you to know that you're very special to me, and that I hope we can spend some time together when I'm home on spring break. I know we can't really have a serious relationship, our lives are so different now. But it would be nice to get together now and then, don't you think? Anyway—just wanted you to know you were on my mind. Give Rosie a kiss for me. Love, For old time's sake, Art.*

I read it three times. Not ready to be tied down to a baby? Did he think I *was*, at sixteen? Girls are stronger than boys? Give me a break! She's cute and I love her? He didn't have a clue about what loving a baby meant. Let him stay up all night with her, with croup. Let him change her dirty diapers and hear her first laughs. Let him arrange his life around her and be charmed by every new little thing she learned to do. Then he could use the love word. His dad loved Rosie, but Art? What an idiot. Absolutely—an idiot. His letter sounded like some little junior high school kid. And—get together now and then—what did that mean? He wanted to drop over for quick sex when he was in town? Did he think I'd go for that? No way!

I tucked the letter away in my dresser drawer, next to the heart pendant. It would be good for me to take it out and read it now and then, in case I ever felt myself falling into the love trap again.

$\mathbf{M}$rs. Werly called me into her office near the end of May. She had my portfolio spread out before her, with my grade reports on top.

"Well, Emily, I must admit you've done much better than I expected. You've kept your grades up, but your attendance leaves a lot to be desired."

"I don't have anyone to take care of my baby when she's sick. She's had a couple of bad colds, and she was sick for a while when she was teething. I always make my work up, though."

"I see you dropped Spanish III."

"I got behind in the conversation assignments when the baby was sick. Mr. Diaz wouldn't let me make up the work—he said he couldn't rearrange his schedule to accommodate my needs—so I dropped it at the semester."

"And what did you replace it with?"

"I'm taking an advanced parenting class with Mrs. Bergstrom at the Infant Center."

"Two parenting classes—ten units at the Infant Center? I'm afraid that won't look very good on your record. It's fine if you're not planning on college. I know a lot of the young mothers take those classes for easy units, but you need *academics*, Emily."

"The homework for advanced parenting requires as much writing as for my honors English class," I said. "And really, what's more important than being a good parent?"

Mrs. Werly peered over her little half-lens reading glasses with a blank stare, like maybe I'd just said something to her in Russian or Swahili. (How would *that* look on my academic record?)

"Well, Emily, perhaps Mrs. Bergstrom at the center has set high standards for you. But we're talking now about how things look on your record. You must finish Spanish III. How about summer school?"

"I have to work this summer. I owe my mom money."

"Well, let's go over your portfolio," she sighed, frowning.

We did, from my ninth grade hopes of everything from a forest ranger to a singer, to the yellow-highlighter narrowing Mrs. Werly had done when she first got word that I was pregnant, to the modified goals I had written at the October Project Hope meeting.

"I suppose you'll need to attend a local college. Project Hope doesn't include housing for dependent children."

I thought of the Sonoma State campus, the giant trees, the duck pond, the split-level dormitories named after Northern California wineries. I saw myself at the duck pond, reading the poetry of Emily Dickinson. I saw all of those images I'd conjured up, when the world was open to me. And then there was Rosie, in our front yard, laughing with delight as she took her first, tentative steps toward me and fell into my arms.

"Yes. It needs to be local," I said.

"Of course, a major part of the college experience is living on campus," Mrs. Werly said, as she crossed out each of my top three choices—Sonoma State University, University of California at Santa Cruz, and Duke University. My dreams. Why did she always redline my dreams?

She read my top choices of majors: Liberal Studies, Music, Environmental Studies. "None of these is what you would call practical," she said. Had she said that to Becky about Art History, or did she only say such things to girls with babies?

"Here, take these catalogs home for the weekend and see what looks good to you. Come back on Monday and we'll revise your portfolio. Remember, as a Project Hope student, your tuition and books are paid for, and you're assured a Work Study position which will provide you with fifteen hours of on-campus work. As I mentioned earlier, absolutely no provisions are made for dependent children. Project Hope is *not* in the business of encouraging teen pregnancy."

I shoved the catalogs into my already bulging backpack. "Thanks," I said. "I'll get them back to you." I practically ran from Mrs. Werly's office. I knew she was trying to help, and I needed the information, but between her redlining my dreams and frowning about dependent children, I'd had enough for one day.

When I got back to the Infant Center, instead of going right in for the afternoon parenting class, I went in to the Teen Moms building.

"I saw your car here," I said to Camille.

"Yep. I'm trying to get caught up with reading the girls' journals and putting news clippings up on the current events board—you know."

"Maybe I should leave you alone?"

"Oh, no, girl. You know I didn't mean that. I always like to do a little conversing with one of my favorite exes. I saw your little Rosie when I was at the Infant Center the other day. She's about got her legs goin' it looks like. She had her walkin' shoes on."

We laughed. "She's walking a little, and I think she said Mommy the other day."

"How old now?"

"One year last week."

"She's going to be a smart one," Camille said. "It's a good thing she got her mama's brains."

I told Camille about seeing my dreams redlined. "Of

course I'm not going to pack Rosie up and take her away to
some college. Too many people love her here—Art's dad
would be heartbroken—and David, sometimes I think she
likes him better than she likes me. And even my mother
plays with her and makes her laugh."

"Yep. She needs all that lovin' up. And you need people
who really care to share her with, too. You know, all that
extended family stuff we talked about in class? That's not
just talk, that's really important."

"I know. But it's hard. I don't want to turn off my brain,
or my future, just because I'm a mom."

"Oh, Em—stop that talkin' like some kind o' fool. You got
to turn your brain on full blast bein' a mom—don't even
think about turnin' it off. And your future? That's double
important now. What kind of dog poop are they fillin' your
head with over there at Hamilton High School?"

"Well, maybe I just can't figure out how everything fits."

"It don't, Baby. It's not supposed to be easy—it's supposed to be a *challenge*. And so far in your life, you're doin'
just great in the challenge department."

I laughed. How could I not laugh with Camille? Another
thing I liked about her, besides that she made me laugh, was
that she had a lot of experience with challenges. Her
husband left her when her third child was only six months
old. He took all their money and their car.

"I decided right then and there, I wouldn't never depend
on no man again. So, I got me a little no-account job, but it
fed us, and I moved in with someone who was in about the
same mess I was in. We helped each other out baby-sitting,
and I started night classes.

"And here I am, a professional woman, my kids all doing
great in school, and I've got me a good man now, too. But I
don't *depend* on him, no matter how good he is. I love him.
He's the cream in my coffee. If something happened to him,
I might just up and die of grief, but it wouldn't be starvin' to
death because of no money and it wouldn't mean my kids
would be reduced to poverty . . . Ooooh, Girl, you got me

goin'. I can be a long winded somethin' or other, can't I?'"

"Well . . . I needed some down-to-earth talk."

We sat for a long time, talking about alternatives and the practical stuff—meeting the challenges and juggling the choices. She had lots of ideas for me to think about. When I heard the van drive in, I stood up to leave. Camille walked me to the door and gave me a hug.

"Don't worry about those redlined dreams. Dream new dreams."

I walked over to the Infant Care Center to get Rosie. She was standing by the door, looking forlorn. She couldn't tell time, but she sure seemed to know I was overdue. I picked her up and she nuzzled her head in the crook of my neck.

"Hi, Baby Rosie," I said, kissing her, then turning to Mrs. Bergstrom.

"I'm sorry I'm late. I was talking with Camille. I'll make up the assignment tonight."

"The assignment is no problem, Emily, but remember our agreement—I need to know where you are at all times, in case of an emergency with your baby."

"But I was right over there," I said, gesturing toward the Teen Moms' building.

"But *I* didn't know it. I know you're very responsible, and this is the first time you've been late without contacting me, but it can't happen again."

"Okay. I really am sorry." I got Rosie's diaper bag and went out to the van.

"She was upset with you," Veronica said when I sat down beside her.

"I know. It was stupid of me—I had a lot on my mind, and I guess I just wasn't thinking straight."

"Well, be careful. That's how Stacy and her baby got kicked out of the program, remember? Now she doesn't have anyone to take care of her baby, and she's dropped out of school and everything."

"Yeah, but she did it all the time. And she wasn't going to school half the time, either. She'd drop the baby off and then go party. I'm not like that."

But I thought about it all the way home. Mrs. Bergstrom came in early every morning so I could participate in the Harmonics. She went out of her way for all of us. But on that one rule she was unbending. "Emergencies come up," she explained, "and I *must* know where to reach you."

I vowed to be extra careful about following that rule. If Rosie and I lost our spot at the Infant Center, I didn't know how I'd manage school, or life. I couldn't do it without the center.

Over the weekend I pored over catalogs. I mulled things over and made lists and talked with Mom and David. I tried to do some of the imaging exercises they'd taught us to do in Project Hope. If I wasn't imaging myself at Sonoma State, I'd find another imaging place. By Monday, when I returned the catalogs, I had new images. I'd dreamt new dreams.

29

"**W**hat do you mean, you're not going to be at Hamilton next year. Are you crazy?" Tammy said. "Becky? Pauline?" she looked at the others sitting at our usual table at Benny's Burgers. "Help me here. A person doesn't just give up her senior year—the whole best year of high school."

"She's right," Becky said. "Think of all you'd miss."

"And the prom, and Senior Ditch Day, and Grad Night."

"And graduation on stage . . ."

"I know, I thought about all that. But look, I might not even be able to stay in Harmonics next year."

"But that's stupid," Becky said. "Mr. Michaels is always telling you how good you are . . ."

"It's not that. He's been great and I know he'd take me back again. But think about the Christmas schedule. The Harmonics are out singing three or four nights a week during December. I couldn't leave Rosie that much. Even in the daytime, I miss performances sometimes because she's sick."

"Well, your senior year is kick back and party, and you're nuts to miss it," Tammy said.

"I've decided, anyway," I said. "I'm going to take the California High School Proficiency Test. That will give me the equivalent of a high school diploma. And then I'll start at Hamilton Heights Community College in September."

"What if you don't pass the test?" Pauline said.

Tammy rolled her eyes. "Are you serious? This girl has

never failed a test in her life, except that one a while back
on methods of birth control."

I threw my sandwich crust at her.

"We'll miss you, Em, that's all," Becky said.

"It's not like I'm leaving town. I'll be around."

"It won't be the same."

"It's not the same now."

I passed the test and started classes at H.H.C.C. in September. Because I was a full-time student, Rosie still qualified
for the Hamilton Heights Infant Care Center.

When I first told Mrs. Werly of my plan, she said Project
Hope was for students who went to four-year colleges. But
then, after making me sit through her standard lecture of
where I'd gone wrong, she came through for me. She talked
with a counselor at H.H.C.C. and sent all of the Project Hope
forms over in time for my appointment.

Things worked out. Through Project Hope, all of my
books and fees were paid for and I got a job, twenty hours a
week, in the C.C. library. I made enough for clothes for Rosie
and me, and, sometimes, a few extras.

When I turned eighteen, I took $4,000 from the money my
gramma left me and bought a six-year-old Honda. I kept the
other $2,000 in the bank for emergencies. David helped me
find the car. He checked it all out in Bobby's dad's shop.

"It's not the coolest car on the road, but it should be
reliable."

"I don't care about cool," I said, though I secretly envied
the beautiful little red Miata Tammy's parents gave her for
graduation.

Every payday I bought a new toy for Rosie. She loved
books and puzzles and musical toys. I only got paid once a
month, on the first, so it wasn't like she was overwhelmed
with new toys. The money Mr. Rodriguez gave me I mostly
turned over to my mom for food and added utility costs.

David gave Mom money every paycheck now, too. It was
fair. And it was nice not to have to listen to her complaints

about how much we were costing her and how we didn't appreciate anything. She still drank too much, and we were always arguing about her smoking in the house. But things were better than they used to be. I really wanted me and Rosie to be in our own place, but I couldn't even think about that until I was through with school and had a real job.

After my first year at C.C., I got a scholarship—not a lot, but it helped. As much as the money, it helped knowing someone believed in me. I managed to get through the first two years of college at H.H.C.C. without borrowing money. It wasn't easy. I wore the same four outfits all the time. It seemed like I had to think twice about every penny I spent. Like, could I really afford a new lipstick from Thrifty's? And already it seemed like it was practically time to be saving for Rosie's education.

I started at C.C. with a major in Liberal Studies and not a clue about a career, except that I wanted and needed one. I thought about everyone I knew. What did they do on their job? Would I like it? Could I handle it? How would it fit with being a mom?

I wondered about teaching in a Teen Moms program, like Camille. She had helped me a lot, and I admired her. Or teaching music, like Mr. Michaels. Or being a nurse. I even thought about studying horticulture and working at an arboretum. Art's dad had taught me to love plants and gardens so much, and to be in awe of the huge variety of life that the earth could produce . . .

Then, one morning toward the end of second semester, while I was helping a student find information on the early life of Herman Melville, I opened my eyes and looked around and knew I was where I wanted to be. So I decided to major in Library Science. I think I may specialize in Children's Literature in grad school.

It's not easy finding time to study and write papers. Rosie just turned three, and she's full of energy. On Saturdays, when the weather is nice, I take my books and Rosie's fingerpaints outside. David built an easel for her, and she loves smearing the paint around and making "pictures." She has a great imagination—two-headed blue dogs and horses on wheels. Of course, nothing looks like what she says it is, but it all looks beautiful to me. Her pictures are hanging all over our room.

On our "outside" days, I usually get a half hour or so of studying out of two or three hours. And I get another forty-five minutes during Sesame Street. But my real study time comes between nine at night and six-thirty in the morning. I get really tired sometimes, and then I get discouraged. Like maybe I should just take a job as a receptionist and forget all this school stuff.

Bergie, where Rosie still goes for day care, tells me, "Don't give up. You're halfway there. Think how great it will be to have a good paying job, and benefits, and retirement."

That always makes me laugh. I haven't even started yet and I should be thinking about retirement?

"Anyway, you owe it to yourself and Rosie to make the best use possible of that brain of yours."

So then I manage to get a decent night's sleep, and I get a paper back with an "A" and a good comment from the teacher, and I get all jazzed again.

I just started California State University at Los Angeles last September. It costs a lot more than H.H.C.C. did, but so far the Project Hope funds are coming through. I heard a rumor that the governor might do away with the whole Project Hope program. I'm not sure what I'd do then. I just walk around with my fingers crossed that the program will last.

But Cal State L.A.? It's huge, and stuck at the intersection of two freeways. I have to drive the freeway now to get to school. And I carry a can of mace with me because there've been several rapes lately, some even in the middle of the day. It's not quiet and serene, like my images of Sonoma State were.

The average age in my Literature for Children class is thirty-seven, and that seems pretty typical. The racial mix is phenomenal—African-Americans, Hispanics, East Indians, American Indians, Chinese, Vietnamese, Thai, Japanese, Korean, Russian, Bulgarian—all in just one class. (I learned that when the professor had us introduce ourselves and state our ethnic backgrounds.)

I like that Rosie is in the college day care because she gets to play with all different kinds of kids. I don't ever want her to be prejudiced.

Some people, like Mrs. Werly, look down their noses at "commuter colleges." But I'm proud of the education I'm getting at Cal State L.A. I appreciate the diversity.

I suppose I did miss something by not being able to go away and live in a dorm, with lots of people near my own age. And I always have to arrange my schedule of classes according to Rosie's needs, so sometimes that means not taking my first choice of a class or teacher. But if I lost something by taking that path, I gained a lot, too.

Robert Frost wrote, "Two roads diverged in a yellow wood/And sorry I could not travel both . . ." I chose the Rosie road, and I'll never know where that other road, with the freer life, would have led. And I hope Rosie will not have a baby at the age of sixteen. It is too hard. But I'm not sorry about the choice I made, because I got Rosie.

I'm doing my best to keep my promises to her. She has never had to tiptoe around the house until four in the afternoon, waiting for me to sleep off a hangover. I am a better mother than my mother was/is. But then, she is better as a grandmother than I thought she'd be. Not great, but not bad. I haven't had to deliver on my Brownie leader promise yet. But when she's old enough, if she wants to be a Brownie, I'll be there for her.

Art? He's taking a year break from school—couldn't take the pressure, is what I heard from Bobby. He comes around now and then, but he's not much a part of our lives. He took Rosie to Disneyland once this past summer. It's more like he's a casual acquaintance than a dad, though. I wish she had a dad who loved her as much as I do, but she doesn't.

I read a newspaper article last week that said children from single-parent homes are 100 percent to 200 percent more likely than children from two-parent families to have emotional and behavioral problems, and about 50 percent more likely to have learning disabilities.

Sometimes those statistics scare me.

David says I'm stupid to worry about that stuff. Rosie has lots of people who love her, and her life is much more stable than ours was. And then he adds with a laugh, "Look at us."

He's right, though. Rosie is not lacking in the love department. She and Mr. R. spend every Wednesday afternoon together. He takes her with him on a job for an hour or so, then they get ice cream, or whatever else Rosie wants. They go back to his house and work in Rosie's own special garden plot for a little while. She has dinner with the Rodriguezes, and Mr. R. brings her home in time for bed. I let her go over there with her grampa because Mrs. R. finally called me, about a year ago, and asked if it would be okay.

It's funny. Rosie talks about Great-gramma and Grampa, but she never mentions Art's mom. If I ask how Gramma R. is, Rosie says "fine" and goes on to talk about one of the others. Maybe she's a natural-born good judge of character.

David is a wonderful uncle. They roughhouse and tickle, and he teaches her to make disgusting faces, but when she is unhappy, he is very gentle with her. And Bobby and Rosie are good buddies, too. And Tammy. As soon as Rosie was potty-trained, Tammy became her best friend.

Tammy works at Nordstroms. Her folks wanted her to go to college but she was determined to put school behind her and "start a real life." Anyway, she gets great discounts, and sometimes she brings a new outfit to Rosie. She likes to dress her up and then take her home and show her off to her mom. I'm afraid she's going to make Rosie conceited, but so far so good.

My love life? Well . . . Between school, and papers, and research, and statistics, and work, and Rosie, sometimes it feels like I barely have time to breathe. But a while back when I was working in the library, I ran into Carl Saunders, from the old Harmonics group. We talked for a long time. He told me about singing in Mr. Michael's church choir. I remembered how Mr. Michaels used to tell us about his church choir and the great music they performed.

"I'd love to be in a choir again."

Carl fished around in his pocket and pulled out a beat-up card with Mr. Michael's phone number written on it.

When I called, Mr. Michaels said, "We always need more good singers. Come join us."

So I did. I was real ill at ease, being in a church and not being religious. But I loved singing again. So I've been going every Sunday. Rosie goes to Sunday School while I sing. Last Sunday Carl and Rosie and I got a bite to eat and went to Griffith Park so Rosie could ride the ponies.

I don't know. I was never attracted to Carl in high school, but look what happened with the guy I *was* attracted to. And I like Carl. He's a very nice person. He's majoring in computer science, and he's got a good part-time job. We laugh a lot, and he has an easy, natural way with Rosie. But I'm in no hurry. We'll see.

ABOUT
THE AUTHOR

Marilyn Reynolds is the author of numerous essays which have appeared in the *Chicago Tribune, Los Angeles Times, Dallas Morning News, San Francisco Chronicle,* and other national newspapers. Her work has also been published in literary magazines, professional journals, and anthologies. *Telling,* Reynolds' first young adult novel, is the story of a 12-year-old girl who is sexually molested by the father of the children she babysits.

Reynolds teaches English at an alternative school in Los Angeles county. Her students help her keep in touch with the realities of today's teens, realities which are readily apparent in her novels. Both *Telling* and *Detour for Emmy* have been inspired by a mixture of Reynolds' own experiences and the experiences her students have shared with her.

Reynolds lives in Southern California with her husband, Mike. They are the parents of three grown children, Sharon, Cindi, and Matt, and the grandparents of Ashley.